CHRYSALIS 8

EDITED BY ROY TORGESON

ZEBRA BOOKS
KENSINGTON PUBLISHING CORP.

ZEBRA BOOKS

are published by

KENSINGTON PUBLISHING CORP.
475 Park Avenue South
New York, N.Y. 10016

CONTENTS

INTRODUCTION

Roy Torgeson

Welcome to *Chrysalis,* the unique science fiction and fantasy original anthology series. Just in case you have not visited with us before, let me explain what we are all about.

The word *chrysalis* describes something in the stage of development, more specifically the third stage in the development of a butterfly. Taken together these definitions capture the essence of what I envision for the *Chrysalis* series and each volume in it: a constantly developing and changing series with each volume giving birth to beauty—in the form of *good* stories.

Chrysalis is an eclectic, one could say, idiosyncratic science fiction and fantasy series. That is, it looks and often tastes like science fiction and fantasy (whatever these are; for they still await tight definitions), but the stories are not bound together by any particular theme, style, mood, et cetera. Nor are they representative of any specific category of speculative fiction. Their only common bond is that I think that they are damned *good* stories. As Theodore Sturgeon wrote about an early volume of *Chrysalis:*

> Here at last is a book you can trustingly sidle up
> to and say, "Hey. Tell me a story." And the book
> will say, "Why sure. Sit right down. Once upon a
> time there was this dragon . . ." And off you go.

The writers whose stories appear in the *Chrysalis* series are as richly varied as their stories. Like all preceding volumes, *Chrysalis 8* contains stories written by men and by women; by long-established professionals and by brilliant newcomers; by older people and by young writers who weren't even alive when I had already been reading science fiction and fantasy for almost two decades; by happy, carefree spirits and by brooding cerebral types given to somber and agonizing soul-searching; and by people I consider my close friends and by others I think of as good friends whom I simply haven't met as yet. My approach to editing the *Chrysalis* series is quite simple. Through specific correspondence, general announcements, and word of mouth, I let it be known that I am looking for *good* stories of all kinds. The stories come, I then select the ones I like best, and we all wait for your critical judgment.

Editing a wide-open continuing anthology series is much like holding an open house every third Tuesday evening of the month. You never quite know who will drop by, what mood they will be in, or just how the evening's dialogue will develop. However experience has taught this editor-host that a good group of fascinating writer-guests will be represented and that the give-and-take which develops will be richly varied and gloriously phantasmagoric. Trust me friends, the *Chrysalis 8* get-together is a science fiction and fantasy happening well worth experiencing, whatever your literary preferences may be.

Now for a few words about the authors and their stories:

The lead story in *Chrysalis 8* is "You Are My Sunshine" by Tanith Lee, and it's a honey. The "scientific" idea for the story is similar to the fantastic speculations about the effects of cosmic radiation on human beings, which so frequently appeared in the pulp magazines during the early years of science fiction. Tanith, however, does things with this idea that the old pulp writers never dreamed of. She has breathed new life into what I thought was a thoroughly worn-out, if not moribund, science fiction idea, and she has done this with her usual fine sense of style. After reading "You Are My Sunshine" the old song of the same name will never seem the same again, and you just may find it impossible to get the tune and lyrics out of your head. I've been humming the song to myself now for almost two months: "You are my sunshine, my only sunshine. You make me happy when skies are gray. You'll never know, dear, how much I love you, so please don't take my sunshine away. The other night, dear . . ."

Mike Resnick's "Beachcomber" appeared out of the blue in the mail one day, and it wasn't until much later that I discovered that Mike and I have the same literary agent. It's a small world. Then Mike and his wife, Carol, dropped in from Cincinnati last week and, sure enough, we were all good friends who simply hadn't met until then.

"Beachcomber" is a poignant little story about Arlo, a supersophisticated robot whose programmed "enthusiasm" gets the better of him. The story is only 1,700 words long; Arlo is not at all human in appearance and says only 118 words, plus he is described by a most unsympathetic narrator. Nevertheless, you will come to know Arlo and feel for him. The memory of Arlo, the run-away robot travel agent, will stay with you for a long time. By the way, Mike Resnick is the only writer to win the American Dog Writers Association Award for a science fiction story, appropriately titled "The Last Dog." I couldn't resist sharing this piece of information with you. Sorry about that, Mike.

"Emily Dickinson—Saved from Drowning" could only have been written by Barry Malzberg. The title alone tells me that Barry wrote it and the story itself is pure Malzberg. Did you know that Sigmund Freud was murdered in Vienna? Or that Emily Dickinson dreamed of President Kennedy's assassination? Or that Emily and Samuel Clemens had an unsatisfactory love affair? No? Well then, you'll simply have to read about this and much more in Barry's latest story.

Jayge Carr is a very talented new writer who takes some unusual positions on current social issues. In "The King Is Dead! Long Live—" she deals with the issues of sexual freedom and choice, which are then related to broader social forces. Subtly written, "The King Is Dead! Long Live—" contains a number of little surprises while providing the reader with a very different perspective from which to view an age-old social/sexual issue, one which has been with us since the dawn of human history. Jayge's "solution" to this "problem" is indeed unique, and its social ramifications will leave you with a lot to think about.

"Hart's Hope" by Orson Scott Card is a superb example of what can happen when an imaginary world and its people come alive in the typewriter and simply refuse to be confined within the original boundaries set by their creator. Planned as a 10,000-word novelette, it quickly grew into a novella more than three times this length. And, I'm happy to report that it is *still* very much alive and well on its way to becoming a novel. Written in modern-day prose, "Hart's Hope" is high fantasy set in a richly detailed imaginary world populated with larger-than-life, yet magically real, people. Orem Scanthips, King Palicrovol, Queen Beauty, Urubugala, Craven, and Weasel are memorable characters whom you will come to know intimately and emotionally.

Margaret St. Clair! Yes, *Chrysalis 8* contains a new story by Margaret entitled "Wryneck, Draw Me." I don't know how far back you go, but Margaret used to write a lot for the magazines during the forties and fifties. She then dropped from sight for a long, long time, and I didn't know what had happened to her until a few months ago when two St. Clair manuscripts magically arrived in the mail. I felt as if I had suddenly been transported more than twenty years into the past, to when I was an avid teenage science fiction and fantasy fan reading *Startling, Thrilling Wonder, Other Worlds, Imagination*, et cetera. Talk about a "blast from the past."

"Wryneck, Draw Me" is quite different from anything I remember Margaret writing in the old days. Hell, it's like nothing I've ever read by anybody! Oh sure, it is about an insane universal computer called Jake who, like the computer in *I Have No Mouth and I Must Scream* by Harlan Ellison, has taken over the entire world. But Jake's lunacy is something else! "Wryneck, Draw Me" has to be one of the most outlandish, wacky, funny, downright bizarre stories you will ever read. And the imagery, well . . . words fail me.

Technically, "The Cathedral in Dying Time" by Sharon Webb is probably not a *story*. That is, it does not seem to contain a clear-cut beginning, middle, and end. It is a fragment, a vignette, or better yet, a *mood piece*. Using a mere 1,400 words, Sharon has created a hauntingly eerie mood which will lurk in the back of your mind for a long time. However you classify it, I think that you will agree with me that "The Cathedral in Dying Time" is disturbingly *good*.

I published Paul H. Cook's first two science fiction/fantasy sales and, with the inclusion of "Proteus" in *Chrysalis 8*, I have the honor of publishing sale number three. I know that "tooting my own horn" may not seem too cool, but I'm very proud of Paul's stories and I think that he is one of the finest new writers to turn up in our field since I began editing anthologies.

"Proteus" is a chilling fantasy about a "man" who can change his total appearance, seemingly at will. This talent allows him to lead dual lives as two very different people, each with his own job, wife, child and so on. Then, one day on the subway he senses that *something is wrong*. What follows is quietly chilling in more ways than one.

By the way, much of the story takes place at a women's club buffet dinner, and I think that Paul has written the most vivid description of this type of real-life horror I have ever read. For me, it is the most frightening part of the entire story.

It has been only a couple of years since Somtow Sucharitkul's first story appeared in *Unearth Magazine*, and now his science fiction and fantasy stories are popping up all over the place. And well they should, because he is enormously talented. "Angels' Wings" is a beautiful and very different kind of first-contact story in which humanity is called upon to perform its most noble deed: to truly be on the side of the angels. Individually, we are all terribly flawed and, collectively, we are even more imperfect, but . . .

* * *

A few months ago I purchased a couple of stories for my original fantasy anthology by a new writer named Steve Rasnic. Just before the book went to press I received a letter from Steve informing me that he was getting married, needed money, and was changing his name to Steve Rasnic Tem. I congratulated him, sent him a very small amount of money, and changed his name in the book. I know the connection between getting married and needing money, but I still do not understand how getting married and changing one's name are connected. When I told this story to a fellow editor a few weeks ago, she immediately came up with an intriguing and plausible explanation. She suggested that both Steve and his wife-to-be chose a brand-new last name so that both of them could take a new identity upon their marriage. It makes sense and I can't help hoping that this is what really happened.

Right now I have four stories by Steve in my files. They are equally excellent and I intend to publish them all. "Filmmaker" is my selection for *Chrysalis 8* because it was the first story to arrive. It is an incredibly skillful blending of photographic techniques with the art of story-telling. Please take your time reading it. It is a complex, unpleasant story which demands your close attention.

Anyone familiar with the *Chrysalis* series knows that I am addicted to *lafferties* and suffer withdrawal symptoms unless I can include one in my current anthology. This time around R. A. Lafferty is represented by a zany piece entitled "Crocodile." Technically, "Crocodile" is not an "original" story for it appeared ten years ago in a small fanzine, *Phantasmicon*. Still, very few people have read it and it is a true *lafferty*.

Do you remember Isaac Asimov's *The Three Laws of Robotics?*

> 1—*A robot may not injure a human being, or, through inaction, allow a human being to come to harm.*
>
> 2—*A robot must obey the orders given it by human beings except where such orders would conflict with the First Law.*
>
> 3—*A robot must protect its own existence as long as such protection does not conflict with the First or Second Law.*

HANDBOOK OF ROBOTICS,
56TH EDITION, 2058 A.D.

Well, in "Crocodile," Lafferty *diabologically* refutes them. I don't know if he is successful, but it's a lot of fun anyway.

Leanne Frahm is another brilliant new science fiction writer whose first two stories were published in the *Chrysalis* series. She lives on the other side of the world, Australia, but when Terry Carr introduced me to her work, it blew me away. Like her previous two stories, "Barrier" is smoothly, almost gently, written, but it is loaded with power. Leanne writes emotionally charged stories, but her sense of power is beautifully controlled.

"Barrier" tells of three most unusual aliens who are suddenly confronted with a race of maniacal beings poised to spill their malignant insanity out into space. It is the story of their first encounter with human beings—whose madness goes beyond their wildest imaginings. Powerful stuff!

* * *

As always, I thank the authors for allowing me to share in their remarkable creativity. And special thanks to Pat LoBrutto, Science Fiction and Fantasy Editor for Doubleday, for allowing all of us to do our things, in our own eliptical ways.

ROY TORGESON
New York City
March 1980

You Are My Sunshine

by TANITH LEE

(Tape running.)

—For the record: Day two, Session two, Code-tape three. Earth Central Investigation into the disaster of the S.S.G. *Pilgrim*. Executive Interrogator Hofman presiding. Witness attending, Leon Canna, Fifth Officer, P.L. Capacity. Officer Canna being the only surviving crew member of the *Pilgrim*. Officer Canna?

—Yes, sir.

—Officer Canna, how long have you been in the Service?

—Ten years, sir.

—That would be three years service in exploration vessels and seven in the transport and passenger class. How many of those seven years with Solarine Galleons?

—Six years, sir.

—And so, you would know this type of ship pretty well?

—Yes, sir. Pretty well.

—And was the *Pilgrim* in any way an unusual ship of its kind?

—No, sir.

—Officer Canna, I'm aware you've been through a lot, and I'm aware your previous record is not only clear, but indeed meritorious. Naturally, I've read your written account of what, according to you, transpired aboard the Solarine Space Galleon *Pilgrim*. You and I, Officer Canna, both know that with any ship, of any class or type, occasionally something can go wrong. Even so wrong as to precipitate a tragedy of the magnitude of the *Pilgrim* disaster. Now I want you to consider carefully before you answer me. Of all the explanations you could have chosen for the death of this ship and the loss of the two thousand and twenty lives that went with her, why this one?

— It's the truth, sir.

— Wait a moment, Officer Canna, please. You seem to miss my point. Of all the explanations at your disposal, and with ten years intimate knowledge of space, the explanation you offer us is, nevertheless, frankly ludicrous.

— Sir.

— It throws suspicion on you, Officer Canna. It blots your record.

— I can't help it, sir. Oh sure, I could lie to you.

— Yes, Officer Canna, you could.

— But I'm not lying. Suppose I never told you this because I was afraid how it would reflect on me. And then suppose the same situation comes up, somewhere out there, and then the same thing happens again.

— That seems quite unlikely, Officer Canna.

(A murmur of laughter.)

— Excuse me, but I don't think this thing should be played for laughs.

— Nor do I, Officer Canna. Nor do I. Very well. In your own words, please, and at your own pace. Tell this investigation what you say you believe occurred.

The girl came aboard from the subport at Bel. There were thirty-eight passengers coming on at that stop, but Canna noticed the girl almost at once. The reason he noticed her was that she was so damned unnoticeable. Her clothes were the color of putty, and so was her hair. She had that odd, slack, round-shouldered stance that looked as though it came from a lifetime of sitting on her poor little ass, leaning forward over a computer console or a dispensary plate. Nobody had ever told her there were machines to straighten you out and fine you down, and vitamins to brighten your skin, and tints to color your hair, and optic inducers to stop your having to peer through two godawful lenses wedged in a red groove at the top of your nose. Nobody had ever presumably told her she was human either, with a brain, a soul, and a gender.

Watch it, Canna. A lost cause is lost. Leave it alone.

Trouble was, it was part of his job to get involved.

P.L.—Passenger Link—required acting as unofficial father, son, and brother to the whole shipload; sometimes you got to be priest-confessor and sometimes, lover too. It took just the right blend of gregariousness coupled to the right blend of constraint. Long ago, the ships of the line had reasoned that passengers, the breadwinning live cargo that took up half the room aboard a Solarine Galleon, were liable to run amok without an intermediary between themselves and the crewing personnel topside. The role of P.L. was therefore created. Spokesman and arbiter, the P.L. officer knew the technical bias up top, but he represented the voice of the nontechnical flock lower side. He related to his flock what went on behind the firmly closed doors of the Bridge and Engine Bay. If he sometimes edited, he took care not to admit it. He belonged, ostensibly, to the civilians, and that way he stopped them rocking the boat.

To do this job at all, you had to be able to communicate with your fellow mortals and they had to be able to communicate with you. In that department, Canna did excellently. Sometimes better than excellently. Dark, deeply suntanned, as were all Solarines, and with a buoyant, lightly sardonic good humor, he had found early on that women liked him very well, sometimes too well. This had been one of the score of reasons that had driven him off the exploration vessels, where for one or two years at a stretch, you rubbed shoulders with all the same stale passions and allergies. The EVs took on no passengers to provide diversion, stimulus and, in the most harmless of ways, fair game. Conversely, the Solarines had a low percentage of female crew: since women had realized their intellectual potency, they tended to go after the big-scale jobs which pleasure cruisers didn't offer. However, the passengers provided plenty of female scenery, women who came and went, the nicest kind. For the rest, the grouses of transient passengers, Canna could easily stand because next stop the grousers got off. Canna's trick was that he found it easy to be patient, appreciative, and kind with all birds of passage.

So there was that little gray dab of a girl no one had ever been kind to, creeping into the great golden spaceship. Canna reminded himself of the story of the man who would go up to drab women on the street and hiss suddenly to them: "You're beautiful!" For the strange ego trip of seeing the dull face abruptly flare into a kindling of brief surprised loveliness: the magic a woman would find in herself with the aid of a man. Watch it, Canna. There were two day-periods and a sun-park of twenty before they turned for Lyra and this live cargo got off.

S.S.G.s operated, as implied, on stored solar power. Their original function was transport, and with a meton reactor geared into the solar drive, they had been the hot rods of the galaxy. The big suns, any of a variety of rainbow dwarfs, provided gas stations for these trucks. Parked in orbit around the furnace, shields up and Solarine mechanisms gulping, the truck became a holiday camp. The beneficial side effects of S.S.G.s were swiftly noted. Golden-skinned crews, whose resistance to disease was 99 to 100 percent, gave rise to new ideas of the purpose of the galleons. Something about the Solarine filter of raw sunlight acted like a miracle drug on the tired cells of human geography. Something did you a world of good, and you might be expected to pay through the nose to get it. From transport trucks, S.S.G.s became the luxury liners of the firmament, health cures, journeys of a lifetime, the only way to travel. The Solarina sun decks were built on, the huge golden bubbles that girdled the ship, wonderlands of glowing pools, root-ballasted palms and giant sunflowers, lizardia blooms and lillaceous cacti, through which poured the screened radiance of whichever sun the ship was roosting over, endless summer on a leash.

The sun between Bel and Lyra was a Beta-class topaz effulgence, a carrousel of fire.

The third period after lift-off, the "day" they settled around the sun, the little gray-putty girl was sitting in the sun lounge that opened off the entry-outs of the Solarina. Not sitting precisely, more crouching. Canna had checked her name on the passenger list. Her name was Hartley. Apollonia Hartley. He had guessed it all in a flash of intuition; though if he was right, he never found out. The guess was someone had died and left her some cash, enough to make a trip some place. And someone else had said to her: Gee, Apollonia honey, with your name you have to have a Solarine cruise. Appollo's daughter, child of a sun-god (they must have maliciously predicted she'd turn out this plain to crucify her with a name like that), could bask in the sun under the ballasted ballsy palms and fry her grayness golden. Except that she wasn't doing that at all. She was sitting—crouching—here in the lead-off lounge, with a tiny glass of champazira she wasn't even sipping. A few people were going in and out, not many. Most of them were placed to grill like tacos within the outer-side bubble.

"Hi, Miss Hartley," said Canna, strolling up to her. "Everything OK?"

Apollonia jumped about ten centimeters off her couch and almost knocked her champazira over.

"All right, thank you," she muttered, staring at her knees.

It was a formula. It meant: Please go away; I'm afraid to talk to you. That was a professional slight, if nothing else. People had to *want* to talk to Leon Canna. It was what he was there for.

"Had enough of the Solarina for today?" he asked.

"Oh yes. That is—yes," said Apollonia. She must be seeing something about her knees which no one but she ever would.

He sat on the arm of the couch beside her.

"You haven't been out there at all, have you?" Silence, which meant go away, go away. "Why's that?" Silence, which had become an abstract agony. "Maybe you've got sun fright. Is that it? It's quite common. Fears of strong radiation. But I can assure you, Miss Hartley, it's absolutely safe. Do I look sick, Miss Hartley?"

Inadvertently, she glanced at him. Her eyes got stuck somewhere on the white uniform casuals, the sun blaze over the pocket. Black hair and eyes and cleft golden jaw and the golden hands with their fine smoke of black hirsuteness, these she avoided.

"I'm not," she said, "that is, there are so many—people out there."

She might have said lions, tigers.

"Sure. I know," he said. He didn't know. People to him were a big fun game. "But I'll tell you what, you

23

know when it gets really quiet in the Solarina?"

"When?" Whispered.

He liked that. He understood what was happening. Fascinated by him, she was beginning to forget herself.

"Twenty-four midnight by the earth clock below. Come back then, you'll get a good three or four hours, maybe alone." She didn't speak. "Or I might come up," he said. Christ, Canna, what did I say to you? He could see her breathing, just like a heroine in an old romance, bosom, as they said, heaving. "Why don't you drink you champazira?" he said.

"I don't—I only—"

"Ordered it for something to play with while you sat here," he said. "I didn't see you at dinner the last two night-periods."

"I ate in my cabin."

"Oh, Miss Hartley—Apollonia, may I?—Apollonia, you'll get the *Pilgrim* a bad name. You're supposed to get something out of your voyage. Come on, now. Promise me. The Solarina at midnight. I have to make certain our passengers enjoy themselves. You don't want me to lose my job, do you?"

Startled, her eyes flew up like birds and collided with his jet-black ones. Her whole face stained with color, even her spectacles seemed to glaze with pink.

"I'll try."

"Good girl."

Good God.

He told himself not to go up to the Solarina after midnight. Of course, he'd met women out there before, who hadn't. But not women like Apollonia.

At twenty-four thirty by the earth clock, he walked through the sun lounge. The passenger section of the ship was fairly still at this hour, as he had assured her.

The Solarina was empty except for its flora and its light. In the sun lounge, Apollonia was huddled on her couch, without even the champazira to keep her company.

"I didn't think—you would come. I was," she said, "afraid to go through on my own. Is it—all right?"

"Sure it is."

"Will the doors open?"

"I have a tab if they don't."

"It looks so—bright. So fierce."

"It's like a hot shower, or the sea at Key Mariano. You ever been there?" He knew she had not. "Just above blood heat. The fish cook as they swim. Come on." She didn't move, so he moved in ahead of her, into the glowing summer, sloughing his robe as he went. He understood perfectly what he looked like in swim trunks. If he hadn't, enough women had told him, using the analogies of Greek heroes, Roman gladiators. "The harmful rays are filtered out by the Solarine mechanism," he said. Encouraged, mesmerized, she slipped through, and the wine water closed over her head.

She wore a long shapeless tunic. Probably just as well. She would be nearly as shapeless underneath.

"Will this do?" she said. "I didn't know what—"

"That's fine. The filtered sun soaks through any material. The tan is all over, whatever you wear. I just like to get directly under the spotlight when I can."

They folded themselves out among the palms, which threw down coffee-green papers of shade. The warmth was honey. You felt it osmose into you. You never grew bored with it. The walls of the bubble, sun-amber hiding the actual roaring face of the sun, pulsed very faintly, rhythmically, sensually, with Solarine ingestation. The Galleon was a child, given suck by a fiery breast. All this to fuel a ship. Man oh man.

"It's beautiful," Apollonia said.

She lay on palm-frond shadows. Her eyes were wide behind the spectacles. Her putty-colored hair was ambiguously tinged, almost gilded. Her lips were parted. He hadn't noticed before, she had a nice mouth, the upper lip chiseled, the lower full and smooth, the teeth behind them even and white. He leaned over her and gently lifted the spectacles off the red groove in her nose. He was completely aware of the cliché — Oh, Miss Hartley, now I see you for the first without your glasses. . . .

She made a futile panicky little gesture after the spectacles.

"Relax," he said.

She relaxed, closing her eyes.

"I can see. But not so well. But I can see without them."

"I know you can."

"I never felt the sun, any sun, like this before," she said presently. He saw it often, every journey in fact, how they grew drunken, wonderful solar drunks, with no morning after.

An hour later, one-thirty earth time, he looked at her again. There was something changed. Already, her skin was altered. Long lashes lay like satin streaks against her face. The red groove had faded, become a thin rose crescent. OK Canna, so you're Pygmalion. But the Solarina sun had got to him also, as it always did. He leaned over again, and this occasion he kissed her lightly on the lips.

"Oh," she said softly. "Oh."

"Baby," he said. "I have to go back to my quarters and put on tape for my captain what 976 people find wrong with S.S.G. *Pilgrim this* trip."

She didn't stir. He thought she'd gone to sleep, perhaps (fanciful) melodramatically passed out at the fragile kiss.

He left her to the Solarina, and when he closed the door of his cabin he found himself carefully locking it, and the sweat between his shoulder blades had nothing to do with the sun.

He didn't see Miss Hartley next day-period. This was partly deliberate and partly luck. There were plenty of things to do, reports to make, two hours' workout in the gym. Then some crazy dame lost a ruby pendant. He took a late dinner in the salon—as P.L., he had a place at the coordinators' table, alongside his flock. The golden wash was spreading over them all, just as usual. Then he saw the girl.

Something had happened to the girl.

She was tanned, of course, enough tan that she must have been back to the Solarina during the day, or else she'd stayed there all night. Or maybe both. But it wasn't only the tan. What the hell was it?

He couldn't stop staring, which was bad, because any moment she might look his way. But she didn't look. She wasn't even wearing her spectacles. She finished the tawny liqueur she was drinking, got to her feet, and walked unhurriedly out of the salon. She didn't move the same way, either.

"I don't remember that girl," said Fourth Officer Coordinator Jeans.

"Apollonia Hartley."

"Not the right mixture for you, Canna."

"Help yourself," said Canna.

After dinner there was the report to make on the rediscovery of the lost pendant. It looked like it was going to be one of those runs with a lot of desk work. Around midnight there was cold beer and nothing much left to do except wonder if little Miss Hartley was on the sun deck.

There were girls, and there were girls. Some girls you had to be wary of. Even birds of passage could turn around and fly straight back, and some had nest-building on their minds, and some had damn sharp claws. This girl now. She might be grateful. She might have taken it for what it was. Then again, she might not. And for godssakes anyway, what was there for him to be interested in?

At one o'clock earth time, Canna went up to the Solarina. No robe and trunks now, but the rumpled uniform casuals he'd had on all day. The sun lounge was empty. Canna went to the entry-out and glanced through the gold-leaf tunnels of shine under the lizardia. Miss Hartley was lying face down on a recliner, about thirty meters away. Her hair poured over onto the ground. He couldn't see her that well through the stripes of the palms, but enough to know that, aside from her hair, she was naked.

He stepped away from the entry-out noiselessly and walked soft all the way back to his cabin. Oh boy, Canna.

You're beautiful! he said to the plain woman. Her face kindled, she opened her mouth and swallowed him whole.

Ten o'clock next day-period, Jean's jowly face appeared on the cab-com.

"Priority meeting, all officers non-Bridge personnel. Half an hour, Bridge annex."

"What's going on?" Canna asked.

"Search me."

"No thanks."

"OK, funny guy. Usual spiel to the mob, OK?"

"Sure thing."

"Usual spiel" was, as ever, necessary. Somehow, your passengers always knew when something was up, however mild, however closely guarded. Passing three groups on route topside, Canna was asked what emergency required a Bridge annex meeting. Usual spiel meant: "No emergency, Mr. Walters. *Pilgrim* always has an annex meeting third day of sunparking." "But surely, if everything is going smoothly?" "Nothing ever goes quite smoothly on a vessel this size, Miss Boenek." "Then there *is* an emergency, Mr. Canna?" "Yes, Mr. Walters. We're all out of duck pâté."

"Sit down, gentlemen, if you will," said Andersen.

He had been captain of the *Pilgrim* since Canna had started with the ship, and Canna guessed he respected the man about as much as he'd ever respected any extreme authority. At least Andersen didn't think he was God and at least he sometimes got off his tail.

"Gentlemen," said Andersen, "we have a slight problem. I'm afraid, Mr. Canna, yours, as ever, is going to be the delicate task."

"You mean it involves our passengers, sir?"

"As ever, Mr. Canna."

"May I know what the problem is?"

"We have some excess radiation, Mr. Canna."

There was the predictable explosion, followed by the predictable dumb show that greets the distant tolling of that bell, about which ask not for whom. Spake, Bridge Engineer Galleon Class, waited for the bell.

"With your permission, sir? OK, gentlemen, it's not big business. We have it under control. Every cubic centimeter of this tub is being checked."

"You mean," said Jeans, "you don't know the hell where it's coming from."

Andersen said: "We know where it isn't coming from. The meton is sound and there's no bleed-off from the casings. That's our only source of internal radiation. Ergo, it can't be us. Therefore, it's coming in

29

from outside. From the sun we're parked over. As yet, we don't know how or where, because every shield registers fully operational. According to topside computer there's no way we can have a rad-bleed at all. So naturally, we're double checking, triple checking until we pin the critter down. Even if we can't figure it, and there's no reason to suppose we eventually can't, all we have to do is weigh anchor and move out of sun range. Meantime (and here, Mr. Canna, is the rub), the most obvious danger zone is the Solarina."

Canna groaned.

"What you're saying, sir, is that we're going to put the Solarina off limits to the passengers, and I have to find some reason for it that won't cause an immediate panic."

"You know what passengers are like when radiation is involved," said Andersen.

"Mention the word and they're howling and clawing for the life launches," said Jeans.

"What's the rad level?" Canna asked.

Engineer Spake looked at the captain, got some invisible go-ahead, and answered: "At three o'clock this morning, point zero one zero. At nine o'clock, point zero two ten."

There was a second round of expletives.

"In other words, it's rising?"

"It appears to be. But we have a long way to go before it reaches anything like an inimical level."

"I guess that's topside's hang-up, not mine," said Canna. "My hang-up is what story I tell lower side."

"Just keep it simple, Mr. Canna, if you would."

"The simplicity isn't what's troubling me, sir."

"You'll think of something, Mr. Canna."

At noon by the earth clock, when nine hundred odd persons were shooed from the Solarina, Canna guided

30

them into the major lower-side salon, and told them about the free drinks, courtesy of *Pilgrim*. Then, standing on the rostrum with the hand mike, gazing out at the pebbled-beach effect of cluster on cluster of grim, belligerent, nervous faces, Canna found himself reviewing the half a dozen times he had been required to make similar overtures; the time the number twenty Solarine Ingestor caught fire, the time they hit the meteor swarm coming up from Alpheus. A couple of those, and a point zero two ten radiation reading was a candy bar. And then he remembered the girl, and for five seconds his eyes ran over the crowd, and when he couldn't find her, he wondered why the mike was wet against his palm.

They were making a lot of noise, but they quieted down when he lifted his hand. He explained, apologetically, humorously, that *Pilgrim* needed to make up a fuel loss, caused by a minor failure, now compensated, in one of the secondary ingestors. Due to that, the ship would be channeling off extra power through the ship's main Solarine area, the sun deck. Hence the closure.

"For which inconvenience, folks, we are truly sorry."

Now came the questions.

A beefy male had commandeered one of the floor mikes.

"OK, mister, how long's this closure going to last?"

"A day-period, sir. Maybe a couple of days, at most."

"I paid good cash for this voyage, mister. The Solarina's the main attraction."

"The beneficial solar rays permeate every part of the ship, sir, not only the Solarina. The sun deck's function is mostly ornamental. But the company will be happy to refund any loss you feel you've suffered, when we reach Lyra."

"If the goddamn Solarina's only ornamental, how can closing it affect the ship's power?"

"That's kind of a technical query. The Solarine pipe ingestors run out over the hull, you recall, and the Solarina's banks are the nearest to the outer surface—"

"OK, OK."

A pretty young woman miked from the other side of the room:

"Is there any danger?"

"Absolutely none, ma'am. We're just tanking up on gas."

"Well, then, let's tank up," someone yelled, and the free drinking began in earnest.

The *Pilgrim* had got off lightly, Canna thought.

He met Jeans near the bar, downing a large double paint-stripper. Grinning broadly for passenger benefit, Jeans muttered: "Guess what the number game was ten minutes ago?"

"Thrill me." Canna also grinning.

"Full point one."

"Great," said Canna.

"And you know what?" grinned Jeans. "Still climbing."

Far across the room there was a sort of eddy, a current of gold like a fish's wake in sunset water. He thought of a woman baking in the yellow-green cradle of the palms, her arms and her hair poured on the floor.

"The max is fifty, right?"

"Right, Canna, right."

The woman with the ruby was approaching. Miss Keen? Kane? Koon?

"I think it's just lovely," she giggled to Canna. "These marvelous ships, and they still get caught with their pants down." She tried to buy him one of the free drinks.

The golden current had settled, become a pool of molten air. Where the girl was. Apollonia. She'd dyed her hair, the color of Benedictine. He couldn't be sure it was Apollonia, except there was nobody else who looked like her now, as none of them had looked like her before.

When he escaped from his flock and got back to his cabin, a slim sealed envelope had come in at the chute with the lower-side stamp over it. Canna opened the envelope.

I waited for you. That was all she had written, in rounded, overdisciplined letters. *I waited for you.*

Sure you did, baby.

He felt sorry for her, and disgusted. She'd improved herself. Perhaps he could palm her off on Jeans. No, he couldn't do that. He'd understood she was trouble the first moment. He should have left her alone. God knew why he hadn't been able to.

At four, Spake came through the cab-com.

"Thought you'd like to hear it officially. The count is now point fifteen zero five."

"Jesus. Got a fix yet?"

"Nothing. It's everywhere lower side, from the Solarina to the milk bar."

"Not topside?"

"Sifting through."

"Then the source has to be down here."

"According to the computer, nothing leaks, nothing's bleeding off. Unless one of your sheep has a stash of plutonium tucked in his diapers . . . It's got to be coming *in*, but the shields are solid as a rock."

"Maybe you're asking the computer the wrong questions."

"Could be. Know the right ones?"

"What does Andersen say?"

"He wants another meet, all available personnel, midnight plus three."

"Three in the *morning?*"

"That's it, Canna. Be there. And, Canna—"

"What?"

"Complete passenger drill tomorrow. Launches, suit-ups, the whole show."

"That'll certainly lend an atmosphere of calm. I'll get it organized."

Just then, the cabin lights faltered. The clear sheen of the Solarine lamps went white, then brown, steadied, and flashed clear again.

"What the hell did that?" Canna demanded, but Spake was gone. Somewhere there had been a massive drain-off of power. That could mean several things, none of them pleasing. Already he was spinning a story for the passengers, a switchover of batteries as the fabricated weak ingestor was shut down. You stood there with the smoke billowing, and the walls red-hot and screaming people everywhere, and you told them: It happens every trip. It's nothing. And you made them believe it.

Canna went out of the cabin, strolling toward the lower-side salon, taking in the three TV theaters on the way. The flock came to him like filings to a magnet. He was amazed they'd noticed the lights faltering. It was only the spare ingestor shutting down. They believed him. Makes you feel good, huh, Canna?

But where was Canna when the lights went out? In the goddamn dark.

He opened his eyes. It was half past one, the cabin on quarter lamp. Over by the tape cabinet, fastened to its stanchions, the grotesque survival suit stood, blackly gleaming, like a monster from a comic rag. He'd been checking the suit for the demonstration tomorrow and then lain on the bunk to snatch an hour's sleep before Andersen's meeting. What had awakened him?

The door buzzer sounded again. That was what had awakened him.

Two thirds of the way to the door, he knew who it was, and hesitated. Then he opened the door.

There in the corridor stood Apollonia Hartley. But it was not the Apollonia Hartley who had come aboard at Bel. The whole corridor seemed to shine, to throb and glow and shimmer. Maybe that was just the effect of full light after quarter lamp. Then she stepped by him into his cabin, and the throbbing, glowing, shimmering shine came in with her.

"I waited," she said quietly. "And then, when you didn't come, I realized you meant me to come here."

"Did I?"

She turned and looked at him. Without her glasses, there was a slight film across her eyes, making them large, enigmatic. Not seeing him quite so well seemed to make it easier for her actually to look at him. Her Benedictine golden hair hung around her, all around her, and all of her was pure gold, traced over by the briefest swimsuit imaginable. And she was beautiful. Shaped out of gold by a master craftsman, Venus on a gold medallion.

"You look fine," he said. "What have you done to yourself?"

"Nothing," she said. "You've done this for me, Leon," she said.

He thought, Christ, no woman could make herself look like this in two days, not starting on the raw material Apollonia had started with. Not even with the Solarina.

"You," she said, "and the strange wonderful sun. No man ever looked at me before, ever kissed me. I've never been this close to a sun."

As she breathed, regularly and lightly, planes of fire slid across her waist, her breasts, her throat. And the cabin gathered to the indrawn breath, spilled away, gathered, spilled—

"Can you let me into the Solarina, Leon?" she murmured. "I can do it this way, but it's better there."

He tried to smile at her.

"Sorry, the Solarina's out of bounds, Apollonia—Miss Hartley—until—"

"Leon," she said.

When she spoke, the room was full of amber dust and the scent of oranges, peaches, apricots; and volcanoes blazed somewhere. Then she put her hand against his chest, flat and still on the bare skin. Here he was, Leon Canna, with the best-looking lady he'd ever seen, and he was holding her at arm's length. He stopped holding her that way and held her a better way and she came to him like flame running up a beach.

Over by the cabinet, the black survival suit for tomorrow's drill rattled dully, as if sex vibrated the cabin.

When he opened his eyes the next time, it was with a sense of missing hours. He felt dizzy and the cabcom was bawling. The girl had gone.

"Canna!" For some reason no picture had come over to fit Spake's shouting.

"Yes. I'm sorry. I'm late for my very important date with the Bridge, right?"

"No, Canna. Canna, listen to me. The radiation count in your cabin is point forty-two, and rising."

Canna straightened himself, his eyes and brain focusing slowly.

"Canna, are you there, for Christ's sake?"

"I'm here, Spake."

"We have a firework display over the panel here for the whole of lower side, centralized on your level, and through to the B entry-out to the Solarina."

Canna saw the suit, black as coal against the wall.

"I've got a demo suit with me, Spake."

"*Good*, Canna. Get it on in two seconds flat."

"Don't make any bets."

"*Canna*, it's forty-two point zero nine. *Forty-three, Canna.*"

"Why no alarms?" Canna inquired as he shambled over to the survival suit, cracked it open and began to load its myriad pounds onto himself.

"The alarms are out, drained. This com. is working on emergency. Get suited-up, then get as many of the passengers suited as you can. You've got about ten minutes to do it before it goes above fifty in there. Oh, and, Canna, with the power shrinkage, half the autogears are jammed, including those of the Bridge exit and the seven lifts through from topside. That's why you're on your own. That's why we can't unpark this truck. Something's just eating up the Solarine, and we're glued over the bloody sun."

Now he was a black beetle. The casque clacked shut and he hit the suit shields and they came on all around him. Did he fantasize the sudden coolness. His skin felt tender, blistered, but he forgot it.

Beyond his cabin everything was quiet. Innocently, the lower side of *Pilgrim* slumbered or fornicated, unaware that death lay thick as powder on every eye and nostril, every limb and joint and pore. Yet the lights were flickering again, and presently somewhere a dim far-off yelling arose, more anger than fear, the ship's insomniacs, God help them. He wasn't going to be in time. And then he ran at the door and it wouldn't shift.

"Spake," he said, "I'm suited-up, but I can't get the

door open."

But the com. was beginning to crackle. Through the crackle, Spake said to him excitedly: "There's something happening in the Solarina—(yes, I have it on screen, sir)—"

"Spake, will you listen, the door—"

"My God," Spake said, in a hushed, low, reverent voice, "it's a woman, and she's on fire."

Canna stood in his cabin in the black coffin of the survival suit. He visualized Apollonia, her fingers in the pocket of his uniform casuals, the authorization tab, the entry-out of the sun deck softly opening.

He saw her, as the bridge was seeing her, lifting her amber arms, her golden body into the glare of the topaz sun. And the sun was shining through her, and like the bush on the holy mountain she was burning and yet not consumed.

A shock of sound passed through the ship. From the suit it seemed miles of cold space away. And then he felt the wild savage trembling like the spasm of an anguished heart, and the tapes and papers on his desk were smoking. The whole cabin was filling with steel-blue smoke he couldn't smell, like the heat he couldn't feel.

The screaming seemed to come all on one high frozen note, two thousand voices melted into one, as the ship bubbled like toffee in a pan. And then the screaming became in turn one with a long roar of light, a blinding rush of noise, and silence, and the dark.

The third time he opened his eyes, he was in a black box with white stars stitched over it. A few bits of unidentifiable wreckage went by, lazy as butterflies. Vast distances below, *Pilgrim's* charred embers fell into the pinpoint of a sun.

Automatically, Canna stabbed on the stabilizers in the suit which had saved his life, anchoring himself firmly to a point of nothing in space. The suit could withstand almost anything, and had just proved as much. It had liquid food and water sufficient for several day-periods, air for longer; it could probably even sing him songs. He had only to wait and keep sane. Everytime a ship died, a red signal lit up on every scan board from Earth to Andromeda. Someone would come. He only had to wait.

If he could have got to any of his flock, he'd have had company. They had suits on the Bridge, of course, but they'd had the jammed doors too. And Bridge was right over the meton reactor. Even a suit couldn't take that on.

He drifted about the anchor point using up any foul words he could think of, like candles. He started to hurt. As all survivors did, he stared at the stars and wondered about God. He thought about the pretty girl in the salon who had asked if there was any danger, and he cried. He thought about Apollonia Hartley, and then the pain came, and he started to scream.

When the search ship found him two day-periods later, his voice was a hoarse wire splinter from screaming, and he spat blood from his torn throat.

(Tape running.)
—Thank you, Officer Canna. I think we are all in the picture. I should now like to analyze this vision. Or would you prefer a short recess?
—No, sir. I'd like to get this finished.
—Very well. Whatever you wish. Officer Canna, I hope you'll forgive me when I say, once again, that this story is preposterous. Having heard your account firsthand, I fear I must go further. You've somehow managed to turn a naval tragedy into an exercise in masculine ego. This tale of yours, the man who tells the woman she's beautiful, at which she magically

makes herself beautiful for him. Can it really be that you credit—and expect us to credit—the notion that the sexual awareness you brought to this pathetic, rather unbalanced girl, triggered in her an unconscious response so enormous that she attempted to make herself beautiful by absorbing and eventually fusing with a solar body, becoming a fireball which consumed S.S.G. *Pilgrim?*

—I don't know, sir. I only know what I saw and what I heard.

—But what *did* you see and hear, Officer Canna? You saw an ugly girl, who for some perverse reason attracted you, who then prettied herself for you, tanning quickly, as do all travelers on the Solarine Galleons, dyeing her hair, using a slimming machine. A girl who eventually offered herself to you. Coincidentally, there was a shield failure which the computer of *Pilgrim* failed to localize. The computer may already have been affected by the loss of power from the Solarine system, hence its inability to identify the source of the trouble. A vicious circle ensues. The shield break degenerates the Solarine bank, the bank is unable to supply sufficient power to stem the break. On the other hand, assuming your bizarre hypothesis to be true, the computer should surely have traced the source. Do you agree, Officer Canna?

—A computer can't think on its own. You have to feed the right questions. Bridge was asking the computer to check for a specific *leakage*, in or out.

—Very well. I don't think we'll split any more hairs on that, Officer Canna. My comments on this phenomenon are amply recorded. The other phenomena you describe are due to the experience itself, but seen in the retrospect of your guilt.

—Excuse me, I don't like what happened, but I don't feel guilty. There was no way I could guess.

When I did, there was nothing I could do.

— Perhaps not, but you were wasting precious hours with a female passenger when you might have been able to help your ship.

— I didn't know that at the time.

— Lastly, the woman on fire in the Solarina, by which garbled fragment you seem to set great store. With the radiation level where it was, and so near the outer surface of the ship as the sun deck, spontaneous combustion of tissue was not only possible but predictable. Er — Mr. Liles? Yes, please speak.

— As the witness's counsel, Mr. Hofman, I would respectfully draw your attention to the note appended to Leon Canna's written statement.

— This one? To do with the radiation burns Officer Canna received? But I would have thought such burns inevitable. After all, the exposure —

— The rad level in the cabin before Leon Canna suited-up was insufficient to cause burns of this magnitude.

— Well, I see. But what —

— Excuse me, Mr. Hofman. Leon, are you sure you want to go through with this?

— I'm sure.

— Mr. Hofman, I'm setting up here a view screen, and on the screen I'm going to present to this investigation two shots of Officer Canna, taken before he underwent treatment and tissue regeneration. Lights, please. Thank you. Shot one.

(A faint growl of men unaccustomed to seeing raw human flesh.)

— Mr. Liles, is this strictly —

— Yes, Mr. Hofman, sir. And I'd ask you to look carefully, here and here.

— Yes, Mr. Liles, thank you.

— This is the frontal shot of Leon Canna's body.

The second shot is of the hind torso and limbs.

(Silence. Loud exclamations. Silence.)

—I think you will take my point, gentlemen, that what might be a curious abstract in the first shot becomes a rather terrifying certainty when compounded by the second.

(Silence.)

—Mr. Liles—Officer Canna—gentlemen. I think—we must have a recess after all. Someone please stop that blasted tape.

(Tape stopped.)

Appendix: Two photographs.

1st Shot: A naked man about thirty-six years of age and of athletic, well-proportioned build, badly burned by a class-8 radiation strike across the lower face, chest, arms, palms of the hands, pelvis, genitals, and upper legs.

2nd Shot: The same man, also nude; hind view. Burns of similar type, but small in area and fragmentally scattered across the shoulders and buttocks. Across the middle to upper region of the back, definitely marked as if with branding irons, the exact outline of two female arms and hands, tightly and compulsively pressed into the skin.

Beachcomber

by MIKE RESNICK

Arlo didn't look much like a man. (Not all robots do, you know.) The problem was that he didn't act all that much like a robot.

The fact of the matter is that one day, right in the middle of work, he decided to pack it in. Just got up, walked out the door, and kept on going. A few people must have seen him; it's pretty hard to hide nine hundred pounds of moving parts. But evidently nobody knew it was Arlo. After all, he hadn't left his desk since the day they'd activated him twelve years ago.

So the Company got in touch with me, which is a euphemistic way of saying that they woke me in the middle of the night, gave me three minutes to get dressed, and rushed me to the office. I can't really say that I blame them: when you need a scapegoat, the Chief of Security is a pretty handy guy to have around.

Anyway, it was panic time. It seems that no robot ever ran away before. And Arlo wasn't just any robot: he was a twelve-milion-dollar item, with just about every feature a machine could have short of white-walled tires. And I wasn't even so certain about the tires; he sure dropped out of sight fast enough.

So, after groveling a little and making all kinds of optimistic promises to the Board, I started doing a little checking up on Arlo. I went to his designer, and his department head, and even spoke to some of his coworkers, both human and robot.

And it turned out that what Arlo did was sell tickets. That didn't sound like twelve-million dollars' worth of robot to me, but I was soon shown the error of my ways. Arlo was a travel agent supreme. He booked tours of the Solar System, got his people into and out of luxury hotels on Ganymede and Titan and the Moon, scheduled their weight and their time to the nearest gram and the nearest second.

It still didn't sound all that impressive. Computers were doing stuff like that long before robots ever crawled out of the pages of pulp magazines and into our lives.

"True," said his department head. "But Arlo was a robot with a difference. He booked more tours and arranged more complicated logistical scheduling than any other ten robots put together."

"More complex thinking gear?" I asked.

"Well, that too," was the answer. "But we did a little something else with Arlo that had never been done before."

"And what was that?"

"We programmed him for enthusiasm."

"That's something special?" I asked.

"Absolutely. When Arlo spoke about the beauties of Callisto, or the fantastic light refraction images on Venus, he did so with a conviction that was so intense as to be almost tangible. Even his voice reflected his enthusiasm. He was one of those rare robots who was capable of modular inflection, rather than the dull mechanistic monotone so many of them possess. He literally loved those desolate worlds, and his record will show that his attitude was infectious."

I thought about that for a minute. "So you're telling me that you've created a robot whose entire motivation has been to send people out to sample all these worlds, and he's been crated up in an office twenty-four hours a day since the second you plugged him in."

"That's correct."

"Did it ever occur to you that maybe he wanted to see some of these sights himself?"

"It's entirely possible that he did, but leaving his post would be contrary to his orders."

"Yeah," I said. "Well, sometimes a little enthusiasm can go a long way."

He denied it vigorously, and I spent just enough time in his office to mollify him. Then I left and got down to work. I checked every outgoing space flight, and had some of the Company's field reps hit the more luxurious vacation spas. He wasn't there.

So I tried a little closer to home: Monte Carlo, New Vegas, Alpine City. No luck. I even tried a couple of local theaters that specialized in Tri-Fi travelogs.

You know where I finally found him?

Stuck in the sand at Coney Island. I guess he'd been walking along the beach at night and the tide had come in and he just sank in, all nine hundred pounds of him. Some kids had painted some obscene graffiti on his back, and there he stood, surrounded by empty beer cans and broken glass and a few dead fish. I looked at him for a minute, then shook my head and walked over.

"I knew you'd find me sooner or later," he said, and even though I knew what to expect, I still did a double-take at the sound of that horribly unhappy voice coming from this enormous mass of gears and gadgetry.

"Well, you've got to admit that it's not too hard to spot a robot on a condemned beach," I said.

"I suppose I have to go back now," said Arlo.

"That's right," I said.

"At least I've felt the sand beneath my feet," said Arlo.

"Arlo, you don't have any feet," I said. "And if you did, you couldn't feel sand. Besides, it's just silicon and crushed limestone and . . ."

"It's sand and it's beautiful!" snapped Arlo.

"All right, have it your way: it's beautiful." I knelt down next to him and began digging the sand away.

"Look at the sunrise," he said in a wistful voice. "It's glorious."

I looked. A sunrise is a sunrise. Big deal.

"It's enough to bring tears of joy to your eyes," said Arlo.

"You don't have eyes," I said, working at the sand. "You've got prismatic photo cells that transmit an image to your control center. And you can't cry, either. If I were you, I'd be more worried about rusting."

"A pastel wonderland," he said, turning what passed for his head and looking up and down the deserted beach, past the rotted food stands and the broken piers. "Glorious!"

It kind of makes you wonder about robots, I'll tell you. Anyway, I finally pried him loose and ordered him to follow me.

"Please," he said in that damned voice of his. "Couldn't I have one last minute before you lock me up in my office?"

I stared at him, trying to make up my mind.

"One last look. Please?"

I shrugged, gave him about thirty seconds, and then took him in tow.

"You know what's going to happen to you, don't you?" I said as we rode back to the office.

"Yes," he said. "They're going to put in a stronger duty directive, aren't they?"

I nodded. "At the very least."

"My memory banks!" he exclaimed, and again I jumped at the sound of a human voice coming from an

46

animated gearbox. "They won't take this experience away from me, will they?"

"I don't know, Arlo," I said.

"They can't!" he wailed. "To see such beauty, and then have it expunged—erased!"

"Well, they may want to make sure you don't go AWOL again," I said, wondering what kind of crazy junkheap could find anything beautiful on a garbage-laden strip of dirt.

"Can you intercede for me if I promise never to leave again?"

Any robot that can disobey one directive can disobey others, like not roughing up human beings, and Arlo was a pretty powerful piece of machinery, so I put on my most fatherly smile and said: "Sure I will, Arlo. You can count on it."

So I returned him to the Company, and they upped his sense of duty and took away his enthusiasm and gave him a case of agoraphobia and wiped his memory banks clean, and now he sits in his office and speaks to customers without inflection, and sells a few less tickets than he used to.

And every couple of months or so I wander over to the beach and walk along it and try to see what it was that made Arlo sacrifice his personality and his security and damned near everything else, just to get a glimpse of all this.

And I see a sunset just like any other sunset, and a stretch of dirty sand with glass and tin cans and seaweed and rocks on it, and I breathe in polluted air, and sometimes I get rained on; and I think of that damned robot in that plush office with that cushy job and every need catered to, and I decide that I'd trade places with him in two seconds flat.

I saw Arlo just the other day—I had some business on his floor—and it was almost kind of sad. He looked just like any other robot, spoke in a grating monotone, acted exactly like an animated computer. He wasn't much before, but whatever he had been, he gave it all away just to look at the sky once or twice. Dumb trade.

Well, robots never did make much sense to me, anyway.

Emily Dickinson—Saved from Drowning

by BARRY MALZBERG

a.

Emily Dickinson sits poised in her bedroom on the second floor of the building at 280 Main Street, Amherst, in the state of Massachusetts, and considers her latest poem. She has finished it just this afternoon. The year is 1862. She is a widely published poet, a frequent contributor to *The Atlantic Monthly, Scribner's,* and *Harper's Magazine* and her first book, published last year, has sold well with excellent reviews, but she still has a feeling of insufficiency in regard to her work.

Probably—she thinks—it has to do with the long years of struggle when she worked in anonymity. She has never deserted a sense of failure, even though her work has improved enormously and, of course, recognition has come in its wake.

The war is going badly. That is the innerspring for her newest poem; the war is going badly for the Union. It was her intention to contribute as best as she could to the staggering northern cause with a frail bit of verse. Emily despises the Confederacy. She despises the institution of slavery. She despises for that matter the institution of war to which the nation has been committed, but she knows that it could have been no other way. Harper's Ferry must carry through, slavery must be abolished. At the center of the war gutters the flame of old John Brown's abolitionism—part madness—and yet even the mad can speak true.

Emily decides that she will send her new poem to the *Globe*. The newspaper has been asking her for some verse. It has elements of the journalistic, and poetry must be used to sway the people the right way in the contemporary struggle or what be the use of poetry at all? Emily Dickinson thinks. It would be an arcane and dreary art that did not work for difference.

b.

For all who know the Chain
Or the Oppressor's Might
The Struggle must seem Constant—
Life Itself a Night—

But that small Flame of Freedom
In fire's Forging Well
Will soon Ignite the Nation
And teach the Slave to Kill

c.

It is 1848. Kansas is bleeding but Fillmore cannot attend. Industrialism and the fragmentation of the culture lie decades in the future, but Emerson, her neighbor, is already delivering thunderbolts to theocracy. Emily Dickinson, unaware of this, regards herself in a mirror, looking at her red hair, her dark, intense eyes, the arresting tilt of her cheekbones which strike her more and more as being dramatic.

She will be leaving for studies at Mount Holyoke in a few hours. Her second year strikes her as being dangerous and exciting and on this September morning she feels close, in imminence, to that sense of intention which has haunted her off-center for years. I am different, she thinks; there is something very special about me. This explosion of pride makes her blush; she sees in the dumb mirror the imprint of shame on her cheekbones and yet she will not allow shame, pride's sister, to drive from her that knowledge. I will be a poet, she thinks; I *am* a poet and will use the medium of verse to inflame and inspire. I will tell the truth, she thinks; I will give them the truth.

Poetry beats within her like a bird: she feels those hot, dark flutters moving under the resistant surfaces of the skin. Soon I will write, she thinks, a sense of mission stealing upon her. First, however, I must perceive myself, this room, the world, the steeples, all the angles of life which conjoin as if by a carpenter's hand in my angle of sight. Fully, richly, darkly. There will be freedom, she thinks.

Blood fills her cheeks, scalps her heart, and she feels an instant of giddiness subsumed in darker intention which leaves her drained yet full.

d.

Four years after the death of Emily Dickinson in 1886, her surviving brother, William Austin Dickinson, becomes interested in the writings and reputation of Sigmund Freud, a German medical practitioner whose insights into the function of the mind in physical disease fascinate him. Austin is by this time several degrees insane; a ruinous marriage and the deaths of his parents and younger sister within a span of half a decade have stripped his mind. His letter to Freud, composed during a spell of lucidity is, however, a precise and well-structured document. He gives his background as member of a distinguished New England family, explains his acquaintanceship with Freud through mutual friends in the medical profession, discusses how some of his writing fell into a layman's hands. He then outlines the interesting career of his late sister who was, of course, one of America's most popular versifiers, her reputation several years after her death still very high.

"My question, respected doctor," Austin concludes, "is to know whether or not my sister's career was *pathological in nature,* that is to say whether or not her poetry was an outcome of the *extreme isolation* of her later years and whether perhaps if she had lived a more social and fulfilled existence. And also, concommitantly and if this were true would it have been better for the world if she were *happier* and the poetry *not existing* or does only the work itself matter?"

Austin posts the letter hoping for a reply. Weeks and weeks glide by, however, and eventually he forgets about his inquiry. By that time his own incapacity is fully advanced and he dies unhappily half a decade later, not only his letter but his younger sister already forgotten. Emily Dickinson's poetry at this time has already begun to slide from popular favor. Oncoming technology and the more brutal social partitioning of the twentieth century will relegate her to the position of minor, sentimental effusionist, not atypical of her time.

When Freud is murdered in Vienna, his files are sealed. Years later his heirs go through them. Austin Dickinson's letter is there, alphabetically filed. Freud had made no mark upon it. It is not understood why he did not reply. His reaction is a mystery. There is some doubt as to whether or not it was read, although Freud was very thorough about correspondence, in the main.

* * *

e.

After the initial rejections, after the bewildered or hostile editorial reactions to her first stumbling efforts to master the poetic faculty, Emily Dickinson resolves to assimilate technique and to compose in the tenor of her times. First publication in 1858 in the *Globe* leads to larger opportunities. She begins to appear in the national magazines. The distraction of the war, its terrible onset and equivocal conclusion, strips her (she comes to understand later) of the huge earlier success which might have been hers but delay is not denial. By 1880 she is recognized as the American successor to the richly honored, if unfortunately deceased, Elizabeth Barrett Browning. Emily Dickinson embarks upon a series of lecture tours which take her through the eastern part of the nation. Her platform manner, alternately confidential and declamatory, is thrilling. Through her travels, Emily Dickinson meets many other famous people including the highly successful Samuel Langhorne Clemens with whom she has a brief, unsatisfying affair.

f.

The year is 1873. Emily Dickinson is forty-three years old and successful. She receives in the post a long communication from the demented rustic Walt Whitman of whose poetry she has had little previous knowledge. Whitman writes of bitter landscapes in an unwholesome manner and is rumored to possess unusual sexual appetites. She has little respect for poets of this sort, whose work rather than an attempt to uplift is—she has always felt—an attempt to degrade.

"You have wrecked your promise," Whitman writes, after a brief salutation. "You have become a symbol of the wreckage of America. We could have transcended circumstance in this country," he writes in a childish and uncontrolled scrawl, "this country might have been the first in the history of all civilization to have subsumed its madness: the dreams of the preachers, curses of the slaves, bowels of the Republic, whine of machinery, the great and terrible engines of desire stroking and stroking us all, finally fused in a terrible purpose which would have made our condition refractive of mankind but *you*, Emilia, Dickinson, *you*—"

You what? He cannot even espy her first name correctly and yet this oaf presumes to assault her very being. Horrified she reads on. "You with your trite and sentimental verse, your deliberate flattening of all that which moves in the embittered blood and sunken organs of this disastrous America, you express only that which is cheapest and therefore the most vile in our spirit and I hold you to blame, Emilia Dickinson, because of all the popular poets you were the one who had talent, who might have done better. You could—"

She could *nothing*. She will read no further. She refuses to have anything more to do with this. Her hands shaking, she destroys the Whitman letter and hurls its remnants in the wastebasket of her sumptuous bedroom.

Whitman disgusts her. She cannot imagine why people read him. His opinions are nefarious and vile. Here in Amherst even she, a gentlewoman, knows the real name for men such as he, but she will not speak it. She will not write that name. She will consider this no further.

g.

At the special commission of President Ulysses S.

Grant, Emily Dickinson composes a poem for the Centennial. She is known as the unofficial poet laureate of America and in that ambiguous function has, during the Grant administration, written many poems for special occasions, but this one summons forth her most special powers and the height of intention.

Sometimes she is overwhelmed by her little gift; the force which it can possess. But she is humble in its power. She knows that she is merely a vessel.

h.

From force of all divining
There came a driving dream
Of justice hope and Brotherhood
How splendid it did seem!

Begun in Boston's harbor
Moved Eastward from the shore
Overtook the South and then the West
As the dream came to the Fore!

Until in all its colors
A Century today
The Dream no longer but a dream
But a great Reality!

i.

It is 1864. It is a year of vast events; the South has begun to fall. Amherst itself seems shaken by the war. In the night, Emily Dickinson awakens screaming from a nightmare that President Lincoln has been shot. In the dream he has been shot in the temple and carried to a room; now he lies drooling like an infant in the bed, the bones of his great head smashed, the blood moving unclotted from the ruined circumference of his face.

She finds herself gasping in terror from the force of the dream. It seems to explode the trap of her head, moving upward in the air, bolting her upward from the pillow and she sits in the darkness of her room, shaking. This is unlike her. This is not like her at all. She has always been unaffected by extrinsic political or social events, but now this war has assaulted her and her sense of isolation collapsed. Daguerreotypes of the President glimpsed in newspapers have apparently given her a great unconscious apprehension of him. In the dream he is dying. The after-impression, the vivid aspect of the rushing blood and caved-in skull, persists. Emily Dickinson sits stunned in the New England night. Hours pass. Further hours pass. Still she remembers. This cannot be, she thinks. I cannot save him. He lives yet. It is all a dream. She wills herself back to sleep. The President lives. She sleeps.

Awakening at noon she has only the dullest recollection of the dream. It has fallen from her like a discarded robe. Days later she recollects nothing.

j.

In the course of her last years as traveler and celebrity, Emily Dickinson has affairs with men of great circumstance and small; men of the bar and of medicine, men of political heft and bearing. The collision with Samuel Clemens on a tangled evening in Chicago in 1893 proves, however, to be the most memorable. Clemens entraps her with words, staggers her with his need. She finds it difficult to forget him. She does forget him, however. She will not commit herself to any one man, believing that the essential conjoinment of the poet must be to the Muse. She was a virgin until twenty-seven when she did it with Judge Otis Lord, eighteen years her senior, on a stable floor. At the time she had been in love with Lord, with the Lord as she called him, but that was romantic nonsense. She became far more sensible in later years.

Still, in his way, Clemens reached her.

k.

In the last year of her life, 1908, Emily Dickinson regularly has dreams of violated Presidents. She dreams once more of Lincoln and of McKinley shot on the stand, his earnest features contorted by grief. She also dreams of another, unknown President, younger than the other two, a President with an unrecognizable face who is slain in a gleaming, highly powered horseless carriage in the South. The dreams fill her with remorse. They are of no inspirational content and depict the most morbid frame of mind. She attributes it to her advanced age, seventy-eight by his time, and depressed state of ill health. She does not confide the dreams. She is a rich, eccentric poetess, once laureate, who lives in isolation in a mansion in New Jersey with servants who are well paid to care for her and make her last years comfortable as she dies slowly of Bright's disease. Her kidneys have been slowly failing her for years; she is resigned to her condition.

"*I* did it," she says to her companions in her high, intense voice. "I did it, don't you understand, I did it, I did it. Whitman was right," but they do not know who Whitman is or was, and they plump the pillow beneath her graying head and calm her to sleep with pats and hugs and winks. "But I *did* do it," she cries. They turn off the lights.

It is this moment (and not an instant earlier) that Emily Dickinson comprehends that it is not easy for a poet to be taken seriously in America.

l.

"We do nothing," Samuel Clemens says to her as he takes her in his arms in Chicago in 1893. His visage seems to dissolve aginst him. "Oh, what will Lavinia think?" Emily Dickinson says. She refers to Samuel Clemens' wife, of course, although it is an object of ironic interest to both of them that Emily Dickinson has an older sister of the same name. "What would she think if she knew?"

"She will know nothing," Samuel Clemens says. "And if she did she would not think, she would only react. There is no thought in this country; there is only reflex. Reflex like pigs straining toward or against the trough depending upon its contents." Clemens, despite his reputation as a humorist, has a brooding view of human nature. He takes her in his arms and makes violent love against her. Thunder in the room. She falls upon the floor. Clemens pursues her. She rises to meet him; he falls in descent, they collapse against one another. All America seems to move hugely through their passage. Later she thinks she may write a poem about this but she cannot find the language.

m.

In her last moments, sisters, nieces, nephews, group around her. Emily Dickinson has a moment of clarity. It occurs to her that she has at last an answer for the demon, Whitman. "Bring me pen and paper," she says. Margaret, her niece, rushes to obey. "I will tell him we made nothing," she says. "I will tell him that we changed nothing, we had no effect, bad, good, dense, patterned, trite or of grace, *the world must remake itself,*" but before Margaret can return Emily Dickinson has lost speech, then reason, then breath, then sight and distance and is borne at last to a place where she sits with the faceless President of one dream and the known Presidents of the others, all of them perfectly reconstructed, and there they discuss much throughout eternity and then again they may talk for a much reduced period of time but of this duration nothing is known.

n.

He fumbles with your Soul
Like players on the Keys—
Before they drop full music on—
Then-stuns-you-by-degrees

No, Emily Dickinson says. No. She crumples the page. The year is 1856. She disposes of it. It is time to make something of my life, she thinks. I must write in the tenor of the time.

Firmly, her hair a firmament, redheaded Emily Dickinson takes a fresh sheet of paper and reconstructs the universe.

The King Is Dead! Long Live—

by JAYGE CARR

It was my own bloody fault, really, I got into trouble. I hadn't paid enough attention to the orientation lecture droned out by the chief steward the night before we landed. After all, I'd been to America before, right after the Commonality was formed, and it couldn't have changed that much in ten years or so, chassies or no chassies, could it?

I found out the hard way, it bloody well could.

I wanted to watch them unload my solo. All right, so I'm a bit half cracked about that bird. I've reason to be. It's a Taiwan Phoenix, special ordered, and I went to the factory myself and bird-dogged every bloody step of the assembly. All this guffo about the inscrutable Oriental. Piffle! They're bloody well scrutable when you cross their yellow palms with plenty of yellower gold. Bloody marvelous workers, too, a real pleasure to watch. They put my Phoenix together with the precision of a computer, and I've kept it running smooth as cream since.

Fact is, my Phoenix is the reason I took this slow boat crossing instead of hopping a 'Cord. And if they as much as scratched its gleaming chrome hide, I was going to sue.

Heart in mouth, I watched that thousand-plus kilos of careful engineering swaying slowly down at the end of what looked like the merest thread. But down it came, slow but sure, and the unloading crew laughed good-naturedly at my nervous hovering.

A good-looking bunch, that crew, young and lithe and sparkling with good health, moving like the carelessly arrogant animals so many Americans seem to be these days—yet as much a precision tool as my sweet-running Phoenix. They were all sun-bronzed, skin in all shades from gold to ebony moving smoothly over svelte muscle, and their shoulder-length hair was in natural colors (I'd heard that was the latest American fad) glowing in the sunshine.

My own hair was in a soft teal-blue shade, chosen after much soul-searching and consultation, for a proper contrast to soft robin's egg skin dye and brilliant apple-green contacts. But seeing those richly colored, shining manes caressing bare shoulders, I was tempted to let my own grow out a bit and go natural. But I decided not. Only the young can carry off that sort of effect properly, and though no one can deny I'm a bloody fine specimen for my age, still, I'll never be a carefree twenty-five again.

When you pass thirty, it's best to opt for polished elegance and a careful program of exercise to keep up the old muscle tone.

With everything piled up on that wharf the way it was, it was pretty tight quarters. I can't deny I might have bumped into one of them first—I don't know whose fault it was, it probably didn't matter, anyway. But we both laughed and moved apart, as much as we could, in that narrow space.

I think I laughed the second time it happened, too.

But it really wasn't necessary to crowd and jostle like a packed underground, was it?

Then one of them blocked my way completely, a short, slender type with golden skin begging to be touched, supple body packed into skin-tight jeans.

"You look awful familiar, you a holo star or

somethin'?" the voice was liquid gold, as though the shining hair had somehow been distilled into sound.

"Just a common, garden-variety working citizen," I smiled, not displeased by the compliment. "To be exact, I'm here to see about some new products for an import-export firm."

My business was shrugged off. "You from—where?"

"England—but it's all part of the Commonality, now."

The docker looked me up and down, a bold aggressive stare that stripped my clothing off to assess the body underneath. I stiffened. I'd heard about the New Americans, about the many changes caused by the chassies, illegal in England, but I hadn't believed a tenth of what I'd heard. Now—I believed.

"If you'll get out of my way," I said, through tight lips, "I'd like to take my bird through your Customs."

"Don't worry, we can take care'f't for you. Lee!"

"Yo!" from a tall, painfully thin brunette.

"Run the bird through the red tape, eh, kid."

"Can do." Before I could protest, Lee had swung into the seat of my Phoenix and engaged the hover. But not before giving me the same up and down look as the blonde.

"Lee knows the ropes," the blonde confided. "You'd take forever wranglin' with those Customs clydies. This way, see, you got lots more time to spend in li'l ol' New York, heh, English."

Though the docks were almost deserted, except for this young crew, I suddenly felt surrounded.

Piffle! A menace—this good-looking crop of youngsters?

Then the blonde took a single step toward me, a movement so sensual, so loaded with sexual overtones that I involuntarily—to my deep disgust—took a step backward.

It wasn't what *I* was used to; it bloody well wasn't!

"My name's Jojo," the golden voice deepened and throbbed. "And I like older types, special when they're as smarsh as you, dollface." I couldn't believe it. Just as though I'd gone to a singles bar to announce my availability, I was being picked up! "So let's us meet Lee when your bird's all through the red tape, and the gang and I'll show you what our town's got to offer cuties like you, dollface."

Well, *really!*

"I have an appointment," I said. Not that I mightn't have enjoyed a date, with *one* of them, but— I hadn't been frightened of a so-called member of the opposite sex since I was fourteen and just learning how opposite the opposite sex was; but now suddenly, with just those few words spoken, I was frightened. It was the way they moved, the knowing grins, the unconscious air of natural superiority, the easy confidence—

The blonde's eyes narrowed. "Hey, now, English, you aren't—blue, are you?"

"Bloody well not!" I exploded before I thought. Maybe if I'd said I was, they'd have left me alone. But something about the tone the word "blue" had been uttered in told me I'd been in far worse trouble if I'd said yes.

"Well—ll, then," the sensual, seductive air was back, "nothing so important it can't be put off a bit, eh, English? We'll give you the short tour, if you're in that much of a hurry."

"No, thank you. I'm sorry, but—"

"But I'm sure," the golden voice positively purred, "that after the—ahhhh—short tour, you'll want more. . . ."

I'm ashamed to admit it, but my nerve snapped. The nearness of that half-naked young body, the stories I'd heard . . . "Let me by, if you please!"

"Oh, listen, so polite," the blonde crooned. "So—oo polite. Let's hear you say please again in that funny accent, English."

I looked around. It was late afternoon, the sun sinking into the pollution, no one near but my dozen tormentors.

"*If* you please!"

"Lo—ove that sound. Say please again, English."

"No. Now—*let me by.*"

"Really smarsh, rea-eally smarsho, right kids?" A chorus of assents. "Too late for appointments now, English, way too late. It's comin' evenin', and evenin's time to howl, right, kids? Right, English? And you're gonna howl, English. You're gonna howl!"

I did what I should have done sooner. I smashed a fist into Jojo's bare, golden solar plexus, right above the tight jeans, kicked backward and heard an anguished yell, swung on the black next to Jojo, pushed, swung—and *ran.*

Somebody managed to trip me.

After that, it was all confusion, until somebody landed a hard fist under my chin, and I saw hideously bright flashes, and then nothing. Nothing at all.

I awoke to dimness and stink, surrounded by shadowy crates and blades and at least a dozen of those New Americans.

Not a doubt what they intended, either.

A bloody orgy, with yours truly laid out for the bloody *pièce de résistance.*

I was flat on my back, naked as a jay, and pinned down good and proper by warm weights of bodies on my wrists and ankles.

Bloody *damn!*

There was just enough light to see by; they were laughing and passing around bottles, and there was a sweetish smell that meant not all the lit cigarettes were tobacco.

I tried to cautiously slide an arm or a leg free.

Jojo loomed over me, swaying slightly. "You are 'bout—'bout to have 'sperens of your life, Eng—Engilsh." Hiccup. "Be a nice smarshy li'l bu'ercup, an' we might even letchew have clothes back."

I stopped trying to be cautious. I wanted to land one—just one!—right in the middle of Jojo's dentifrice-ad grin.

My futile struggles caused no little amusement.

"Um-um, nice," the black had one eye swollen half-shut. "Nice, nice. Me second, huh, Jojo, huh?"

"LET ME GO!" Hands on me, all over, crawling, *knowing* hands.

"Louder, Eng-Engilsh."

"HE—ELP!!!"

"Nobody gonna come, this time-a night. Save your yellin' for when you *need* to yell, Engilsh."

I never felt so bloody *helpless* in my life.

Jojo knelt over me and slowly slid down the tight, tight jeans.

"I'll kill you for this you bloody ass-holes," I snarled.

"Temper, temper," punctuated with a drunken giggle. "I thought you Eng—Enk—ish were posed to be calm an'—an' collect-lected."

I cursed and heaved, not at all calmly and collectedly.

"This gonna hurt you more'n me, Enkilsh." Another giggle. "Sorry 'bout that!" I *almost* got a knee free. "But not much!"

And then there was light.

"All right, gangos," an amplified voice rumbled through the sudden brilliance. "That's enough of that for tonight."

Jojo twisted around with an animal growl and I saw my rescuers. Correction. Rescuer. One. On a lit hover, smiling thinly down. Some kind of uniform—a bobby.

But only the one.

"Vivyan Penderrick, I presume," said the bobby.

It was a bloody miracle. One second I was surrounded, smothered by a dozen bloody young devils, and the next—butter wouldn't melt in their mouths. Innocent lambs, the lot of them. Just a bunch of high-spirited—*kids*.

"Get away from me," I growled, utterly furious. At myself, for getting into such a bloody stupid sticky wicket. At those fucking kids. Even at the bobby, for finding me in such an awkward, embarrassing—

"OK, gangos, let's let our friend from across the water up," commanded the bobby, swinging the hover lower, until it was almost within our cozy circle. One hand went out, palm up. "Clothes," the bobby snapped and to my surprise they were slapped into the outstretched hand. "With our apologies," the bobby smiled. "I'm sure you'll make allowances for youthful exuberance. . . ."

"Bloody likely." The weights had rolled away, and I scrambled awkwardly to my feet, almost literally growling myself. "Bloody flaming likely!" I snatched my clothes, yanking them on any which way. I caught Jojo's eyes, smiled grimly. *You'll get yours!* that smile promised.

"If you wish to make a complaint," the bobby said, eyes fixed somewhere over my head, "I have a holo of this entire scene, plus ident recordings of all present. But if your complaint comes to trail, that holo will have to be shown in open court."

I ground my teeth. Bloody! A few years in Wormwood Scrubs, or whatever the American equivalent was, would teach these bloody young animals a well needed lesson.

It would almost be worth it.

Almost. If the news services picked it up, I'd never live it down.

Never.

"Awwwww," Jojo showed white teeth in a sheepish grin and stuck out a grimy paw. "No hard feelin's, Enklish. We din't mean no harm."

"Yeah, we was only kiddin'," seconded the black.

"We wouldn't've hurt ya none," added a third.

Bloody flaming *liars!*

But I wasn't hurt—thanks to the bobby. And they might even get off with a suspended sentence. I'd heard that in American courts, despite the pendulum swing to strict punishment, juveniles still got off lightly. And these were, after all, merely kids.

Of course, a kid with a blob of plastic explosive can take out a fair chunk of territory, and a kid with a gun can kill as efficiently as any adult.

Kids!

But *I'd* be bloody well ruined.

I had connections, even in America. There were other methods of revenge besides the Scrubs. I could wait.

I was still shaking—fury and reaction, actually—when the bobby escorted me to my hotel room and waved the bellboy away.

"You'll feel better for a good night's sleep." And the bobby turned to go.

"No, wait." I was confused and emotionally battered and oddly—or not so oddly—reluctant to be left alone. "I—I need some information. Can you spare me a few minutes?"

The bobby hesitated, then nodded. "Sure. If it'll make you feel any better."

I felt a lot better with a mug of beer. (Ugh! Warm beer, the bobby grimaced.) I leisurely examined my rescuer, lounging around my suite, innocently curious at how the other (i.e., richer) half lived.

The view alone was worth the price. Looking down together at the lights of New York, I suddenly realized what was so strangely familiar about the bobby. The gangos. Add ten years to any one of them, maturity strengthening that healthy self-confidence, leaven with an air of authority, and top with a generous seasoning of good looks, charm, and ye olde animal magnetism—ummm, yes. Bobby—*yum!*

Whether it was reaction, gratitude, or what, the old libido was definitely stirring.

Mature wine has the subtlest savor.

"I haven't thanked you properly," I said. "And I don't even know your name."

"All in the line of duty"—a broad grin—"and I like the way you say bobby."

"I liked the way you took care of that gang of young toughs. You snapped your fingers and they toed the line."

The grin widened. "Progress deserves the credit. When all you have to handle a mob like that is a gun and a nightstick, it's not so easy. But the new stuff—I'm loaded for crowd control. If one of them had made a wrong move, I'd've zapped the lot of them, and they all knew it. And while you may or may not have filed a complaint, and there may or may not be a trial—sometime—and they may or may not have gotten a sentence, nobody—nobody!—argues with a crowd spray. It's here and it's now and it's—'bloody' "—somehow I didn't mind the mimicry—"unpleasant. Which is why I don't like to use it unless I have to."

"I wish you had."

"Sprays don't discriminate. Did you really want to spend the next twelve hours heaving your guts out?"

"When you put it that way . . ." The libido was

definitely stirring. "Care for a beer," I offered. "There should be ice here. Or something stronger if you prefer."

"Not on duty. Thanks anyway."

"Coffee, then. Or—tea?"

"Coffee, then, please. Black." A shrug. "We practically live on the stuff."

"I imagine." There was a coffeemaker set up on the small serving bar; I adjusted it as strong as it would go and turned it on. "I'll wager gangs like those keep you pretty much hopping. You know, I was here a few years ago, and I can't get over the changes. They say England and America are a lot alike and march pretty much together, but—I suppose chassies are the root of the differences now. They were just being introduced when I was here before, strictly for the rich only, and now, I understand, they're pretty much universal."

"Just about," Bobby nodded. "You don't have them at all in England, do you? Didn't your Parliament pass a law . . ."

My turn to nod. "Chassies are classed as a drug. Strictly forbidden."

"And that's that, eh?"

"Well—"

"You can't stop progress."

"You call those bloody, rotten little animals progress!"

"In the first place, Penderrick"—I must have touched a raw spot; Bobby was slit-eyed angry—"chassies didn't cause 'animals' like that. We had kid gangs long before we had chassies."

"Kid gangs like *them?*"

"In spirit, if nothing else. Look, Penderrick"—a long forefinger thrust into my midriff—"chassies are an effect, not a cause. Liberation, power movements have been going on for decades. Racial, sexual, religious nondiscrimination. Chassies have just taken the element of force, of fear, out of some personal relationships."

"Not bloody likely. They were forcing *me*, and I was bloody afraid, let me tell you!"

"You had the right to be. You could have gotten badly hurt. They were pretty mad at you, and anger and fear hormones set the chassies off. But it's only pain, you know, no permanent damage at all; it's only nerve stimulation."

"I've heard that when a chassie bites, it feels like being dipped in molten metal."

"It's all subjective."

"All sensations are if you want to be technical about it. Under the circumstances, I'm bloody glad you happened along."

"I didn't just 'happen' along. Those pretty green eyes of yours made quite an impression on the First Officer." I couldn't help smiling smugly. The impression had been quite mutual, and I seriously doubted that it was my *eyes* the First Officer so fondly remembered. . . . "Anyway, when that shiny toy you bragged about so much came through Customs without you . . ." Cinnamon-colored eyes twinkled at me over the coffee mug. "There were six of us looking for you; I was just the lucky one."

"No, I was the lucky one. I can't say I liked my introduction to your American progress."

"I'll say it again, Penderrick. The chassies are an effect, not a cause. All right, the pendulum has swung a little the wrong way, but it never quite balances, ever, does it? We've hundreds of years of repression, slavery whether it had the name or not, of force and threat always lurking to make up for. Can you blame us if, now and then, someone overreacts to their new freedom à little?"

"Look here now! Are you blaming *me* for what my ancestors may have done? Let me tell you, here and now, that I've never—"

"What, never? No, never! What, *never*? Well—hardly ever!"

My hand clenched into fists and I consciously relaxed them. "All right, Bobby, let's get personal *You've* never abused the power of that uniform you wear? Nor the power of those weapons so close to hand? Your psychological advantages of—"

"All right, Penderrick, you've made your point. But, don't you see, you made mine, too. Wherever there is power, there will be, sometimes, abuse of that power. Historically, power is spreading to more and more of the mass of the people. Chassies are just helping that spread." A thoughtful pause. "Thanks for the coffee, Penderrick. And now, I've duties to attend to."

My libido positively screamed. "I think I still need protection, Bobby."

"Penderrick," Bobby started—and then got the message. I got the same up-and-down look I'd gotten from the gangos. But this time I didn't resent it, probably because I was returning it—with interest. "I'm off duty in another half hour, Penderrick."

"Protect me until you're off duty, Bobby. And afterward, that offer of cold beer—or anything else you might want—still holds."

Suspicious. "Not out of gratitude, Penderrick?"

"Not bloody likely! What do you take me for? Haven't you looked in a mirror lately, Bobby my pet? And—my name is Vivyan."

Bobby flicked a glance into the entry mirror, smoothed down a lock of hair that looked—I thought—nice enough where it was. "I like the funny way you say Bobby. And they wouldn't use you to scare babies with, either—Vivyan."

I couldn't help grinning. "Nicer when it's mutual, eh, Bobby pet."

"No fear, no force, no threat, no mention of pay for favors—just good old chemistry, between a man and a woman. You'll see, Vivyan, what you've been missing. It's a whole—a whole new—you'll see!"

Things went along swimmingly after that. Bobby went off duty and called in to report same, accepted an American martini. We had supper for two sent up to my suite. . . .

I remembered that bloody flaming chassie just in the bloody nick and I do mean nick!

"Bobby!"

"Mmmmmmhm?"

"That chassie. Have you turned it off? I mean—" I suddenly realized I wouldn't know, one way or the other. Maybe it was *already* off.

"Viv dear, I *can't* turn it off. That's the whole point of the chassie, that it *always* protects me. Why, if I could turn if off, I could be made to turn it off, gun or knife or even hands at my throat. This way—"

"Get the flaming hell away from me, you bloody—you think I want to fry my—Go on, get away, dammit!" I shoved and, I'm not ashamed to say, not gently, either. I'd *heard* about what those chassies did!

Instead she sat up laughing, which did unmentionable things to her gorgeous bod, and my insides twisted just watching her. "Viv, you poor dear, you don't know, you really don't know. Viv, they aren't *chastity* belts, not really. They—"

"It may not be a chastity belt for you, Bobby girl, but *I'm* not going to—" What else had we men talked about on the trip over, besides the good-looking dishes aboard, but the American chastity belts? What they did to the unlucky male. No permanent physical damage, but all damage isn't physical, no, sir! Pavlov's dog and all that. I'd had too much pleasure in the past to want it ruined in the future. Thank you, but no thank you! No thank you!!

She was laughing so hard she could barely talk. Moving away from her was one of the hardest things I ever did in my life, but I did it. I was halfway off the bed when she caught my wrist and held it. "Viv, listen. Nobody'd use something that prevents them from ever— The chastity belt only prevents me from being *forced*. If I *want* it . . ."

I knelt awkwardly on the edge of the bed, my wrist still imprisoned by her hand. "That doesn't make sense. If I held a gun on you, you'd want it all right, eh, Bobby girl. So how can your fool chassie protect you?"

"The chassie monitors my hormones. I might say I'd do what your gun ordered, but inside I'd be angry or frightened or both. And the chassie'd *know*. And so would you, when the time came." She lay back, smiled. I groaned. A Lucullan feast tantalizing a starving man! "I can't shut the chassie off, Viv dear. But—my body can. When the hormones are right. When I'm—enthusiastic—enough." She pouted, the kind of pout begging to be kissed away. The hand round my wrist moved to stroke other pieces of skin, and rockets went off inside. "I'm all upset, now, Viv," she teased—oh, that mouth! "But I'm sure we could both be enthusiastic—together—"

I never could resist a challenge.

And—she was right. Mutual enthusiasm—and I made bloody sure she was flaming enthusiastic, let me tell you!—added a—a—a whole new—dimension.

I stood, smoking a languid cigarette and watching the sun come up over the Manhattan skyline, and tried to balance what Bobby and I had had, with what had almost happened to me on the docks. If those girls had managed to rape me—and I was a normal male; there was a point past which I couldn't have controlled myself—then their chassies would have fried me. Only subjectively, as Bobby claimed, but even subjective frying didn't sound too pleasant. I wasn't sure it was worth what Bobby and I had had, superior as it was. After all, I had gotten plenty of pleasure from the old-fashioned method, hadn't I?

But—you can't hold back progress.

And Bobby said—and I thought she was probably right—the chassies were an effect, not a cause.

England and the United States had always marched together, but now they were out of step because of the chassies. But—which was right?

A rustling noise made me turn. Bobby rolled over, and our eyes met—there was plenty of enthusiasm left in both of us.

And I knew, as I went back to her, that my decision was made, too.

Whether chassies were good or evil or, as I suspected, a mixture of both, I was going to complete the arrangements I had come to America to make: to smuggle chassies into England and the Commonality. I had the doctors all lined up, all I needed were the chassies themselves. You can't prevent people from getting what they want with mere legislation. The English girls wanted chassies, just like their American cousins. And she who wants will pay, and I enjoyed living in the manner to which I had become accustomed.

And after all, we men had had our own way for a long time, a long, long time, and maybe it was only fair to give the women their day.

Besides—if I didn't, somebody else would.

Hart's Hope

by ORSON SCOTT CARD

Orem was in Banningside when King Palicrovol came. It was high summer, and so Orem was not needed on his father's farm. As the seventh son, Orem's future was well marked. He might become a cleric or a soldier, but farmer he would not be. His father's farm was small enough that only the oldest three sons, already married men, could have each of them a parcel. There was no secret made of it: from the time Orem was small he knew he would not inherit. And because as a young child he had been pious, praying many times without being bidden, he was bound over to the cleric during high summer and all winter long, in hopes that he might become educated and holy and perhaps become a priest of God in his own right.

"But you'll never be a priest, will you?" sighed Halfpriest Dobbick on the day King Palicrovol came. "Your father, your mother, they come to holidays, they keep the five prayers and the two songs, but at heart they're still superstitious. They still make offerings to the Sweet Sisters, don't they?"

Orem shrugged. Of course they did. But then, what farmer would be fool enough to forget the Sweet Sisters? And what housewife would neglect the hunger of the household goms and leave herself open to spilled soup and lost children? God's single eye was little help about the house.

"You even know some spells, don't you?" Dobbick said.

"Some," Orem said. "But they never work."

"Well, it isn't your superstition I worry about, anyway. It's your cynicism. I've seen you yawn at prayers."

"They're always the same."

"Not to believers."

Orem had heard it before. When Halfpriest Dobbick stopped his lessons and his stories and began with his attempts at stirring up a lively fear of God in Orem's soul, Orem could only endure patiently. He had learned over the years that silence brought punishment and argument brought interminable discussion, while quiet compliance made poor Dobbick frustrated to the point of despair.

"Orem, you're my brightest student. How does it look, when the brightest student in all Banningside isn't a God's man?"

"I'm a God's man," Orem answered. But his voice was infervent, and he looked out the window, down from the monastery walls to the street below. There was a stir, a hurry about the people passing back and forth, and it wasn't even a market day. And then trumpets in the distance, getting closer. Was King Palicrovol coming early, then? Orem had to see him, for it was tragic King Palicrovol who searched all Burland for brave men who could stand with courage against Queen Beauty's terrible magic.

Orem did not know whether it was Palicrovol himself who intrigued him, or the fact that Palicrovol was a hero on God's errand, fighting the Queen, who, it was said, had more power than all the wizards in the world.

"You seem drawn to the window."

Downplay it, Orem told himself, or the priest will close the shutters. "Oh, just the preparations for the King's coming. Caught my eye."

"And your heart. God's single eye can see you deep, Orem. You have studied everything here, and yet you refuse steadfastly to take the slightest vow. Why, with a simple vow you could be introduced to the Tales of Water and the Tales of Wind, to the Burden of Amasab and the Obligation of Many Fingers."

Outside the window, the gate of the town's stockade was opening—yes, the King was coming, for outside the gate were soldiers ahorse and soldiers afoot, shining with steel breastplates and helmets. It was a dazzling sight, but soldiers held little glamour for Orem; it was the magic that drew his dreams and it was King Palicrovol, who battled daily with the Queen, that he had to see.

"But what is God to you, is that it? You want to serve the King. Do you want to be a soldier?"

"No," Orem said.

"If not a soldier, then what? The King's battle—it's hopeless."

Orem was surprised. "The King fights for God! How can you call him hopeless?"

"The King may fight for God, but does God fight for the King?" Halfpriest Dobbick was smirking a bit, Orem noticed—no doubt feeling triumphant because at last he had drawn Orem's eyes from the street below. Well, smirk away, but tell me this riddle, Orem thought. "Tell me," he said, "why God would not fight for the King."

"King Palicrovol—have they told you the tale of how he won his crown?"

Orem shook his head.

"I should think not. Not a tale for children. But you're, what, fifteen, disgustingly skinny for the age but old enough, no doubt. I've seen you watching the waterwoman's teats when she bends to serve. Old enough."

Orem blushed a little. He had thought no one could see.

"King Palicrovol was not born to be King. He was born to be Count of Traffing; but King Nasilee, he wasn't much of a King. No, he was a hated man, and served God but little and overtaxed and undergoverned, and all in all it was a good thing, a God-blessed thing, when Palicrovol took to the field and won the kingdom of Burland from old Nasilee. Bloody, but he had the trust of the twicepriests in the Great Temple of Hart's Hope."

"Well, then," Orem said, his eyes being drawn to the street again, for the trumpets were now close to the gate and the crowds had come out to line the streets and shout for the King.

"Well then," said Dobbick, "it was right enough except that no man can be King in Hart's Hope until he beds the King's daughter. And King Nasilee was still young. His daughter was only eleven. Only eleven. And her name—she was called Asineth."

Orem was startled. One did not speak the Queen's old name except in whispers, for it was said the Queen could see every corner of Burland with her Searching Eye.

"Yes, Asineth. And only eleven. But Palicrovol felt he must take the crown then, at any cost, or he wouldn't rule well. And so he had her stripped before the whole city, and there on the steps of the Hall of Faces in Hart's Hope he made her his wife, willing or not. And then, when all had witnessed that her inner blood had come out on him, he cast her aside, had her taken and put away in some hidden place. If he had been wise, he would have killed her—his general, Zymas, advised him so. But he was merciful and let her live. And in the fisher's cottage in East Cuts, she was found by the great Wizard Sleeve, who taught her all he knew. She opened the forbidden books. She learned the hated powers. And she overthrew Sleeve and enslaved him, and then came armed with only her hatred and her vile magic and drove Palicrovol out of Hart's Hope and ruled in his place. He fled alone, he did, and she told him then that she would give him the mercy he gave her and let him live to see the kingdom ruled by another."

It was a story Orem had never heard before, but it rang true in his mind. Yes, it was hate and ravishment and usurpation and forbidden powers—the tale drew him, and he turned to see King Palicrovol coming through the gate of Banningside. King Palicrovol, tall on a high saddle on a tall gray horse and on his head the gilded antler crown of Burland. He looked every inch a king. He turned his head not at all, just stared straight ahead as the crowd cheered and threw roses at him.

He came closer, and Orem winced as the sun shone brightly, reflected off King Palicrovol's eyes.

"His eyes," said Orem, and he looked again. No, not his eyes. For where his eyes should have been there were two gold balls, shining in sunlight, so that the King could not possibly have seen anything.

"The King is blind," Orem said, in awe.

"No," Dobbick said behind him. "His eyes are as good as yours, underneath those golden blinds."

"But why does he wear them?"

"He chooses not to see. I've heard it said that the Queen has power over him. When she chooses she can see out of his eyes, see all that he sees. So he covers his eyes to blind her, as well."

"Blind her! But she has the Searching Eye!"

Dobbick seized him by the shoulder, turned him. "Aye, boy, the Searching Eye, and a good deal more than that. But if you had ever learned anything of

God, you'd know that her Searching Eye can't penetrate a temple or a monastery or the seventh circle of the Seven Circles of God. So why do you think King Palicrovol doesn't surround himself with priests to keep her sight out? Because he's black, too, at heart. Because he's the kind of man who'd rape a child on the steps of Faces Hall in order to steal the crown that it was her only gift to give. God has no part of him, Orem. And God will have no part of you, if you keep being drawn to magic like this—"

But now it was Dobbick who stopped the conversation and turned to look out the window. For the crowd had fallen silent outside, and when Dobbick looked he saw that King Palicrovol had stopped, had taken the antler crown from his head, and now held it before him.

Orem leaned out the window, too, and watched as the King turned his blind eyes from one side to the other, as if he could see to search. "No!" cried a strange, moaning voice, and it took a moment for Orem to realize that it was the King. "Oh, Hart's Hope, not here, not through my eyes!" And then the King looked up, and the golden balls seemed to fix on Orem's face, and the King pointed at Orem's heart and cried, "Mine! Mine! Mine!"

Soldiers leaped out of line, and suddenly Orem felt himself being jerked back into the monastery. It was Dobbick, and the halfpriest moaned, "Oh, God, oh, God, oh, seven times seven the dark days that come from incaution. Oh, God, Orem, he wants you, he wants to have you—"

Orem was confused, but made no resistance as Dobbick dragged him up and down stairs, through doors usually locked, and finally into a trapdoor leading along a hidden path. "The monastery is old, from the dark days before God had His victory over all the strangers and all the powers. This path comes out near the river, well outside the stockade. Go home. Go to your father's farm and bid good-bye to your family, and then get away. Far away. To the sea. To the mountains. But where the King can't find you."

"What does it mean!" Orem demanded.

"Mean? It means the King has some use for you in his battle. And you can trust this—it will be to your cost. Everything has a cost, but a man like Palicrovol hasn't lived his two black centuries by paying his costs himself. In the games of power, there are only two players, and all the rest are pawns. Oh, Orem—" and the halfpriest hugged the boy at the gate of the monastery. "Orem, if you had only stepped within the seven circles, just a step. God knows I hate to let you go."

"What's happening to me?" Orem asked, frightened as much by Dobbick's sudden expression of love and regret as by what had happened with the King.

"I don't know," Dobbick answered. "But whatever it is, you don't want it."

But I do want it, Orem thought. More than anything I want to make a name for myself, and find a place, and earn a poem. And now, when I verge on finding something—

"You're fifteen, you're only a child." And then Dobbick took Orem's face in his hand and drew the seven circles on him with his finger. "Ah, yes. I was not wrong. You're no tool of Palicrovol's war, Orem. You're God's tool."

Orem shook his head. "I'm not a—"

"Oh, we all are tools, we are, every one of us. You don't want to be a servant of God, do you? Well, serve yourself, Orem, and I think you will end up serving God anyway."

And then it was God-be-with-you and gone, the

gate closing behind him and Orem tramping down a short run of what looked like sewer but wasn't, and then a struggle to clamber out of the end of the pipe, where it was fouled and tangled with silt and shrubbery. He heard the halfpriest call to him down the pipe: "Orem! Anywhere but Hart's Hope!"

Anywhere but Hart's Hope? Oh, no, Orem answered silently. *Only* Hart's Hope for me. He was glad to answer his own fear by fleeing King Palicrovol now. But whatever the King's pointing finger might have meant, it did mean this: Orem had a poem in him, and he meant to earn it out; and if Hart's Hope was where God's man thought he must not go, then Orem knew that it was Hart's Hope that called him.

He followed the halfpriest's instructions except for that, however; Dobbick was no fool, and Orem meant to leave nothing to chance. He went home and bade good-bye to his mother and father, who were sad enough to see him go, but not much surprised by it. "You're so young," his mother said as she packed him some meat and bread and cheese in his shirt, and dipped water from their own spring into his field flask, and kissed him seven times. She did not say anything about love because she had never thought much about love and never heard it mentioned except a few times before her marriage when her husband had spoken of it.

Orem did not feel any pain at separation when he left the cottage and trod the field for the last time. He had spend too many days away from the farm already to miss it much—it was only a place where he labored for his brothers' bread, not his own. One of his brothers—it was too far away to see which one— waved at Orem. Orem waved back, jauntily, feeling very much his own man as he walked west to the River Banning.

Perhaps, he thought with pleasure, perhaps King Palicrovol is still searching for me back in Banningside. Then he remembered the golden eyes that stared at him and felt a chill. But it soon passed. It was still only afternoon of that very day, and already he felt the poem growing.

Near sunset a grocer bound downriver took him aboard his raft.

"How far are you going?" Orem asked cheerfully. The grocer only eyed him skeptically for a moment, then turned to study the current, using the long pole of the raft to keep the rough barge in the center of the current. Orem was a basically cheerful person; he did not know that the river customs did not admit questions, and so he marveled that such an unfriendly man would have taken him aboard at all.

Night came quickly from behind the eastern trees, and when the last light was going, the grocer slowly poled the raft nearer the shore, though not closer than a hundred yards from the bank. Then he took the three heavy anchor stones from the rear of the raft and dropped them overboard. The current soon drew them from the stones until the three lines were taut.

Orem watched silently as the grocer crawled into the tent and pulled out a large clay pan. In it the grocer built a fire of sticks and coal and placed on it a brass bowl, where he made a carrot-and-onion soup with river water. Orem was not sure whether he would be invited to share and felt uneasy about asking. So he opened his bundle and took out two lumps of salt beef.

"Want to turn a soup into a stew?" he asked, more timidly than the last time he had spoken.

The grocer looked him in the eye and nodded.

They ate together in silence, spearing the lumps of

carrot and meat with their knives and taking turns drinking the broth from the brass bowl when it had cooled enough. The meal over, the grocer rinsed the bowl in the river, then dipped his hand to bring water to his mouth.

"I have water from my father's spring," Orem offered, holding out his flask.

The grocer looked at him sternly. "Then you must save it," he said, the first words he had spoken to Orem.

"What for?" Orem asked. "Isn't there water where we're going?"

"When you get to the Little Temple, you must pour in the water from your home and take out God's Water."

"To drink?"

"To pour into your father's spring. What, is God forgotten on your father's farm?"

Orem flushed. It was doubtless something Dobbick would have taught him if he had allowed it. "We pray the five prayers and the two songs."

The grocer nodded. "All right, then. But save the water. It can save your life."

They sat in silence as the wind came up, brightening the coals in the clay fire dish. So we're going all the way to Hart's Hope, Orem thought. It was the likely place for a grocer to be headed, and it was the only place outside Orem's own neighborhood that he had ever wanted to go. And this grocer had been there before, plain enough. "I'm going to Hart's Hope," Orem said.

"Good thing," said the grocer.

"Why?" asked Orem.

"Because that's the way the river runs."

"What's it like there? In Hart's Hope?"

"That depends, don't it?" the grocer answered.

"On what?"

"On which gate you go through."

Orem was puzzled. He knew gates—the market at Banningside had a stockade, and there was the castle, of course. "But don't the gates all lead to the same city?"

The grocer shrugged, then chuckled. "They do and they don't. Now, I wonder which gate you'll go through."

"The one that's closest, I expect."

The grocer laughed aloud. "I expect not, boy. No, indeed. There's gates and *gates*, don't you see? The South Gate, now, that's the Queen's own gate, and only the parades and the army and ambassadors uses that gate. And then there's God's Gate, but if you go through there, you get only a pilgrim's pass, and if they catches you out of Between Temples, they brands your nose with an *O* and throws you out, and you never get in again."

"I'm not a pilgrim. Which gate do *you* use?"

"I'm a grocer. Swine Gate, up Butcher's Road. I get a grocer's pass, but it's all I want. It lets me go to the Great Market and the Little Market, to Bloody Town and the taverns. Aye, the taverns, and that's worth the trip alone."

"There's taverns in Banningside," Orem said.

"But they doesn't have Whore Street, does they?" The grocer grinned. "No, there's no place else in the world has Whore Street. For two coppers there's ladies'll do you leaning up against the wall; they ups their skirts and in three minutes you fill them to the eyes. And if you've got five coppers there's ladies'll take you into the rooms and you have fifteen minutes, time to do twice if you're lively, which I am." The grocer winked. "You're a virgin, aren't you, boy?"

Orem looked away. His mother and father never talked that way, and his brothers were swine. Yet this grocer seemed well-meaning. "I won't be for long," Orem said, "once I'm in Hart's Hope."

The grocer laughed aloud, and darted a hand under Orem's long shirt to tweak his thigh perilously near his crotch. "That's the balls, boy! That's the balls!" And the grocer began regaling him with tales of his sexual exploits on Whore Street. Apparently Orem had passed some kind of test; and they were friends until the grocer yawned abruptly and as suddenly stood up, stripped off all his clothing, and bundled it into a pillow and pushed it ahead of him as he crawled into the tent.

Orem caught a glimpse of the inside as the grocer crawled through, and there wasn't room for him. The grocer took no further notice of him, so Orem curled up out on the deck, nestled against the leeward side of the grocer's load. It was chilly, but not too bad.

In the morning, the silence reigned again, but this time Orem began silently to help, bringing the grocer water to drink now and then, and sharing his own small bread for nooning. The grocer seemed more agreeable, and that night they cast the anchors over the side together. And after supper, the grocer again got merrier and merrier, though he touched no beer, and he told Orem more and more about Hart's Hope.

"There's Asses Gate, but you're no merchant. And Back Gate is only for them as lives in High Farms, which you don't and never could, those families being older than the Queen's own tribe, and near as magical, they says. No, boy, for you there's only Piss Gate and the Hole. For Piss Gate you get a three days' pauper's pass, and if you don't find work in those three days, you have to leave again, or they cuts off your ears. Second time they catches you on an old pass, they gives you a choice. Sell you as a slave or cut off your balls, and there isn't as many free eunuchs as there is horny slaves,

I can tell you!"

Three days. That wasn't much of a chance to find work.

"What about the Hole?"

The grocer suddenly got quiet. "The Hole, now. That's closed, and there isn't passes. Not from the Guard. But there's ways through the Hole, and ways to get around in the city from there, but I don't know them. No, I'm a God's man, I am, and the ways through the Hole are all magical, them as isn't criminal. No, take your chances with Piss Gate and the three days' pass, and when you don't find work, go home. No good comes from the Hole. It's magical black and God hates it."

Magical. Well, there it is, thought Orem. They say Queen Beauty's a witch, and magic flies in Hart's Hope, even though the priests do their best to put it down and the laws are all against it. Maybe I'll see magic, thought Orem, though he knew that God wouldn't truck with wizards, and there were seven foreign devils to take your soul if you did the purchased spells. The clean spells of the farm, that was different, though truth to tell they never seemed to work on Orem's father's farm. The Hole was magical. Maybe Orem needed to enter Hart's Hope through the Hole, to find the city he wanted to see.

"I don't like the look of your face," the grocer said. "You're not thinking witchy thoughts, are you?"

Orem shook his head. "I'm on my way to find a place for myself and make a name. And earn my poem, if I can."

The grocer relaxed. "There's poems to be had in Hart's Hope. I met a man there whose poem was long as his arm—I mean it true, he had it needled right in-to his skin, and a fine poem it was." Suddenly the grocer was shy. "I have a poem, given me by three singers in High Bans. It's no Hart's Hope poem, but it's mine."

Suddenly the mood of the night became solemn. Orem knelt on the hard logs of the raft, and reached out his hands. "Will you tell me your poem?"

"I'm not much for singing," said the grocer. But he put his left hand in Orem's hands, and his right hand on Orem's head.

He sang:

> *Glasin Grocer, wanders widely,*
> *Rides the river, drifting down,*
> *Turns to north, town of Corth,*
> *Feeds the frightened Holy Hound.*

"You," said Orem, in awe.

Glasin Grocer nodded shyly. "Here on my shoulder," he said, baring himself so Orem could see the scars. "I was lucky. It was the Hound's first day, and he took little enough before he went back to the Kennel."

"Weren't you afraid?"

"Peed my pants," Glasin said, chuckling. Orem laughed a little, too. But he thought of how it must be, the huge black Hound coming out of the wood without a sound, and fixing you with his eyes that froze you to your place. And then to kneel and pray as the Hound came and fixed his teeth in you, and took as much flesh as he wanted, and you hadn't the power to run or the breath to scream.

"I'm a God's man," Glasin Grocer said. "I didn't scream, and the pain was taken from me, it was. They carried me to the city and the singers gave me my song. Best crop ever, that year."

"I heard about that year. They said the Hound took an angel."

Glasin laughed and slapped his thigh. "An angel! I never!" Whenever Glasin laughed, his breath took the odor of his rotting teeth in foul gusts to Orem's nose, and Orem would have turned away but for the failure of respect. And Glasin was worth it now—only one bite from the Holy Hound, and a good crop, too. "You were the Corthy price," Orem said, shaking his head.

Glasin punched Orem in the shoulder. "An angel. They don't."

"Oh, they do," said Orem, and Glasin sang his song again. He sang it many times on the way down the river, the two weeks as Banning turned into Burring, and they passed the great castles of Runs, Gronskeep, Holy Bend, Sturks, and Pry. There were times, in fact, that Orem wished devoutly that he and Glasin had not become friends, for the silence was preferable to the endless repetitions of the same tales. Glasin had had a small enough life, after all, to be contained in only a few nights' talk, and Orem had to force himself not to say, "But your whole song is because by chance the Holy Hound found you, and you were clean. Being clean is just a list of the things you've never done." An empty sort of life, after all; and Orem thought, I will have a poem so long and fine that I will never have to sing it myself, but others will sing it to me because they know the words by heart.

And then one morning Glasin began to talk even as he poled the raft back out into the current. "These woods is the Ainn Woods, and there, up there, you see that low hill, that's Ainn Point, and the creek just beyond." Other rafts and even boats had begun crowding the river the past week—Orem saw and heard the same excitement rising on the other rivercraft. "Clake Bay!" cried a woman. And then they rounded a bend and there was Hart's Hope itself, a high stone wall bright with banners, and below it the docks of Farmer's Port, and rising high behind it the great walls of King's Town—no, *Queen's* Town—and the gaunt Old Castle highest of all. Glasin named all the places until he nearly missed his turning and only made one of the last slips of Farmer's Port.

They tied to a post at the slip, and Orem was all for jumping ashore, but Glasin glared at him and ordered him to stay. They waited, and soon several men in gaudy clothes came to eye them and their raft.

"A weaky ship," said one.

Glasin turned away from that man and faced another. "All oak," he said,

"Bound with spit and catgut?" the man retorted.

"Good only for lumber," said a third. "And three days' drying to boot. A cart in trade."

"Cart and twenty coppers," said another.

Glasin snorted and turned his back.

"Cart and donkey," said the man who had called the ship *weaky*.

Glasin turned around with a smile. "That and two silvers gives you raft *and* tent."

"What do I want with a tent?"

Glasin shrugged.

Another man nodded. The third turned away, shaking his head. The first man, who had the eye of a hawk, staring open always even when the other closed, raised his hands. "God sends thieves downriver in grocers' clothes," he said. "Two silvers, a donkey and cart, and you keeps the tent."

Glasin glanced at the other bidder, but he was through.

Hawkeye looked at Orem. "Boy for sale?" he asked.

For sale? Orem was appalled—how could anyone take him for a slave? He had no ring in his nose, had he? But there was the man asking, and the grocer not saying no, but standing, thinking.

"I'm a freeman," Orem said hotly, but Hawkeye made no sign of having heard, just kept watching Glasin. Glasin at last shook his head. "I'm a God's man, and this boy is free."

The buyer said nothing more, just tossed two gleaming coins to Glasin, who caught them deftly so they didn't slip down between the logs to get lost in the river. The buyer waved, and four men came up, one leading a sad-looking donkey and cart while the others quickly unloaded the raft and put all that would fit into the cart, piling the rest on the dock.

Orem mounted the dock and stood near the pile of the grocer's goods. Not that the grocer had anything more to do with him. Orem simply did not know where he should go next. The wide space fronting the river was crowded with carts and men and some women, shouting and cursing; other rafts were being unloaded at other slips, and Orem had only been ashore a few moments when the buyer's men had the raft unloaded, including the tent, and already were poling it farther downriver.

"They takes it to Boat Island," the grocer said in his ear. "They trims it into boards and builds sea ships with it. From Boat Island on out to the sea, the big ships comes and goes. Half my profits is from the raft. Now, boy, you stay here and watch my things, don't let any be taken, and when I come back with my stall, you get five coppers. Fair enough?"

Orem nodded, and the grocer immediately took off with his cart loaded high with carrots and onions, peas and apples.

Around him Orem watched the other grocers as they sized each other up and began trades. Most came alone, and so the trip to the markets to get a stall was a risk, for none had a cart to hold more than half their goods, and some had only their backs for porting. They would pick a man they thought they could trust and leave their piles side by side, the one going to pick two stalls and hire them, the other waiting on guard. The system seemed to work well enough, except once, when the grocer left on guard accepted a bag of coin from a buyer and turned his back as four workmen quickly loaded all the goods from both piles into a wagon and took off. It was done in only three minutes or so, and then there was no sign that piles had been there, and another craft was already pulling into the slip, and the grocer who had stolen the other man's goods took off running toward Swine Gate, with the other men at the dock spitting and throwing vegetables at him.

Such a thing would never have happened in Banningside, and it made Orem a little afraid. Hart's Hope was a big place, and the stink of the stockyards and pens and stables was strong, and men did dishonesty right in the open. And why not? There were fifty thousand people in Hart's Hope or near it, or so said the travelers who came to Banningside. A thief could hide among these crowds and who would hope to find him?

Yet the feeling of danger only made Orem more intrigued, more eager to get inside the walls.

It was well past noon when Glasin returned, smiling broadly. "Got a place in the Great Market," he said, "and I don't have to give the pick to anybody." Then Orem understood that the man who waited on guard got to choose which stall he'd get inside; by hiring Orem to do his waiting, Glasin hadn't had to give up the choice. The five coppers were counted into his hand ungrudgingly. Orem guessed that Glasin would have been willing to pay more, if Orem had known enough to bargain. Well, Glasin had given him free passage, and that was worth much, even if he had worked and provided company and shared good beef from his father's farm.

"Piss Gate," the grocer said. "And don't buy anything outside the gate. Don't buy anything from anyone who offers to sell. They'll spot you as a farmer from the first second, and they'll up their price by tens." It was all the wisdom Orem was likely to get, and because the grocer didn't ask, Orem didn't help him load the cart for the second trip into the city. Instead, he plunged into the crowd, and after a dozen dozens of jostles and bumps he came out where the carts and wagons and porters waited in four lines to pass the Guard at Swine Gate.

The Guard wore mail shirts that came well down the thigh, and their weapons were in plain sight and looked brutally efficient, as did the faces of the men who wore them. There were archers on the towers that flanked the gate, and it was plain to Orem that sneaking through was out of the question. There was no place that wasn't watched.

"No use looking, farmer," said a voice behind him.

Orem turned and saw a weaselly-looking man near four inches shorter than he, smiling at him.

"I'm not a farmer," Orem said. It was the truth—he was determined never to farm again.

"Then you'll not get through Swine Gate, will you?" asked Weasel.

"I'm looking for Piss Gate."

The man nodded. "They all are, boy, they all are. Well, when you're done with Piss Gate, you find old Braisy here, and he'll get you through. He'll get you into Hart's Hope for a very small fee of five coppers and a favor, he will." And then Braisy was gone; because he was not tall, he quickly disappeared in the sea of heads moving in every direction on Butcher Street.

It took few enough questions for Orem to find that Shit Street, which ran between the stockyards, would lead him north to Piss Town, and he could find the gate from the towers. Of course he got lost—Shit Street quickly became narrow and kept turning away from the main path of traffic. But he spotted two towers, a sure sign of a gate, and headed for it.

There was no gate. Instead, rambling tall houses lined a narrow street that dead-ended near where the gate should be. There were no soldiers on the towers, and if there was a gate it was permanently shut, for the houses leaned on the stone arch as firmly as they leaned on the stone walls.

A few guards lounged in the narrow street nearest the towers. Otherwise the street was deserted, the window shuttered, the place as empty as market at midnight.

"Ho, boy!" said a guard. "Ho, what do you want here?"

"Trying to pass the Hole in daylight?" asked another.

Orem didn't know what to say; this was obviously not Piss Gate, and he had no business here. From what Glasin had said, Orem didn't expect guards at the Hole.

"I'm looking for Piss Gate," Orem said, and then decided to play farmer after all. "I'm here for the first time. I'm lost."

"Where you from?" asked a guard, as they surrounded him.

"A farm. My father's farm. Upriver, near Banningside."

The guards glanced at each other. "An illegal person is near Banningside," one said to him.

Illegal person—it could only be the King. How should he answer? He knew nothing of the politics of

Hart's Hope, or what could or could not be said.

"I left weeks and weeks ago. I've been working my way downriver."

The guard with white in his hair studied his face. "He's just a country fool," he said. "A spy'd know better than to try the Hole in daylight."

"I say question him," said another guard.

"I say eat shit," said the white-haired guard. "Get on, boy. Follow the north road closest the wall always. It'll take you to Piss Gate. Or better yet, go home. There's nothing in Hart's Hope for you."

Orem nodded, trying to look as stupid as possible, and took off up the road. He stumbled once and tried to pretend to himself that it had been part of his act.

Behind him, a guard was saying, "Why'd you let him off?"

"No need to pick on children," came the answer, and then Orem was lost again in the maze of streets.

The houses in Beggarstown—the settlement outside the west walls—were all wood, crowded together and extending out over the street farther with every story. Between tall houses were shanties; where a gate opened into a courtyard, filth raised the ground level by several feet, and often there was a building snugly fitted inside the courtyard, so that no inch of ground that could hold a house went empty. The farther he got from the Hole, the more crowded the streets, but not with the grocers and butchers of Farmer's Port. These people wore elegant clothes, but all faded and worn; and many were wearing only rags of absurdly fine satins and silks. No one was curious. No one looked at him. There was only a dullness in the eyes, as if something in Beggarstown took the mind out of the head, and they went through their daily chores with out being conscious of them at all. It was an ugly place, and Orem quickened his pace until he fairly ran through the streets, hunting for Piss Gate.

And then there it was, its twin stone towers looming over some of the poorest and nastiest neighborhoods Orem had yet seen. Smaller towers had been set between the stone ones, so that the gate itself was only a few feet wide, and the gates were guarded by a heavy troop, including six men ahorse. As with Swine Gate, there was a line, only this one was a sad one of miserable-looking people, dressed badly, or coarsely from the farm. Like Orem. And while he could not find this group of people attractive, he recognized that this was where he belonged. His people from the farms, though he doubted they were from as far north as Banningside. He took his place at the end of the line, which moved steadily forward. Quickly there were more people behind him. No one spoke; there seemed to be awareness that the line contained no friends. All would be competing for the same jobs, the same chance to get a workingman's pass so they could stay inside Hart's Hope when the three days were up.

As they got close to the gate, the man in front of Orem turned to him and whispered, "First time?"

The man did not look friendly, but at least he had spoken. "Yes," Orem answered.

"Well, take a word. Accept no jobs from the men just inside the gate."

"I want a job," Orem answered.

The man's mouth twisted. "They promise to take you for a year, but in three days they turn you over to the Guard without your permanent pass. How's that? And they don't pay you, either. They just get three days' work out of you for free and turn you out. The real jobs are farther in."

"Where?" Orem asked.

"If I knew, would I be in this line again?"

And they were at the guards. The man in front

96

sullenly answered the questions: Name? Business? Citizenship? Rainer Carpenter, carpenter looking for work, citizen of Cresting. The guard took the man by the chin and turned his face, so he could see his cheek. For the first time Orem noticed the three thin vertical scars on the man's cheek. Two were old and white, but one was still faintly red.

The guard noticed it too. "Still, red, Rainer, dammit, are you blind?"

"Got no mirror," Rainer answered.

"And a carpenter, no less. Sure you are. Get out and come back when the waiting's done."

And now Orem was at the front of the line.

"Name?"

"Orem."

The guard waited, then said impatiently, "Your whole name?"

Orem was puzzled. "That's it. Just Orem."

The guard was amused and looked the boy up and down. "Orem Scanthips," he said, and now Orem could see a clerk just inside the gate writing down the name on a small paper. "Business?"

"Looking for work," Orem said.

"What kind of work?" The guard was getting impatient.

"Any kind, I guess."

"Unskilled," the guard said, and the clerk wrote it. "Citizenship?"

"I'm from a farm near Banningside."

"Banningside." And then, suddenly, another guard inside the gate had him by the arm, and then seized his chin and held it while, with a very sharp knife, he made a quick cut vertically on Orem's right cheek. It bled profusely, staining Orem's tunic, but it hurt very little.

"Mind you," said the guard, "we know from experience when this wound is healed enough that you ought to be back outside. Any guard who sees this scar will have your pass, and if you're overstayed he'll have your ear, too. Understand? Get caught twice, and it's your balls. You have three days. Sundown, clear? And stay off the King's Road. Go on." The clerk stuffed the pass into his hands; another guard was halfway through the same speech with another man whose cheek was also bleeding.

As soon as Orem was five steps inside the gate, there were five or six men around him, shouting about employment, sign your papers, a year's stay for sure, guaranteed, twenty coppers a day starting pay. It sounded good. Orem followed the advice of Rainer, however, and passed them by. They cursed him when he ignored them; the man behind him took the job offer, and Orem wondered if he had been lied to before.

It was a miserable three days. He tried the Markets, first, but all the stalls were filled with grocers who had no power to hire and give workingman's passes. Worse, Glasin refused to recognize Orem—the friendship had ended at the dock.

The taverns had all the staff they needed and didn't like hiring pissers; up Shop Street he was viewed with suspicion, and the shopkeepers shook their heads without speaking when he asked about work. By the third day, discouraged, he followed the advice of many and dodged across King's Road, the only stone-paved road in the city, to see about work in the guilds. A stableman at the arena looked him over and asked if he knew horses. "As well as I know my own self," Orem answered eagerly, but the stableman thought for a moment and looked him over and said, "Sorry, no. Need to start someone younger than you. Can't take 'em over sixteen."

"But I'm only fifteen," Orem said.

"Sure, they all get younger when I tell 'em that," said the stableman, and Orem went away angry because he had been telling the truth. Down in the Exchange the rich men in heavy brocades and furs eyed him suspiciously and wouldn't speak to him, and so the day passed and it neared sundown and the stableman was the best chance he had had. Orem even went back to try again, but a different man was on duty, and he turned Orem away brusquely, saying, "Only the morning man hires, boy, get away, isn't your scar near ripe?"

It was ripe indeed, and a guard stopped him just after he had dodged back across King's Road. For a moment Orem was afraid he was being arrested for having stepped on the road the pissers were forbidden to use, but the guard only checked his pass. "You have an hour," he said. "Better get moving."

Orem got moving, and found a line as long as the one that had led him into the city waiting to take him out. The guards kept this line moving faster, however. It was just a matter of looking at the face, looking at the pass, and checking off the name on the clerk's list as the pass went into the fire.

"Orem Scanthips," said the guard, and Orem was through the gate and back outside. His visit in Hart's Hope was over, and he had neither work nor adventures that even the craziest poet could turn into a poem. The man behind him who had been accepted for work was thrust out of the gate, shouting about how he had been cheated, how he had worked for three days and now they didn't even pay him for that, let alone give him a pass. At least Orem hadn't been cheated; and meals were cheap enough in the pissers' haunts that he still had one copper left. He didn't know that the meals he had eaten should have cost no more than seven stones, and he should have had four coppers three stones left.

And there was Braisy, the weaselly man, plucking at Orem's tunic. "How much do you have left?"

"None of your business," Orem said.

Braisy laughed. "Not so nice now, are you! No, they teach you the language of the city fast in there, don't they? None of your business, is it? Then I take it you're going home to the farm."

Orem shrugged. "Maybe."

"Well, I'll find another customer, then."

"Wait," Orem said.

Braisy waited. "I'm waiting," he said.

"The Hole. I only have one copper left."

Braisy nodded. "Then the price is one copper and a *big* favor."

"What's the favor?"

Braisy smiled. "I won't know till I get you in there, will I? But tell me, boy, what did you see in there that made you want to go back?"

It was a good question, and Orem didn't know. The parts of the city he had seen were dirty enough, dirtier than Banningside, for sure. But there had been the gleaming marble fronts of the houses on King's Road, though he had caught only a glimpse. There had been the rich robes of the Exchangers and the Guildsmen. Yet that wasn't it, for none of that would ever be within his reach. It was something else that he wanted. He wasn't sure what. Maybe just the crowds. That was probably it—there was something pulsing in there, a current running against the ebb and flow of the masses moving every which way yet curiously all together. Under it was a touch of—

"Magic," said Orem. He did not know why the word had come to his lips.

Braisy raised an eyebrow. "Oh, ho. The Hole it is then, boy. Aye, for the Hole, and I know the favor, I do. I know the favor and so will you," and they were off, following the winding street of Beggarstown. In the distance Orem could see the towers of the Hole. But they did not go up the street Orem had seen before. Instead they went into a tavern, a cheap beer tavern that looked filthy and sullen, as did all the customers. Orem headed for the bar, but Braisy pulled him away.

"Don't be an idiot," Braisy said. "This way."

They ducked through a curtain to a back room, where four or five people waited in the shadows. Braisy was known here; he tossed a single copper to a fat woman in a corner, and she motioned him toward a bench. Braisy sat, and so did Orem. "The copper," Braisy said. Orem took the last of his coins from the pocket sewn into the hem of his tunic and gave it to the weaselly man.

Suddenly the middle of the floor sank out of sight. Orem gasped in surprise, then was ashamed as Braisy and several others chuckled at him. All the people in the room lined up and stepped into the trap, where a stairway led down into the darkness. There was no light below—they felt their way and tried to see in the dim light filtering from the room. The walls were stone and there were rats underfoot. One was daring enough to nip Orem's toe where the sandal provided no protection; Orem cried out and Braisy jabbed him in the stomach with his elbow. Suddenly they came to a wall, wooden, this time, blocking the path. "Oh, shit," said Braisy. "The low road this time," and they turned right and went down a steep, uneven ramp. Orem twisted his ankle a little, but it didn't hurt much.

"Quiet now," Braisy whispered as they reached level ground again. "We're going under the street. Right under the guards." Sure enough, there was a sound of marching overhead, and a few passing horses. After a while, however, the sounds faded away, and the path sloped upward, and they were in a room, half underground and half above, with light coming from a single candle.

"Braisy," a woman whispered. "What have you?"

"A darkling boy," he answered softly, "who seeks the Hart."

The woman giggled. "Then come with me."

She led them through a curtained door and up a steep stairway, and then stopped at the top of the stair, though there was no landing. "Strip," she said, and began following her own advice. Orem was surprised, but seeing that Braisy was also shedding his clothing, he did likewise, trying not to look at the woman, whose old breasts sagged down below her navel. Orem had never seen a human female nude before, and he did not like the sight much now.

Their clothes bundled under their arms, they went through the door then, into a room lighted by red lamps, so that it seemed all to be afire. One wall of the room was made of huge stones; Orem realized that it was the wall of the city. Soon enough, though, he had no thought of the walls. A hart lay slain on the floor, its eyes staring and its blood smeared on the stone in a pattern that made little sense to Orem, except that he knew it was not the seven circles of God. The woman suddenly seized him by the thigh and pulled him down to kneel by the hart. "Taste the blood," she whispered fiercely and showed him how, reaching down her finger into the gaping hole in the deer's throat and then sucking it. Orem did likewise and turned to the woman. She looked at him expectantly—something was supposed to happen. Apparently it didn't. Her look turned to one of horror.

"What is the price?" she asked him. "Oh, God, a pilgrim's trap!" And she backed away.

Braisy giggled nervously behind him. "You didn't tell me, boy. Cheater, cheater; God hates all liars." But

Orem did not understand, except that he knew Braisy did not worship God, or the hart's blood would not be on the wall. What did he fail to do? Why were they suddenly afraid of him?

Then a man, not nude, but covered only on his thin shoulders with a deerskin, stepped out of the shadows in a back corner of the room. "No," he said softly, in a voice that seemed adolescent in pitch. "Not a pilgrim, are you? Yet still we see you, when you should have disappeared." And he touched Orem's eye, reached out a finger and set it directly on the boy's eyeball, and Orem did not blink, but just stared at the pinkish black of the man's finger resting on his eye, vaguely aware that the finger burned. Then, suddenly, he saw the whorls of the fingertip, and in them he thought he saw crowds of people, thousands of people screaming, reaching upward to him out of the whorls as if they were a maze, pleading with him to release them.

"I can't," he whispered.

"Oh, but you can," said the adolescent voice, and the finger pulled away from his eye. Now his eye stung bitterly, and he clapped his hand there and rubbed it as the tears flowed to soothe the parched glass of his vision. "Braisy," the man in the deerskin said, "a pilgrim would only stay visible himself, yes? But here you see the hart's lady also naked to the eye. No, indeed, no pilgrim, but more valuable, more valuable. This one's mine. Give Braisy a full purse, lady, a full purse from Galloway Glovehand, but the purse buys silence, complete silence, doesn't it, Braisy? Doesn't it, lady?"

"By my soul," Braisy answered.

But Galloway only laughed and said, "That's foresworn a thousand times over, Braisy. No, by the hart, yes? By the hart." So they swore by the hart, and Braisy left carrying a bag of coins that jingled because he was trembling. Galloway took Orem by the arm, his slim fingers delicate and dry and irresistible, and led him out of the red-lit room by a different way. "What's happening to me?" Orem asked as they both dressed.

"You've been employed," said the wizard.

"For how long?"

"For life, I think," said the wizard. "Yes, for life, I'm sure of it. But don't despair. You'll have the freedom of the city, and the best forged passes that money can buy, with spells on them to blind the best guards, even the God's men. And all you have to do, my boy, is serve me."

"But I only wanted to get into the city."

"And you *are*. Or almost."

"But I don't know if I *want* to work for you."

Galloway only smiled kindly at him before his face disappeared in the mass of his green robe, which fell to reveal a brocade pattern which repeated what seemed to be God's seven circles but was really eight circles, and all broken subtly in odd places. "Why do you think wizards hire at the Hole, boy? I think you've come seeking magic; but in Burland all magic is against the law, punishable by death. The hart was slain to blind the eyes of the priests, who watch always from the Great Temple. But you're already hidden from them, aren't you, boy? And hidden from me, I think. Yes, and even hidden from Queen Beauty's Searching Eye. Oh, you're a good servant, boy. What's your name?"

Orem was reluctant to say it aloud. "Scanthips," he finally said.

"A lie. But your name would give me no power over you, not at a price *I* could ever pay. You have a gift that draws you to magic, yes, and also draws magic to you. A Sink, that's what you are, a Sink, and to think you walked into my own night's hart. Well, that's more than fate. I have the strongest magic on

Wizard's Street, and I shouldn't think you would have come to anyone else, would you? Your clothes are covered with manure from the farm. But I'll get you new clothes, boy. Don't think of betraying me. Your pass will burn up if you try it, and the Guard won't just take your ear, no, boy—they know a magic pass when they see one burning. You won't betray me, and I'll take care of you. That's friendship, isn't it?" And then they reached a place where the only passage was a trap in a ceiling, and they were in an attic that butted against the gate, and when Galloway Glovehand pushed a needle through an invisible opening in the thick wood of the gate, a part of the gate fell open and they slithered through on their bellies.

Two hours later, they emerged from a house on Thieves' Street. Orem was inside the city again, this time to stay, with a wizard holding him by the arm and a terrifying excitement holding his heart in at least as firm and dry a grip.

"What is a Sink? It is a whirlpool in the sea of magic, and spells disappear into a Sink. You're a thief, boy, a thief who steals from thieves. Now listen, and learn from me, and you'll learn the ways to use the gift the Sweet Sisters gave you off in your frozen farm in the north." And day by day Galloway taught Orem Scanthips how to draw the magic to him, how to find it and suck it in where it would disappear.

"What you have swallowed can't be drawn out again," said Galloway. And Orem began to learn how magic tastes and smells, spending his days in the dark high room where Galloway had hidden him, reaching out to see with his closed eyes the way magic cast a glowing smoke that grew brighter and less penetrable the closer Orem came to its source. "Suck it in," he heard Galloway's voice saying, but it was not sucking that Orem did, not at all. It was as though Orem reached out an invisible tongue, just to taste the magic right at its source, to find the cold fire that made all that glowing smoke. And he would taste, and his tongue would burn, and then the cold fire was out and the smoke darkened and disappeared in air.

Orem wondered what was really going on; could only guess that Galloway was using him against other magicians, to undo their magic at its source. Now and then a wizard would find a way to hide the magic, so that Orem's probing tongue tasted only glass or stone. But Orem made the hand signs Galloway had taught him, and sang the songs whose words he did not understand, and the walls and windows dissolved and he put out the fire, its taste all the sharper because of the struggle to reach it.

Orem also found Galloway's walls but knew enough not to try to break them down. Let Galloway think that his servant Scanthips could not undo his magic; and perhaps Orem could not. But he suspected that Galloway was not as clever as he claimed to be. Sometimes Galloway looked at Orem uneasily, as if the boy's uncontrolled power—or rather, uncontrolled negation of power—were a sword with no hilts, just a blade that cut wherever it touched.

"Where did my gift come from? Why am I a Sink?" Orem asked one morning, when Galloway woke him for the day's work.

"Why? I don't know. Sinks are rare enough, and they don't usually live long, not when wizards know where they are. Fools—they usually kill a Sink. But I'm not afraid of power, boy. Besides, you're so easy to kill if you ever get out of line." Galloway patted him affectionately. "Which you'd never do. Let me see the scar." The wizard studied his cheek, where the guard at Piss Gate had cut him. "Fine. Fine, now. Well,

Orem, a day for adventure, I think. How would you like to go outside?"

Orem laughed and sat up, automatically bending over to avoid banging his head against the sloping roof of the attic. "I thought you meant to keep me here forever!"

"You wouldn't have stayed, though, would you?" Galloway asked.

Orem shook his head. "But then, I wouldn't have lived through many tries at escaping, would I?"

"None at all," said Galloway. "I've saved your life, boy. If you lived in this city without what I've taught you, you wouldn't survive your first meeting with a wizard. You would have drawn the power from him, without knowing it—his purchased power—and swallowed it without a price. Now I've made your gifts selective. You only draw in what you want to draw, and from all the rest you're hidden. Remember that—don't ever draw from a wizard you can see, or his eyes will go where his Searching Eye cannot, and he'll nail you to the wall and bleed you like a hart. Do you understand?"

Orem nodded. He knew from the walls he encountered that the other wizards were aware of his power, if not of him. They would be looking for the person who melted their icy flames; Orem had to be sure he seemed to be only Glovehand's shy servant boy.

They went down the stairs together. Orem's legs were weak under him—the attic had not given him room enough to walk, and it had been a month of no more exercise than standing and sitting. He leaned on the banister once, and when he got downstairs his thigh cramped and he lay moaning on the floor until Galloway could massage the cramps out of it.

Galloway's house was large, but mostly empty. Only the attic room, and Galloway's own heavily locked room, where he did his real work, and the main rooms on the ground floor, where customers came, were put to any use.

And Orem began service.

His duties were simple: tea for guests and of course to collect the money from them, since the wizard never touched it in front of customers. And when the customers were gone, the sweeping and cleaning, and bearing all the burdens in the market. And alone in his dark attic room, the searches to find and put out cold fires that burned here and there on Wizard's Street.

"Why doesn't the Temple put a stop to all this?" Orem asked one day, when they came back from market, their purchases in a heavy sack that Orem carried.

"What? Wizard's Street?" And Galloway smiled. "They'd love to, you can be sure. But there's the Queen, you see. Queen Beauty. They have their pilgrims and their revenues, and the guards arrest wizards who are fools enough to do magic Between Temples or in the sight of a priest. Put them to death, too. But the Temple stays silent about the Searching Eye that roams the city from the palace. And when the King's army comes, the priests go deep in the cellars of the temple and hide, while the Queen works her terrors at the city walls."

"Then it's true, that the Queen keeps the King out of the city with witching?"

"Oh, yes, with witching, if you want to call it that." But Galloway's face looked sour. He didn't want to talk about it, that was clear. "The Queen's ways are the Queen's ways, you know."

"Is she very powerful?"

Galloway looked nervous, and plucked at his robe. "Well, you know, if she weren't, do you think the Temple would tolerate her? But it's a fearful price she pays."

"What is it?"

Galloway turned away. "I don't know."

"Come on, now. Of course you do."

And when Galloway turned back, his face was terrible. "I don't know, Scanthips; I don't know and I don't want to know. Is that enough? I hope it's enough, boy, because even a Sink can't pay a price high enough to swallow all the Queen's power, that's so. Not and live. Understand that? Here is a magic you'll never find, that's how strong it is, and if you found it, you'd be wise to lose it again, because if *she* knew about you, boy, I doubt even the Temple's best prayers could save you or even make your death quick."

But Orem was puzzled—if the Queen's magic were that strong, and her Searching Eye roamed all of Hart's Hope and the lands around, why had he never seen *her* bright mist and followed it to the cold fire at its source?

"There's another part to the Queen's balance with the Temple. Just so you understand, Scanthips. And put on the soup, please; there's no reason to stand still when you're listening. The Temple leaves us Wizards alone, so long as we work *here* and so long as we do no great magics."

"Great magics?"

"We can cure warts and other blemishes. We can do love words and vengeances on enemies, and pranks and little spies. We can even keep the hart's blood hot on the city wall and go invisible in the daylight when we have the need. But we do not darken skies or move the hearts of masses in the city. We do not question the Sweet Sisters and we do not shiver the earth. The river's course is beyond our reach and the wind must not be spoken to, and we may not kill the baby in the womb or dry the semen in a man's loins."

Orem was at the pot by the fire, stirring; but his eyes did not leave the wizard's face, for the gaunt man's lips were trembling, and his eyes had glazed. Even speaking of such things had a strange effect on him, and Orem was afraid, yet also drawn to him. The cold fires Orem had tasted so far were not the strongest flavors in the world. There were others, and Orem's tongue slipped in and out between his lips like a snake's, as if searching the air for a taste of the magic Galloway spoke of.

And suddenly Galloway's legs gave way, and he curled on the floor, weeping. Orem dropped the spoon and ran to him, touched him, and the wizard's tight, dry skin was cold. "What is it!" Orem asked.

"We may not—" began the wizard.

"What?" asked Orem

"We are forbidden—"

Orem held the man's arm tightly, as sobs shivered in the thin body.

"We are not permitted to live forever," he cried softly, and he clutched at the boy and held to him, his cold tears soaking into Orem's tunic and, he imagined, freezing into fires on his skin.

After a while the wizard's trembling stopped, and Orem carried him upstairs, discovering for the first time that the wizard weighed little, as if he were just skin stretched taut over desiccated bones. Live forever? It did not occur to Orem that anyone could live forever, except God, and those most blessed who took God's heart as their own and shed their own souls, and so were really dead anyway. But here it was a power denied Galloway, one so real that even speaking of it was enough to weaken him.

Orem could not open the locks to Galloway's room, of course, and so he laid the wizard in the attic bed and watched him for an hour, until there was no more light and Orem himself could not keep his eyes open. He knew that downstairs the soup was getting cold as the fire died untended. But it was not in sleep that Orem closed his eyes; it was in hunger. He had tasted a faint flavor when the wizard spoke, and he wanted to find it again.

At first he found nothing unfamiliar when he went roaming with blind eyes among the glowing mists of small magic. Small magic—it had seemed great enough when Orem first learned to taste it. But now, alerted, he found faint traces of that other flavor, so strong that he could pick it out even at the coldfire heart of the wizard's small spell. Even when the wizard had paid for the spell with a hart's blood, or the blood of a bear spilled living, that flavor of great magic remained, and Orem knew, tremblingly, that it had been there all along; that it was like the blue of the blue sky, which is so common, so all-pervasive that it seems not to be there, but once you notice it you can see nothing else. It is the Queen's magic, Orem realized, the Queen's bright mist, and as he searched for it, it began to gather to him. The flavor was stronger by the moment, and it went to Orem's head. He had never been affected by the fires he had tasted before, for the power had sunk into him immediately, without price. This time, though, the power could not be swallowed all that quickly; it lingered. It touched him. And suddenly it was so strong that he screamed and pulled in his tongue and opened his eyes and the flavor was gone; but before him stood a living hart, which somehow had come into the closed attic room and now regarded him placidly from the space between him and Galloway. Galloway was awake.

"What have you done?" Galloway whispered.

"I don't know," Orem answered.

"O Hart," Galloway said, "who sent you?"

But the hart did not answer. Its eye seemed fixed on Orem, and it raised a gentle cloven hoof and placed it in Orem's open hand. It was warm.

"Have you been searching for the Queen?" Galloway asked fearfully, but Orem hardly noticed him now. All he noticed was the hart's hoof in his hand, and the warmth that slowly crept up the veins in his arms and centered hotly in his chest so that he felt alive as never before.

"What do you want of me?" Orem asked the hart, but without speaking the words aloud.

The hart did not answer in words, either. Instead a vision came abruptly into Orem's mind. He saw Hart's Hope as if he flew in the air, the city teeming with people below him, boats docking and pulling from the shore, the Guard marching here and there along the walls. But as he watched, the city unbuilt itself; its shrank, as if time had come undone and it was a century, two centuries, a dozen centuries in the past. There were no walls; just the huts of fishermen along the shore and behind the shore, forest, unbroken except for one clearing not far from where Wizard's Street would one day run. There in the clearing a farmer worked, pulling the plow his wife guided. It was painful work, and the plot was small. Orem could not see his face.

Suddenly there was a movement at the edge of the clearing; a deer bounded into the furrows, its hoofs plunging deep into the loosened soil. It was frightened, and behind it came four huntsmen with bows and pikes, and dogs that barked madly at the deer. The hart ran to the farmer, who shed the harness of the plow and took the hart's head between his hands for a moment, then let it go. The hart did not move. Nor did it show fear of the farmer, and the hunters stopped in surprise.

The farmer raised his hand, and the deer took a step away from him, toward the forest on the far side of the clearing. As it did, the hunters also moved, the dogs bounding forward a single leap. The farmer lowered his hand and the movements stopped, and all waited for him again.

The farmer turned to the plow. He picked it up, heavy as it was, and laid it upside down in front of the hunters' dogs. Then, behind him, his wife came and took his head in her hands. He knelt, trembling, and placed his throat on the blade of the plow, and drove his neck into it sharply. Blood spurted, and Orem winced with the agony of it, as he watched the wife drive the farmer's head down and down, until the blood gushed and spouted and the blade was almost all the way through the neck.

Then the hunters lowered their bows and did not see as the hart made its escape into the trees. They were watching as their dogs came up and licked the blood leaping from the blade of the plow. The dogs went mad in the aftermath of lapping the blood; they bounded high as if they were dancing and ran from the clearing joyfully, heading in the direction they had come from. The hunters also knelt, marveling, and the wife dipped her finger in the blood and made the sign of seven circles on their faces. The hunters also left.

It was dark, and the moon rose, and the man's body still lay broken over the plow, when the hart returned to the clearing. But not alone. There were a dozen harts and a dozen hinds, and then seven times seven of them, and one by one they came and licked the hair of the dead farmer. When they were through, they came to the farmer's wife, and the hart whose life the farmer had saved led them, and it stretched out its neck to her. There was a knife in her hand, and she cut the hart in the throat as her husband had been cut. The bleeding hart staggered to the man and lay beside him, and their blood mingled on the plow.

Then, as Orem watched, the plow became a raft,

and the head of the man and the head of the stag lolled over the edge, drifting in bright water. The raft flowed against the stream, and suddenly Orem realized that the water flowed from the wounded necks of the two broken animals. Along the banks of the river a million people knelt and drank, each a sip, and left singing.

At last the raft came to rest against a shore, and like waterbags the two bodies seemed empty, and no more water flowed from them. They were mere skins, now. And Orem looked up and saw, standing beside them on the bank, the living hart and the living man, whole again, both naked in moonlight.

And the farmer's face was Orem's face, and the hart was the deer that stood before him in the room.

"What does it mean?" Orem asked silently.

The only answer he got was the face of a woman. It was the most beautiful face Orem had ever seen, a kind and loving face, a face that cried out like a tragic virgin starved for a man's life within her; Orem did not know her, but recognized her at once. Only one living human could have such a face: it was Queen Beauty, and she called to him, and a tear of joy stood out in one eye as she saw him and reached for him and took him into her embrace.

And the vision was gone, abruptly, and Orem and Galloway were alone in the attic room.

Galloway looked at him in awe. "I saw blood come from your neck, Scanthips, and yet there was no wound."

"There will be," Orem answered, and he turned away. "Galloway, how did Hart's Hope get its name?"

Galloway shrugged. "Something to do with the Sweet Sisters. A hart died here, I think. There's a shrine a few streets from here. Kind of a sad place, pretty much untended. If it ever had priests, they're gone now, and no one knows much what sort of thing one should do in worship. It isn't a good place to buy magic with a hart's blood, though, or so I hear."

"Take me there tomorrow."

"There's nothing to see," Galloway said.

"Nothing for *you* to see," Orem answered.

Galloway stared at him, afraid. Orem had touched something Galloway had no power to find—nor, truth to tell, did he much want to find it even if he had the power. Harts had no business appearing and disappearing in a wizard's house, not living harts, and not when a wizard's own servant lay bleeding under the hart's hoofs. That was not the way the magic worked. And try as he might, Galloway could not imagine who had worked such a miracle. It couldn't be the Temple, either. The Temple didn't work in harts.

The Queen, thought Galloway. The Queen has found the boy. I won't take him to the shrine. It must be a trap.

But in the morning the boy was already gone, and Galloway learned from neighbors that he had asked directions to Shrine Street. Galloway ran, using small spells to clear the crowds out of his way. Even so, he got there too late. The guards already had Orem in hand, and as Galloway watched from a distance he could see the guards demanding a pass, and Orem searching for it in vain. The fool lacks his pass, Galloway thought. He forgot it. All I have to do is step forward and say, "He's my servant," and they'll set him free.

But Galloway remembered the hart in the attic the night before, and he was afraid to link himself with the boy. Scanthips is something out of any wizard's control, Galloway told himself. Let him go. Let him go. And pray God he dies without telling anything about me.

The guards bound the boy and led him off toward Little Temple and King's Road, which led to the Castle, where they were doubtless already waiting for the boy in the Gaols. Galloway searched his heart for pity for the boy, and to his surprise found neither pity nor fear. Just relief. The boy was gone, and life could get back to normal again.

"Holy shit," said another wizard standing nearby. "Last night I couldn't do a single spell! Not a single spell! If I find the bastard who's been doing it, be he priest or wizard, I'll have him fried in half a minute. What about you, Galloway?"

"Couldn't do a spell all night, either," Galloway said cheerfully, and they went off to the taverns together to complain about the day.

This time, instead of dodging furtively across King's Road, Orem walked right along, flanked by two guards. There were crowds on King's Road as on any other in Hart's Hope, but these were different. The pedestrians were more often parted by carriages, and there were no sweating oxen drawing wagons. The clothing was richer, the errands more important, and instead of the normal backdrop of wooden houses garishly painted or grayed with weather, King's Road was lined with the five-floor townhouses of the rich, with their stone and marble fronts, their porters and coachmen lounging on the porches, their tiny barred lower windows and huge, breezy upper windows that let out curtains to billow like cream in a moving pitcher.

It was as foreign to Orem as if he had just gone to another country. What went on behind those doors was a mystery. And if a monster or a siren or God himself had leaned out one of the open windows, Orem would not have been surprised.

But then King's Road crossed Low Shop Street, and the great houses were replaced by tenements and the workhouses established through the mercy of a king five generations ago. Deathhouses, they were called among the poor, but the despairing went there because at least the uncertainty would end.

The castle wall towered ahead. Five hundred feet it rose straight up, though half the height was the craggy cliff the castle had been built on. At the end of King's Road, here called High Gate Road, the cliff had been pierced, so that a road two wagons wide plunged upward into the belly of the hill. It turned immediately, and Orem looked upward in unashamed awe at the cliff and stone walls that came so close to meeting at the top that the sky was only a thin ribbon and it was dusky where he walked with the guards.

This was power, to Orem; God had put a hill here, and men had made it into a mountain. But now the power was directed against him, and being a Sink would do him no good here. He had not been caught with an expired pisser's pass. He had been caught with no pass, and new clothes. Slavery for sure, if not worse. Yet the hart had called him there, hadn't it? Or was last night just a dream after all, a strange nightmare shared with Galloway? The world did not move according to the simple patterns of a farmer's life after all. There was more than plow and plant, hoe and harvest. Was even the sun unsteady in the sky? Would the shining eye of the Half-blind Hare fall to earth at the command of a Queen?

And seeing the high, impenetrable walls, Orem wondered at the madness and tragedy of King Palicrovol, who for twenty years had built army after army to attack these walls. Every time he had brought his army to the walls of the city, the Queen's magic had wrought such terror that all in the army who were weak of heart, who did not love the King, were made to flee, so that the army dissipated and never came to battle at all. The first time, only a dozen men still stood with the King despite the fear; each time thereafter a dozen or a score or a crasp of new men would prove their love and loyalty. Now King Palicrovol had near three hundred men he knew he could count on. Three hundred. And yet, even if they withstood the fear, even if somehow they pierced the city wall, what would they do against walls like these? Three hundred brave men, and how blithely would they ride their mounts between these steeply rising walls, to challenge Queen Beauty at the castle gate?

No, Queen Beauty would reign as long as she lived, and there were those who said she had already lived ten centuries and meant to live forever. Could that be true, Orem wondered? He had always dismissed it as a rumor meant to lead the King's men to despair; but Galloway had thought it possible to live forever, and it was certain from all the tales that Queen Beauty never aged.

Will I see Queen Beauty? Orem wondered. The face from his dream danced in his memory, but faded, and he longed to make the vision whole again. Queen Beauty would not visit the Gaols; but maybe she would be in a carriage within the Castle; maybe she would—

They passed within High Gate, a steep stairway that led to the ground level of King's Town—no, Queen's Town—within the Castle's walls. There were great wooden platforms raised by winches pushed by grunting slaves; these were lifting dozens of heavily loaded wagons filled with food. Briefly Orem pictured himself at the rod of the winch, sweating out his life in hot sunlight to raise a hundred wagons a day to feed the Queen. He thought of the bees by the Banning, all of them existing only to bring back honey to the queen bee, who lived only for herself, creating children only to be her slaves. That was Queen Beauty, Orem thought. She sits and spins all day, and all the world comes to her, even her hopeless husband Palicrovol; and everything that comes she eats or uses up until all the world is gone, all the world. And then will she make another?

Rough hands took him through the gate at the end of the stair. "Charge?" asked a clerk. "No pass, new clothes, no friends, at the Dead Shrine," came the answer. That was his identity now — defined by what he lacked and where his want had been discovered. No friends, no pass. Five times he said his name. Five times a clerk wrote *Orem Scanthips of Banningside* and passed him through to other guards. In all his life Orem's name had never been written down except by the register priest in Banningside; since coming to Hart's Hope his name had been put on six lists, and Orem felt as if his virtue were being drawn from him with every flowing of the ink.

But in all the passing back and forth, in and out, Orem did not end up in the Gaols.

He stood before a table where three judges sat, each dressed in fine clothing, all masked. Orem, too, was masked, for justice knew no names and recognized no faces.

"Why did you come to Hart's Hope?" one man asked him.

Why? Unable to think of a good reason, Orem told the truth. "To make a name for myself, and find a place, and earn a poem."

One of the judges chuckled.

"How did you get into Hart's Hope without a pass?"

"I had a pass, through Piss Gate."

"We know that. Your name was on the list there, we are told. But expired months ago. And passed back through before the third day. How did you get into Hart's Hope without a pass?"

"Through the Hole," Orem answered softly.

The judge who chuckled was still laughing in the undertones of his voice when he said, "We didn't think you flew. Do you know the way?"

Orem shook his head. "Tunnels in darkness," he said. "I didn't know the way, or who I met. They told me nothing. I've never seen the people again."

"And who, boy, was your sponsor?"

"Sponsor?"

"Come on, boy, don't waste our time. What you don't tell us freely, the pins will tell us at great expense to you. You had new clothing. And you never pass through the Hole without a sponsor."

Galloway, of course, but Orem hesitated to name his teacher. He had seen Galloway in weakness, weeping. He had held him in his arms and carried him up the stairs gently. The man had no substance to him; he was fragile as a kite. Would he name him to these judges in their silver masks? Orem thought not. No, he decided. He had no friends, for certain; but that did not mean that he could not *be* a friend. It was not in him to break trust so easily.

"He can't speak," said one of the judges disgustedly.

"Damned wizards," said another.

"Spells and spells," said the chuckling judge. "Well, we know from the past that even the pins won't get names from them, not even their own. Someday perhaps we'll get permission to burn out Wizard's Street, but until then, boy, we don't pin them who cannot speak because of the magic on them. There was hart's blood shed, wasn't there?"

Orem nodded. Let them think what they would; no need to tell them that no such spell would work on *him*.

"Well, then, obviously you're guilty. Take off your mask so we can see the face you've earned yourself before we sentence you."

And Orem reached up and removed his mask.

One of the judges gasped.

The one who chuckled had no laughter in his voice now. "The Queen's dream, and brought to us masked. Who would have thought."

"Boy," said another. "You have a wound in your throat. How did you earn that scar?"

Wound? Orem reached up and touched his throat. There was a low welt there, that ran all the way around his neck, except for a few inches at his spine. The only explanation for such a scar was his dream. "I'm a farmer," he said. "I was cut on a plow."

And the judges looked startled. One made as if to stand, while the one who chuckled nodded and his hands trembled.

"Sentence, sentence," said the third, who alone remained calm. "We have no power to sentence you. The Queen saw you in a dream last night, boy."

"Guards," called a judge. "Guards!"

And they gave orders, and Orem was led from the room. Before he reached the door, he asked, "My lords! What was the Queen's dream?" But they did not speak to him, and he was gone with the guards.

They took him out onto the stone-paved square. The palace walls, delicately mosaicked all along their length, opened in broad, well-guarded gates before him. He could see the palace, a gleaming building of polished ivory, it seemed, with so many wings and piles added that it was impossible to find the original structure. It looked like a place of majesty all the same. It was the Queen's hive. He wondered what the bees found when they went home.

At first he did not understand what was being done to him. He was too afraid, certain the Queen had seen him too well last night, certain that she would destroy the Sink who alone could extinguish a part of her Searching Eye and leave her partly blind. And there was the sheer newness of the place. They took him through rooms larger than the town of Banningside, whose ceilings looked as distant as the sky. All the walls were layered seven times in tapestries and metalwork and stone. There was no marble that was not living with the figures of men and animals engaged variously in killing and in coitus. There was no iron that was not silvered, no silver that was not inlaid with gold. The furniture was made of heavy woods, yet all was delicately carved so that there were thousands of tiny windows in the wood and it looked as if the weight of it was borne by dark and insubstantial lace. And through it all no one spoke to him, so that he realized what was happening to him only gradually.

After all, in the villages and farms it was done only symbolically, for they were poor. It was the Dance of Descent, of course, the last thing Orem expected. And it was done for real. He was carried to the palace door in a carriage with twelve wheels, drawn by eleven horses. He was surrounded by ten armored men, their shields marked with nine black stones. His hair was cut in eight passes of the shears, and seven naked women with blood on their thighs immersed him six times in hot water and five times in cold, so that he was washed in menstrual blood each time thinner than before. It was then that he understood, and began to anticipate the steps.

He himself had been one of the Four Virgin Boys at three of his brothers' Dances of Descent. On the farm the Three Oils had been pig fat, sheep fat, and chicken fat, and they had jostled and joked as they anointed him and scraped. There was no joking now. The four young boys who knelt around him as he lay naked on the stone floor were sober and worked strenuously. The oils did not reek of animals; they

122

were delicate yet strong of scent, and the boys rubbed them firmly into his skin, each oil in turn, scraping his body between each oil. They did not even speak to ask him to turn himself over; instead, their thin childish arms reached out and their small hands gripped him firmly, and he was turned abruptly without any volition of his own, and yet without any discomfort, either. The odor of the oils went into his head, and he felt a slight aching between his eyes. Yet it was a delicious pain, and the scraping of his body was a pleasure he was not prepared for. It left him weak and relaxed and trembling, and he reached gratefully for the Two Cups when they were brought to him.

No rough clay cups here. The Cup of the Left Hand was a crystal bowl set in a lacy gold cradle that rested on the top of a thin spiral stem. The liquid in it was green and seemed to be alive with light, yet a smooth light that did not flicker with the dancing of the lamps on the walls. As he reached for the cup with his left hand, Orem was suddenly filled with fear. This was the stuff of poems, but he had not been ready, had not been warned. I am like Glasin the Grocer, chosen by chance for adventures that only the Sweet Sisters could have predicted. I am not ready, he cried out inside himself; but still his hand reached out, and though his hand trembled, he spilled no drop of the green. In the villages it had been a tea of mints; here it was a wine, and when it touched his tongue the flavor went through him like ice, bringing winter to every part of his body, so that he felt it sharply in his fingers, and his buttocks clenched involuntarily. Still he drank it all, though when he was through, his body shook violently and his teeth chattered. Steam rose from the empty crystal cup.

The Cup of the Right Hand was made of stone, plain unpolished stone with no figuring or sculpture on it except that it was cut to make the proper bent curve required even on the farm. The soul of the woman he had drunk, and now he reached down with his right hand to pick up the soul of the man. The stone was not as heavy as he had expected, and he nearly spilled it, but the thick white fluid was heavy and slow as mud and did not slosh easily over the edge.

This time when he sipped, the drink was hot and did not penetrate as quickly as the cold. On the farm it had been milk, and perhaps it was milk here, too; but it was sweet, painfully sweet and hot enough to burn his tongue. Yet he drank the thick stuff down and set the cup aside slowly, relishing the heat as it fought the cold within him and won. He knew that his skin was flushing, that his face was red. He gasped his breaths, and knelt on all fours, his head hanging down nearly to the floor as his body absorbed the heat of the soul of man.

Then the servants bore away the Two Cups, and others led him to a golden chair covered with a thick velvet cloth, where he sat waiting for the One Red Ring. Not made of painted wood, the ring they brought; it was carved whole from a ruby, a thing whose value was so beyond Orem's understanding that it was not until years later that he realized that the price of that ring would have bought a thousand farms like his father's farm, and had enough left over to buy ten thousand slaves to work them.

Which finger? How did his brothers ever decide? All the future would hinge on this one choice.

He raised his left hand, the hand of passion, without much thinking of the meaning of it, only because that was the hand that wanted to rise. The servant picked up the ring between his forefinger and thumb, and waited for Orem to choose. And he chose the one finger no man would ever choose; he chose the last finger, the small finger, the finger of weakness and surrender. He flushed with shame at his choice, but knew that he could make no other. Why? he asked himself.

But he did not know the why of anything today. It was too quick, too strange, too inexorable. He had thought to earn a poem. Instead, he had just completed the Dance of Descent, and somewhere nearby was the woman he was to marry. Marry, at fifteen years of age—or no, sixteen now, he had passed his birthday in the months at Galloway's house. Marry; and with all that had passed in the Dance of Descent, Orem had little doubt who his wife would be. Though it was a thought so outrageous that he would never have dared to name her name aloud.

To his surprise, he was not asked to arise from the chair. Instead, with the ruby ring on his small leftmost finger, he sat in the chair as porters passed rods through rings on its side and lifted him up, bore him from the room. There was no door at that end, but the wall itself parted in a great crack from floor to ceiling, and then slid aside, and he was carried into the presence of the queen.

Behind him the doors slid shut again, and the only light in the room was the moonlight that came through great windows and was reflected off a thousand small mirrors on the walls. In the mottled silver light, he saw her standing alone and naked in the middle of the floor, her bare feet white and smooth as the cold marble they seemed carved from. Her hair was long and full and reached below her waist; the hair of her head was the only hair on her body, and she could have been a child except for the small, perfect breasts that, in their slow and tiny rise and fall, were the only proof that she was alive.

Her face he recognized. It was the perfect,

pleading, loving, inevitable face of the woman in his dream. She was the virgin, begging for his gentlest love. She was Queen Beauty, and she was now his wife.

He stood from his chair, keenly aware of his own thin, unproportioned body, tanned and weathered from the waist; yet he had scant thought for shame at what little he had to offer the only perfect woman in the world. For she had raised her hand, and it was her right hand, and the golden ring she wore was on the impossible finger, the finger he could not have hoped for; the small finger of her right hand, her rightmost finger, and as he walked to her, his hand upraised, the rings on their fingers rested the same distance from the fingertip.

If he had chosen to surrender all his passion, she had chosen to surrender all her will.

"Are you a virgin?" she whispered, her voice soft and urgent.

He nodded. It was not enough.

Impatiently she asked again, "My boy, my husband, my Little King, has your seed ever spilled inside another woman's womb?"

And Orem spoke, though where he found his voice he wasn't sure. "Never," he said, and she leaned forward and kissed him. It was a cold kiss, yet it lingered and Orem did not want it ever to end. As she kissed him, her breasts leaned in to touch his chest, and then they met hip to hip, and her left hand was behind his back and she clung to him. The kiss ended.

"I will never love you," she whispered. "You will never have my heart." But the tones of her voice rang with love, and Orem trembled at the power she had without using any magic at all.

Should he answer? He could not. For he had worn the ring on the hand of passion, and that was a vow to love forever and completely. Yet in his heart he knew, without knowing why, that he would never love her, either. His heart was surrendered, but not to her; her will was surrendered, but not to him.

"We will have a child," she said softly, leading him to the place where the floor gave way to a vast sea of a bed.

"It will be a boy," she said, as they knelt together and her hands softly touched him.

"I will give him all of myself," she said, "and that is why there will be none of me for you."

And they lay together all the night, and the child was conceived, and Orem never knew the Queen's body again. It did not matter. The night's passion was so strong that he dared not think of it thereafter, for when he did his body aroused and lost control and violently spent itself, all in a few moments, from just the memory of it.

Yet Orem knew as no other man could know that none of it was magic. She had worked no spell on him that night. It was merely what and who she was that had so much power over him, and at last he began to understand why King Palicrovol could not forget his obsession with returning to Hart's Hope. He was not coming back to kill the Queen and regain his place in the Kingdom of Burland. He was coming back to regain his place in her bed.

In the morning, sunlight danced from a thousand mirrors. Orem awoke with his body stiff from the unaccustomed softness of the bed. It took him a while to sort out his dreams from reality. For the first time in his life, it was the reality that was less probable and more desirable. The Queen herself had lain with him last night. From a strange dream of a hart in Galloway's cramped attic room to the most powerful and beautiful woman in the world taking his virginity in a sparkling mirrored room in the palace, all in a single day. Here was a poem if there had ever been a poem.

And a place, too. For she had not just lain with him, he remembered. They had done the Dance of Descent, the most sacred binding between man and woman—a greater tie than existed between King Palicrovol and the Queen. I am husband of the queen, Orem thought, and it was so incredibly perfect that he laughed aloud, laughed until the bed bounced and the sunlight seemed to go crazy in the mirrors.

They must have heard his laughter. The quiet servants came in, making almost no sound. At first Orem was surprised and tried to cover himself. But he couldn't find an end of a blanket before he noticed that they were not looking at him. They went about their business without even seeing him. He could have voided his bladder on the bedsheets, and there would have been no comment, he was sure; though he was just as sure that the mess would have been cleaned up the instant he was through.

They dressed him—in clothing cut to fit perfectly, something Orem had never experienced before in his life. It was heavy clothing, but not overwarm; the brocades were layered, and gold and jewels gleamed here and there. Orem took no thought for his family, who could have lived for a year on the cost of such a gown. His delight was complete because it was so innocent. He knew he had not earned his good fortune, and so he did not worry about fighting to keep it. He simply enjoyed it, and there were plenty of mirrors to give him the pleasure of seeing his shoulders suddenly enhanced to look broad and strong, his thin thighs masked so no one could know that an unpowerful boy hid behind the costume of a mighty man.

"I look like a king," Orem said softly to the mirror.

The servants, who had unobtrusively fastened all the hidden fasteners, said nothing. But there was a pretty young girl reaching out her hand to him. Her right; he was not sure what she wanted but reached out his left hand to see if she wanted to lead him somewhere. She did. When their hands met, she gravely curtsied, then took his fingers lightly and led him slowly out of the room, then more briskly down corridors, up stairs, through chambers. Every room was perfect, with doors placed symmetrically, though some were obviously false doors going nowhere; if one room was wood instead of marble, it was a rare and deep-polished wood; if furniture here was light instead of heavy, it was intricately carved so that its value was all the greater; and wherever Orem went, he was surprised again by the great pains that had been taken to make beautiful even corners where surely no one important ever went.

But no; this was not designed to impress important visitors, he realized. This was designed to please only one person, and she might go anywhere.

The Queen was waiting for him in what he later learned was Moon Chamber; great discs of silver were set into the walls, and a huge glass table, also a perfect circle, filled the center of the room. It was the Queen's second court, her private court. The servant girl led Orem to the space between the table and the two white thrones that dominated the head of the room. Orem was conscious, as the girl withdrew, that there were others in the room; he could not see them, for he could only look at the Queen, who arose to greet him.

She stepped forward from her throne and reached out her hand. Orem took it, and he noticed that, unlike the servant girl, whose hand had been under his to lead him, the Queen's hand was over his, as if to be led. Orem would have bowed to her, but he hesitated,

129

unsure of protocol. So it was that the Queen bowed, and Orem heard someone else in the room gasp.

"Beauty has taken a husband," a high-pitched voice intoned with an edge of madness, "to last her all his life. Has she taken him to his bed with poison in his head?"

The Queen lifted her head from the bow and faced the others in the room; she turned Orem in the process. Before her, in the middle of the glass table, sat a black man, a small man, nearly naked, with a headdress of cow's horns on his head and an immense false phallus hanging from his belt. It was he who had recited the rhyme. "What a pretty little king, with a pretty little thing," said the black man, "but will the bee still sing when he finds he has no sting?"

"Shut up," said the Queen beautifully, and the black man turned a somersault and landed, laughing, at Beauty's feet.

"Ah, beat me, beat me, Beauty!" cried the black man, and then he wept piteously. In a moment he started tasting the tears, then retreated to a corner of the room, dabbing at his eyes with the stuffed phallus that dangled longer than his legs.

"As you see," said the Queen, "I have taken a husband. He is a common criminal from the filthiest part of the city, and he is as attractive to me as a leprous hog, but he was given to me in a dream from the Sweet Sisters, and it amused me to follow their advice."

Orem could not sort out the difference between her sweet, musical voice and the acid words she was saying. He smiled stupidly, vaguely aware that he was being abused, but unable to react negatively to the song Queen Beauty sang.

"As you see, he is also quite stupid. He once had a name, but in this court he will be called Little King. And for all that he has the sexual prowess of a dung beetle, we conceived a child last night."

Orem was startled that she could know, for sure, already. Didn't she have to wait awhile? He vaguely remembered something his brothers had said about being sure only when the moon didn't rise for the woman, or something. He looked at her, and she glanced back at him. "You don't imagine such things are left to chance, do you?" She turned back to the others. "You will speak of my child to the others. Spread it as a rumor through all the world. Dear Palicrovol will know what it means, even if you do not, and he will come again and knock at my gates. I miss the man. I want to see him weep again."

There were three in the room. The black fool, who was gnawing on his false phallus under the table; a wizened, withered old man in extraordinarily large breastplate and helmet, like a mockery of a great soldier; and a deformed woman, whose face was pocked and lumped with scars of old sores. Why would the Queen introduce him first to such a bizarre trio? Yet there was an odd note of respect in her voice when she spoke to them, and they were all grave and selfpossessed as they answered her.

The old soldier came first, his step slow and unsteady as he lurched under the weight of the armor. His voice was hollow and soft, full of air. He spoke to Orem first.

"Little King," he said, "I see you wear your ring wisely. Look at it often and follow its advice." Then the old man turned to the queen and looked her in the eyes. Orem was surprised by the force of his gaze — when the old man had looked at him his eyes had been tender and soft, but now they were full of fire. Hatred? This man had power despite his weak body and the large armor that made a joke of it. "Beauty, dear Beauty," said the old soldier, "I give your child a blessing. May your son have my strength."

Orem looked toward the Queen in alarm. Surely she would be angry that the old man would curse her unborn child so. Orem well knew the power of wishes on the unborn—many a dull-wit and cripple had been the product of an ill-thought jest. But the Queen only nodded and smiled as if the old man had given her a great gift.

And then the woman. Closer up she was uglier still. Her walk was canted a bit, so that one step was long, and the other short. Her hands were gnarled and twisted, and when she touched Orem's cheek it felt like her fingers were scaled like fish. She smiled, and Orem realized the dirt on her lip was a scraggly moustache; her hair was also thin and wispy, and she was bald in a few patches. "Little King," she said to him in a voice that grated on him like the cry of a rutting hen. "Be lonely, love no one, and live long." Then she, too, turned to the Queen. "Beauty, I also give your child a blessing. May your son have my beauty."

Again, the Queen accepted the cruel curse as if it were a gift.

Then the short black man waddled up, grinning idiotically. He stopped in front of Orem and pulled down his loincloth to reveal that he had only one testicle in his scrotum, and a penis so small it could hardly be seen. "I'm half what I should be," said the fool, "but twice the man you are." Then he giggled, pulled his loincloth back in place, and darted forward to lift Orem's gown and peer under it. He reemerged from the boy's costume as quickly, laughing hysterically. "Little King, Little King!" he cried. And then, suddenly somber, he said, "The Queen sees all, except that which she sees not that she sees not. Remember it, Little King!" And then he turned away from Orem. But for a brief moment Orem realized that the fool was no fool—or for a moment, at least, seemed to speak with serious intent.

"Beauty, dear Beauty," sang the little black man to the Queen, "I bless your little unborn child on whom all gods but one have smiled: though all his life the lad hear lies, he'll be as wise as I am wise." Then, laughing uproariously, the fool somersaulted backward and sprawled under the table.

Orem was horrified at the bitter gifts they had given the Queen's child—his child, for that matter, though he was far from having much parental feeling for a creature he could not even imagine yet. All Orem knew was that a great discourtesy had been done, and he fumblingly tried to put it right. He knew no blessings for the unborn except the common one used in Banningside and the farm country, the blessing Halfpriest Dobbick had invariably used. Orem turned to the Queen and said, "Queen Beauty, I'd like to bless the child."

She glared at him, but he hardly noticed—he just blurted out his gift in words that almost had lost meaning to him: "May the child live to serve God."

Orem had meant it as a kindness. The Queen took it as a curse. She slapped his face with such force that he fell to the floor; his cheek was cut open by her ring. What had he said? But from his place on the floor he watched as she looked imperiously at the others and said, in a voice dripping with hate, "My Little King's gift has no more power than his little pud." Then she turned to Orem. "Command and bless as you like, my Little King; you will only be obeyed by those who laugh at you." Then the Queen turned and started toward the door. She stopped at the threshold.

"Urubugala," she said firmly, and the black fool suddenly scrambled out from under the table. It must be his name, Orem realized.

"Come here," the Queen said. Urubugala kept crawling, whining about his sad lot in life. He passed close to Orem, who instinctively retreated from the strange man — but suddenly the fool's black hand snaked out and grabbed Orem viciously by the arm and pulled him close. Orem lost his balance, and in the struggle to get up he found the fool's lips against his ear. "I know you, Orem," came the almost soundless whisper. "I have waited long for you."

And then the fool was standing as Orem knelt — they were almost the same height, then — and the fool kissed him firmly on the mouth and put his hands on Orem's head and shouted, "I name you with your true name, boy! You are Hart's Hope!" But as abruptly as the naming ritual had begun, it ended. Suddenly the fool was writhing on the ground, screaming in agony, clutching his head. Is it a show, Orem wondered, or is the pain real?

"His name," said the Queen softly from the other side of the room — softly, but clearly heard despite the black man's screams — "his name is Little King, and he will have no other."

The words finished, she left. Urubugala immediately stopped screaming. He lay panting on the floor a moment, then arose and walked out of the room, following the Queen.

Orem also stood up. His cheek hurt, and so did his elbow where he had hit the floor. He was confused; he understood nothing. The heavy gown felt like a burden he did not want to bear. The door where the Queen had left was closed now. Orem turned to the others, the ugly woman and the weak old soldier. They regarded him with pitying eyes. He did not really understand their pity, either.

"What do I do now?" he asked.

They glanced at each other. "You're king," said the

soldier. "You can do what you like."

"King." Orem didn't know what to make of it. "I saw Palicrovol once."

"Did you?" said the woman. She did not sound interested.

"He covers his eyes with gold balls, so the Queen can't see."

The woman chuckled. "Then he does it in vain, doesn't he? For the Queen sees everything."

"But she can't look everywhere at once, can she?" Orem asked.

"She sees everything, like an orchestra of visions in the back of her mind. She watches always." The woman laughed. "She sees us now. And she is laughing, I'm sure."

It made Orem afraid. If she saw everything, hadn't she seen him with Galloway? Didn't she know that he was a Sink? Did she feel no fear of him because her magic was so powerful that he could not possibly swallow it all? Yet she hadn't even tried to work any magic on him—Was it because the spells would not have worked, or was there another reason? He was grateful for this, at least: Galloway had taught him well, and Orem could hold his strange power in abeyance so that at least he wasn't irritating the Queen in her presence by swallowing any of the magic that he could taste thick in the air in every room he had visited. She filled this place with magic, no doubt to some purpose more than a mere Searching Eye, and it would surely irritate her if he sucked holes in it wherever he went.

He wanted to ask the soldier and the ugly woman whether the Queen knew of his gift; but the asking would give the answer, since she would overhear. He would have to find more subtle ways of discovering what he could and could not do with his inborn gift.

Perhaps somehow it could work to his advantage in this strange place where everything was bent to the Queen's will.

"What am I allowed to do?" he asked.

"Whatever you want to do," the old soldier answered.

"You command everyone," said the ugly woman. "You're the Queen's husband, Little King, and they must obey."

It was a heady thought, and Orem distrusted it. "Tell me your names, then," he said.

"I must beg your pardon," said the ugly woman. "I misspoke myself. You command everyone but Urubugala and us."

"And why not you?" Orem asked.

"Because we do not laugh at you," said the ugly woman.

Orem thought about that for a moment; he remembered the Queen's words. "Then everyone but you and the black man will obey me?"

The ugly woman nodded.

"Because everyone but you and the black man will laugh at me."

"It's awkward for you, I know," said the old soldier. "But I can promise you this—the less you command, the less they'll laugh."

"Don't tell him that, Craven," the ugly woman said. "Little King, command all you like. Your life will be much easier if everyone here keeps laughing. Command all you like. The Queen, too, will laugh."

If the Queen laughs, then do I command *her*, too? Orem wondered. She had worn her ring with a promise to surrender her will to his. But he did not ask the question aloud. Already he sensed that in this palace a wise man said as little about the Queen as he could get away with. Better not to mention her, because then you could not offend her.

"Craven," said Orem. "That is your name? Craven?"

The old soldier nodded. "It is the name the Queen gave me."

"And you," Orem said to the old woman. "What may I call you?"

"I am called Weasel, surnamed Sootmouth. It is the name the Queen gave me."

As the Queen had named him Little King. "I had a name before she named me," Orem said. "Didn't you?"

"If I did," Weasel said, "I don't remember it."

"But you must," said Orem. "Mine is—my name is really—"

But Weasel put her scaly hand to his mouth. "You can't say it," she said. "And if you could, it would cost you dearly. Don't try to remember."

He looked at her wide-eyed. She apparently believed that he could not say his name, or remember it. But he could. Orem, he said in his own mind. Orem Scanthips, or Orem of Banningside. He had only stammered. There had been no magic in his hesitation to speak his own real name. Yet apparently Weasel and Craven were bound by magic and assumed that he was, too. It was a hint to him that perhaps he was immune to the bindings of magic in the palace.

"May I ask you another question?" Orem asked.

"Ask anything," said Craven.

"Why am I here?"

Silence, and the two looked at each other. "The Queen uses great magic," Weasel finally said. "She must pay a price for it." And then she winced and covered her mouth.

"She can say no more," said Craven. "She should not have said that much. You're lucky you know nothing of magic. Don't try to learn."

"I won't," Orem said, and Weasel instantly relaxed, as if a pain inside her head had gone away.

"Thank you," Weasel said.

Orem had another question. "Why don't you laugh at me?"

They looked at each other again. Finally Craven spoke. "We can give only a poor answer to that, Little King. We do not laugh at you because we know the ending of—" And then he stopped, gritted his teeth, and moaned in a high voice, quietly, behind his painful smile.

"Never mind," said Orem. "Please, I'll ask you no more questions."

Craven relaxed and smiled, touched Orem's arm. "Thank you."

"Perhaps," Weasel said, "You would like to be presented to the court."

Orem smiled weakly. "I don't know if I would or not."

"I assure you that you would," Craven said. "Until there's a presentation, no one will know who you are, and until they know who you are, they won't pay the slightest attention to you."

"Besides which," Weasel added, "it will be the easiest way for us to fulfill the Queen's command that we tell the world about you. She wants the word to reach Palicrovol."

"What will happen when he hears?"

Weasel laughed, a hideous sound, and when she bared her teeth Orem saw that many were rotting in her mouth. He had seen teeth like that—he well knew that Weasel's breath must smell like a gutter at noon in the marketplace. "When Palicrovol hears," Weasel said, "he will rage to God and all the gods, and he will assemble his pathetic army of fifty thousand men, as he has before. This time his fury will be more terrible than ever, because someone else is sitting in his throne and someone else is called King. He will bring his army to the gate of Hart's Hope, and there his men will face the Queen's magic, as they have before. It will strike terror in their souls, so that they believe they face the worst thing they fear in all the world. Despite their courage and their oaths and their self-respect, they will almost all flee. Only a few will stand with Palicrovol at the gate then—maybe a hundred this time. Every other time, Palicrovol has shouted hideous oaths and gone away, hoping to build a braver, larger army. But this time—perhaps this time his hate will be so strong that he'll launch his silly group of a hundred men, who are stronger than their worst fear, against the gate."

"Because of you," Craven said. "Because you sit on his throne."

"And this time, perhaps, all the men will be killed."

"Except Palicrovol, of course."

"Except Palicrovol," Weasel corrected herself. "He'll just be sent on his way again. Or perhaps this time the pain will be enough that he'll kill himself. I don't know what exactly the Queen has in mind."

"I'm here to hurt Palicrovol," Orem said, trying to distill the sense from all that they had said.

Weasel and Craven glanced at each other again.

"Then there's something else, something more than that." Orem tried to find answers in their eyes, but they said nothing.

Until Weasel laughed again. "Come with us. Let's go to the stewards and have them send the invitations for a party tonight."

"Tonight? Who could come, hearing of it only today?"

Weasel touched his arm. "When the invitation says

that the Little King invites them, there's not a soul in Hart's Hope who would not come, if he could. Don't you realize, Little King? You're the most powerful man in the city."

Orem shook his head. "I don't even know what to command people to do. What use do I have for power like that?"

Craven looked at him bitterly. "You'll learn."

They left the room together, walking slowly so that Craven could keep up with them. Orem thought of helping the man, giving him support. But he decided against it. Feeble as he was, Craven did not seem the kind of man who would lean.

And as they stood waiting for the stewards all to memorize the invitation so Weasel could assign the lists, Orem closed his eyes and went searching in the magic of the palace. He did not want to find the Queen; it was just as well, for there was nothing in the mists of power to hint where she herself might be. Wherever his attention went, he knew that a small amount of the magic disappeared. He waited, tensely, expecting to feel at any moment the Queen's anger, the stab of—what, pain?—that immobilized the others when they crossed her will. But there was nothing. He became more daring and yet more careful; he began to spread his influence, draw off more of the power, yet he also took his attention beyond the palace, out into the city of Hart's Hope, where the feeble fires of the wizards burned coldly. He tasted one, put it out, and waited. Nothing.

Why had he expected it to be any different? His gift was not magic, it was the absence of magic. At worst, the Queen could only know that here or there she was blind. She did not know where the blindness came from; he left no thread that could be followed. The only way she would discover what he was, he decided,

140

would be if she were to try to work magic on him directly, for she would surely notice if the spell did not work.

So far, Orem thought, so far I am safe.

"The Queen called you a fool. Do you have to prove her right?" Orem opened his eyes, startled, to see Craven looking at him with cold criticism in his eyes.

"I'm—sorry. What did I do?"

"Have the good sense to keep your eyes open, Little King. You've stood here while the mistress of housekeeping instructed her stewards, and yet you haven't listened, you haven't learned. Do you intend to go blind through your sojourn among us?"

Orem shook his head. "I'm sorry. There's—other things on my mind."

"Then take them off your mind and concentrate. Do you think this is going to be a country party tonight? Do you think you'll dance to the scree and maybe have a willing little girl behind a cowshed?"

"I don't know what I think."

"I know what *I* think," Craven said. "I think the Sweet Sisters played us no pleasant prank when they dreamed you into the Queen's life."

"Be easy on him," Weasel said. "He's new to this."

"He'll wreck himself too soon," wheezed the old soldier, "if I'm easy on him now." He turned back to Orem. "Go with Weasel. The Queen has damned you to be a laughingstock, but you needn't leap into the role with such perfect assurance. Let it at least be magic that makes a fool of you, and not your innate inabilities. There is the matter of manner. There is the matter of courtesy. There is also the matter of the abominable slouch you have that gives you the look of a halfwit."

"Craven," Weasel said, from the corner where she talked with the stewards, "I said be easy."

Craven glared at her. He muttered, so she couldn't hear, "Go break mirrors somewhere else."

Surely Weasel had not heard his words, Orem thought, for he had barely heard them. But still she answered sharply, "Haven't you even the courage to speak your insults openly, Craven?"

Craven seemed to wither before her eyes. Where Orem had begun to forget his weakness and be a little frightened of him, he now saw him as the frail, powerless man he really was. Craven looked at him and must have seen the pity in his eyes. "So your cock has filled a Queen, boy? Bloody lot of good may it do you." And Craven laughed—but still led Orem out of the room to instruct him in the manners of the court and what would be expected of him at the party. Orem looked back helplessly at Weasel, who did not watch them go. Why did he expect help from her? She was no better than Craven—a monster—and God only knew why Queen Beauty kept such hideous creatures around her and treated them with such cruel respect.

Then Orem remembered what Weasel had started to say before the Queen had closed her mouth: "Why am I here?" Orem had asked, and Weasel had answered. "The Queen uses great magic. She must pay a price for it."

The price of magic. It was well known what the price of magic was—blood. The blood of an eel for the fisher's spells; the blood of the ox for the farmer, drawn from the healthy, living beast. The housewife shed a chicken's blood. The archer drew from an eagle or a hawk that afterward flew again. The Wizard Galloway had drawn the blood of rabbits, the blood of boars, and for the most powerful of his small magics he had drawn from the hart, and even from the living bear. But the Queen worked great magic. The Queen drew power, and therefore blood, from something greater than an ox or a bear or even a hart, even the sweet hart that had come to him and loved him in a dream. Orem reached up to the welt of the new, unearned scar at his neck. Galloway had seen blood flow from his throat, though no wound had ever been there in all Orem's life. He had a terrible vision of the farmer pressing his own throat into the sharp blade of the plow, and the woman, his wife, pressing from behind, driving him on. I have a wife now, Orem thought. I had no wife, when I dreamed the dream, but now I am married, now I have a scar on my neck.

Why am I here? What do I have to do with the Queen's great magic?

"Don't you learn, boy!" demanded Craven. "We've walked half a damnable mile in these corridors, and you haven't even watched to learn the way!"

Orem mumbled his apologies, but could not pay much attention to Craven's wheezing rebuke. He could only think of his own blood flowing from his throat. I am the price of the Queen's magic. I must . . . I must escape.

He remembered Glasin Grocer, who had been spared from death in the Hound's jaws only because he was clean, a God's man.

"I'm no God's man," Orem said aloud.

"Damn good thing for you, in this place," Craven answered. "Now the matter of eating. Not with fingers. You must learn to lift a knife and spoon to your mouth."

With a great effort, Orem forced himself to pay attention. "Won't I cut myself if I put the knife in my mouth?"

"Not if you're careful." And the lesson began in earnest. Orem cut himself once anyway, and the blood tasted strangely sweet on his tongue.

The party began well enough. Though Orem's head was still a muddle of bows, kisses, knives, spoons, steps left and steps right, he managed to get through the introductions well enough, partly because he was a bright young man in spite of the Queen's abuse, and partly because, being king, whatever he did was right as long as it wasn't too obvious. He even managed to keep his dignity when the Queen herself suddenly appeared to make a short speech in which she made it humiliatingly clear that her Little King was an object of ridicule. "Obey him," she said as she left, followed by the cheers of a crowd that knew enough to cheer without cue.

The crowd. Orem recognized them all. Not individually, of course, for he had seen little enough of the wealthy in Hart's Hope. But collectively, they were the haughty ones borne in litters or seated in carriages, their homes the towering mansions along King's Road, their servants almost as unbearably arrogant as their masters as they ran their errands through the town. There were even a few faces that Orem knew personally. He had taken an aphrodisiac to the home of that one, the tall, effeminate lord, the one introduced to him as Count of Burmouth, though everyone knew Palicrovol held Burmouth—as he held all of Burland more than a day's ride from Hart's Hope. And Orem remembered dousing a spell one magician had tried for the fat but vain wife of the Gamesmaster of Arena—what had the spell been? Orem could not remember. He touched hands, kissed ladies and gentlemen of rank, accepted gifts graciously. But the eyes that met his were not friendly. They were calculating, sizing, measuring. He knew too well what they saw. A child, really, though not an ugly one, certainly, and obviously well past puberty since the

Queen's belly was full. But his face held no force. He was unaccustomed to power, and when the Queen left, there was no hope of his holding things in control.

Of all the things Orem had wondered about the rich, he did not wonder how they amused themselves. He thought he knew. Fun was fun, and it had never occurred to him that the wealthy might not be content to drink good ale and pull sticks and throw darts and wrestle. They might wear gold and velvet, but they were still human beings, weren't they?

But at a party for the Little King, that was not the way it went. At first it was mere conversation, and the clumsiest speaker among them was adroit compared to Orem. "Your Majesty," asked a near woman, "how shall we address you privately?"

Weasel, her face so ugly that only her voice could show additional irritation, answered for him. "You address him privately as you address him publicly."

A soft-spoken lord with the eyes of a man to whom vice was a familiar friend intervened. "But surely Little King answers for himself, and not through the voice of the Lady Housekeeper."

Orem shook his head. "I don't know how it should be done. The Queen said my name should be Little King, and that's good enough for me."

A mistake—he saw it at once in Craven's scowl. But the assembled dignitaries laughed and cheered. "A common sort of Little King," cried the Count of Burmouth, "who does not elevate himself above the rest of us. A cheer." There was a cheer, and then another, and prayers for his happiness, which for some reason that escaped Orem completely seemed hilarious to the other guests.

Drunkenness did not lead to stick-pulling. More like dog-baiting, with Orem the dog, though he did not see it at first.

"Will Little King judge a dilemma for me?" asked one woman, and when he consented, trying to please them, she laid before him a shocking story of her husband's repeated infidelities with barnyard animals, to the delight of the listeners.

"So tell me, Little King, command me—should I take him back into my bed or cut off a good six inches when next he comes at me!"

Orem did not believe her story—he doubted that the giggling man beside her would come near a sow, let alone lie with the beast. "I don't know, lady," he said. At that the husband leaped to his feet.

"I implore you, Little King! Don't make me give up my liaison with Balak! The cows I can part with, and the chickens give little satisfaction. But the sow is my heart, my life, my love!"

Was the story true, then? Orem could not believe a man would willingly tell such a tale on himself, even if it were true. Especially if it were true, in God's name! "You make me sick," Orem said angrily, and the crowd cheered.

"To righteous indignation!" cried a man, and there was a toast all around. They smiled at him, winked at him; he fancied them as friends for a moment and drank the toast.

"But you must decide! What should I do?" the lady demanded.

The husband interrupted. "She uses too much paint. She's greasy and keeps sliding out of bed!"

"Decide!" came the chant, well-mixed with laughter.

Orem looked at Weasel's inscrutably ugly face and could read nothing there. But she had said before that he should command. Keep them laughing, and the Queen will laugh, too, she had said. Very well, "I command you to stay together. I think you're well-suited," he said.

146

It must have been the right thing to say. There were cheers, and the woman wept and said, "I must take you back!" She embraced her husband, and they toppled and fell clumsily against their small table, winding up in the middle of the floor.

"About time!" cried the man, and he lifted her dress and had her on the spot. Orem was horrified—such things would be cause for a public whipping in Banningside. "Stop!" he cried. The startled man withdrew from his wife.

"But I am unsatisfied," he said, sounding miffed.

"Stop anyway," Orem said, "and cover yourself." Was it for this that he left Halfpriest Dobbick back in Banningside? Here again, however, his attempt to restore order only led to more problems. The lord only covered himself with a tablecloth and pranced around making lewd jokes.

Was it Orem himself who suggested wrestling? He could not remember afterward, but he wrestled two old men to submission before a younger man beat him. In the corners of the room, where the lamps were dim, he was aware that worse things were happening. A virgin only yesterday, he was not prepared to see people behave with the indiscriminate self-gratification of animals. He withdrew to his table and drank more wine, watching but unable to stop the commotion. Two wrestlers demanded that he command them to do something more difficult. They ended up wrestling with their arms tied to the other's legs; then another quarrel began, and finally in despair Orem cried to one pair of fighters, "Kill each other, for all I care."

For Orem, the party ended then, for one, laughing brightly, seized something from a table, and a moment later the other lay screaming with a table knife in his throat. The stewards carried out the man who was ruining things with his indecorous agony, and the party went on. But it did so without Orem. He ran from the party, to much applause, and vomited in a corridor.

A steward cleaned it up almost before he had finished, while another held a laver of water for him to clean himself. Orem washed, and then let them lead him, weeping, to his room. It was the mirrored room where he had loved the Queen the night before. All excitement was gone now. This was a black place, where people were not people anymore.

The door opened, and he looked up from where he lay crying on the bed, half hoping to see the Queen. No, not Beauty. Rather her opposite, Weasel Sootmouth, who looked angry.

"I don't want a lecture. I made myself an ass. Did the man die?"

Weasel didn't answer. Instead she came to him and knelt by the bed. She reached out and touched his cheek, where he wept.

"Yes, it's a tear," Orem said bitterly. "And more where that came from. Can I command them to take me back to Banningside?"

Weasel shook her head. "You'd be killed if you tried to leave the palace grounds. Her gift of power does not give you wings."

"In God's name, are there no good and normal people here?" he cried, and she embraced him, comforted him as he wept against her neck. He did not remember falling asleep. He woke up in darkness, needing to piss, and found that he had been undressed and covered in the bed. Had Weasel done it herself? Doubtless not—the stewards were too efficient for her to need to do body service for him. Where was a pisspot? He didn't know where to look in this room, and the other pisspots were in rooms he didn't know how to reach. There was no pisspot under the bed, no pisspot standing in the corner; he wasn't sure the room had corners.

At last he went to the open window and voided himself into a flower garden below. Someone cursed, but Orem did not stop. He thought he would piss forever, but at last the flow ended and he went back inside the room feeling much relieved, as if he had pushed the night's experience out of him and was clean again.

He could not sleep immediately, though. Outside he was vaguely aware of conversation. "Someone pissed on me from that window, by the Queen's own name!" "Hush, fool, that's the Little King's room." And then silence. But Orem did not listen. Instead he closed his eyes and let his attention wander far away. What was he hunting for? He had never strayed outside Hart's Hope walls; there had been no need to, for it was in Hart's Hope that the wizards worked. But now he let himself fly, coasting through the thin mists of the Queen's magic, where her Searching Eye touched delicately every living thing.

Where was he? The landscape was not so simple when Orem searched this way. It was not rivers and roads he followed, but villages and farms, the small cold spells rising as a housewife thrust out a gom or placated one too powerful to control. Here and there a place, a small place where the Queen's sight was weaker—but not gone. Priestly places, where they thought they were invisible to her. They were wrong, Orem knew now.

He wandered thus for a long time; hours, he thought, though it could have been only moments. Nowhere did the Queen's power slacken for long. But at last there was a place where her power increased, palpably strengthened, and Orem realized, suddenly, that he had come to Banningside. He felt it more than saw it; reasoned it out at last. The Queen's vision was keener here because the King—the real King—was still in the town.

King Palicrovol was asleep. Around him a few wizards did not sleep. They were awake, and Orem felt their spells as strong lights burning like ice. They were guarding the King, but to no avail, though they could not have known it. Orem saw—as none of them could see—the Queen's magic was not held back by such slight fences.

In his tiredness, Orem could not resist striking back against the world in some small way. They might laugh at him at the party, and the Queen might think him a nothing, which could be used and then made to dance like a fool for her amusement. But he had a power, and it was stronger in its small, negative way than any of theirs.

One by one he tasted their fires and put them out. He sensed the thin, futile rage; he knew that they thought the Queen was striking at them. Let them think what they would. For now he turned to the Queen's own magic, the mist itself. He swallowed its strong, sickly flavor. It gathered and increased around him, but still he swallowed it, and then it was gone; he himself was panting, sweating on his bed, but the Queen's sight was gone from Palicrovol, perhaps for the first time in years, and any spells she might have put on him were gone. Would she notice? Orem almost hoped so. He knew this: once he had cut a hole in her power, she would have to discover it and remake all the spells that he had taken. Her mist of magic was not like a real fog; it was not carried on the wind. It went only where she put it.

For a long time he stayed there, reaching farther and farther from Palicrovol, tasting, drinking down all the Queen had put there, finding that its unpleasant taste grew tolerable and finally, finally invigorating. Yet, when at last he quit, none of it had stayed with him. It was as Galloway had told him: What he swallowed up

150

was gone forever. It only touched him slightly on the way into him. He could never draw it back again.

He withdrew his attention, opened his eyes. He was alone in the darkness and very tired. The palace was silent, and almost he went to sleep. But before he had dozed off completely, he heard a faint sound, a distant sound in the palace. It was a cry of rage, he thought. And then, as sleep finally did come, he was vaguely aware of servants moving very, very quickly on their near-silent feet, on a hundred errands.

In the morning he did not see the Queen. He asked Weasel, who met him at breakfast.

"You won't see the Queen today."

"Why not?" asked Orem.

"She's very busy." And that was that. Except that once he caught a glimpse of Urubugala, who was waiting outside a door. The little black fool winked a white eye at him and made a grimace and a sign with his hand. It could have meant anything, really. Except that Orem recognized it. It took him a few moments of remembering to realize what it reminded him of. Urubugala had pointed at him with his eyes bugging out, in exactly the same way that King Palicrovol had pointed at him from the street in Banningside. "Mine, mine, mine," cried the fool, cackling with laughter. And he winked again.

Orem turned and ran from him, though in a few moments he stopped and wondered why he had been so afraid. The man was just a fool, the sign just coincidence.

But he knew it was not true. Urubugala, at least, knew who and what Orem was and knew also that it was King Palicrovol who, however accidentally, had sent the Little King to Hart's Hope so many months before. Urubugala knew; but the Queen did not know. The fool was disloyal, then. Well, he had good reason.

151

So, for that matter, did Orem. He had been brought here against his will, and though he hadn't fought his marriage with the Queen, no one had so much as asked him if he would like to wed her; now he knew, or at least suspected, that he was here, not for himself, but for the blood in his veins, for the power that it might give to the Queen in her great magics.

He did not know how he would keep her from taking his life, but he would do it if he could. One thing he *did* know, however, was that until the last breath was drawn in red fire from his body, he would work against her, secretly, in the darkness, by undoing all of her work. All of it, if he could. Was Palicrovol her enemy? Then Palicrovol was Orem's friend, as was everyone who hated her or feared her.

Such as Urubugala. And wasn't it Urubugala who had told him, when they first met, "The Queen sees everything except that which she sees not." The Queen could look at the whole world; but she could not see that she could not see Orem. With her eyes she could see him, but not with the perpetual vision that floated like mist in the back of her remarkable mind.

In the late afternoon, Orem walked in the palace garden because it was green and beautiful and reminded him of the forests of the high Banning Valley, where he had walked all his life until a few months ago. Nearest the palace, the gardens were well clipped and tended, with gravel paths and even a few corduroy carriage roads for lazier guests. But it was not far at all to where the paths faded into many thin trails and the underbrush grew thick and untended and rude squirrels fled the sight of man. Orem walked westward until he came to the palace park wall. High above him a few soldiers lounged, looking nowhere in particular—certainly not at him. The wall was not climbable: the stones were set so close, without mortar, that Orem doubted a knife blade could fit between them, and three times up the wall's height the wall stepped out nearly a yard. There was no escape here.

Still, lost in his own thoughts and facing, in small bits, the fear of certain death that was growing in him, he walked north along the wall until it curved in sharply, and a tower was set into it. He did not know until later that this was Corner Castle, with its Lesser Donjon. But without having to ask anyone, he knew what the place was for. He could hear it only faintly. It could have been a distant cry, even a sound from the city beyond the wall; could have been, but was not. Orem pressed his ear against the stone of the tower and the sound became clear. It was the scream of a man in agony; it was the scream of the worst terror a man can know. Not the fear of death, but the fear that death will delay its coming.

Orem could not conceive of the torture that would arouse such a cry from a human throat. The stone he leaned against was cold, and he shivered. The sun was long since hidden behind the west wall, but now he could see that the sunlight touched only the topmost domes of the palace. It was near evening and getting cooler. He left the tower and the man suffering inside. He wondered if he would ever hear such a sound coming from his own throat. Ah, no, he told himself, shivering again. He who can make such a sound is already far beyond hearing.

He walked back a different way and came suddenly to the Queen's Pool. It was the water from the Baths, of course, the pure spring water that flowed in an endless stream as if God himself were pumping, right in the heart of the Castle. The Baths were public and the water good; but most of the water went somewhere else, went in aqueducts to the Temples, to the great houses and embassies lining King's Road and the even more exclusive Diggings Avenue, went in bronze pipes to Pools Park, where the artists dwelled outside the palace, and went here, to the Queen's Pool, where few ever bathed and the water was pure as a baby's tears. Orem stayed back in the trees, just looked at the water rippling in the breeze, transparent, green, and deep because the sun did not shine brightly from the surface.

Then he saw that someone else had come to bathe. It was a woman, distant across the huge pool, but still easy to recognize—Weasel Sootmouth, and as Orem watched she stepped from her gown and entered the water and began to swim lazily along the surface of the water, lying on her back.

Why does this woman serve the Queen, Orem wondered. Named Weasel by the Queen, but what was her name before? What magic has the Queen placed upon this woman?

And so Orem looked, or rather tasted; and was surprised to find that here the Queen had spent at least as much power as she had used to bind poor Palicrovol. But why? Who was this ugly woman, that the Queen feared her as much as her hated enemy, the true King?

Orem toyed with the idea of breaking all the spells that bound Weasel. But he restrained himself. If it is far beyond the walls of Hart's Hope that the Queen finds her magic undone, that's one thing, he decided. But for her to find such things happening here—it would not do. For now, anyway. At least for now.

It was ungracious of him to watch poor Weasel's bent and shapeless body, he realized. She would surely be embarrassed that a man knew that her breasts hung like empty feedbags and that her legs and knees were gawky and overboned. He turned away from her in pity. And then remembered that she had also pitied him.

Of such feelings are friendships made in this sad place, Orem thought as he left the pool. He took a wide curve around the pool and was quiet. But then he could not resist one last temptation. It was not for lust or even curiosity that Orem turned back. He was drawn some other way. But this time he approached the pool from the south end, as silently as he could; and this time he learned something more than the sadness of Weasel's nudity. For he came up behind the Queen, and she did not see or hear him, because she was also watching the pool, as he had watched. And so both the Little King and Queen Beauty, his wife and owner and executioner, watched as the great stag emerged from the wood, just where Orem had been only a few minutes before, and came to drink from the water's edge. It was an ancient hart, as could be seen from the tremendous rack of antlers that overbalanced its head. As the stag braced itself to lower its head into the water, it became just as clear that if it once lowered its antlers that far it would never have the strength to raise them up. What a monstrous trick the Sweet Sisters play on such a magnificent animal as this, Orem thought, that if he bends to drink, he may never rise again.

And then Weasel Sootmouth was beside the hart, and received its antlers into her hands, and held their weight as it drank its fill from the Queen's pure pool. Drinking done, the stag strained to rise, and Weasel rose with him, lifting the horns high until the weight sat properly upon the great stag's neck and it moved slowly, gracefully, imperiously back into the forest. How old this hart must be, Orem thought, to have earned two dozen points to each antler; and all his life he has dewelled here, in the palace park, surrounded by these ancient walls. Or is this stag so old that he remembers freedom?

And he thought again: how strange that this most

beautiful of animals comes to drink when Weasel bathes here. If the stag needed help today, it needed it yesterday, too; each day, then, Weasel comes, faithfully, the hart's true friend.

It was then that Orem first loved Weasel Sootmouth. Not as a man loves a woman, certainly, for he was not yet old enough that he could forget a woman's ugliness and love the beauty of her soul; few men ever are that old. He loved her as a child loves his good teacher. Perhaps, most of all, he loved her because he had to love someone, and she at least had shown herself capable of being trusted. If she can love this great old stag, Orem thought, perhaps she can love me.

Just in time Orem slipped back almost silently into the trees; he was just out of sight when the Queen turned and walked back to the palace. Orem could see her face, though she did not turn to look at him. The virginal sweetness was not there. Queen Beauty looked angry and beautiful and tired and beautiful and vengeful and beautiful, and it made Orem afraid.

It was dark again. Orem had wasted the day. But he did not waste the night. He went back to his mirrored room and shut his eyes and found King Palicrovol again. The Queen's magic was stronger around him than ever before but, systematically, Orem tasted it all, drowned it all in the deep well within him. And this time he took even more, took it in an even wider circle around the King, so that many miles of land were free of the Queen's Searching Eye. Oh, you will have to lay many a spell tomorrow, Orem silently said to the Queen. Many a spell before you even find old Palicrovol with his golden eyes. And he went to sleep satisfied, hearing once again with pleasure the servants on their errands, and the Queen's dim cry of alarm, of fury, and of fear. Orem hoped, at least, that she felt fear. Let her turn cold inside herself, wondering what wizard challenges her, what power that she cannot find opposes her, he thought. She will never imagine it is her Little King.

Orem dreamed that the Queen came to him in the night and made love to him; he awoke in his moment of ecstasy and wept that it was not true.

The palace was filled with infinite variety, but variety itself soon becomes monotonous. Today the elephant from the northeast nation of Bushmouth, brought by a great barge towed upriver by five hundred slaves; tomorrow a chariot all of gold and ivory, drawn by fifteen horses with one black diamond eye, perfectly matched, a gift of the Prince of Woodrise. The next day naked boys dancing and virtually flying through the air as they wrestled and tossed; and afterward soft hollow candies filled with wine, each a different vintage, or flavored with a different fruit. Orem's place in all these things was the same: to appear prominently, to say little, and to be laughed at whether he spoke or not. Oh, all were polite; all bowed to him and, as Queen Beauty had commanded, everyone obeyed. But it was known that in Hart's Hope, the greatest city in the world, Queen Beauty was pregnant by a farmboy and had made the bumpkin her Little King.

The diversions were all the same to Orem. For a few moments he was interested, but when the novelty was done the palace itself returned; the servants ran their inscrutable errands, the local nobility and nouveau riche came and went, favorites fell and favorites rose; it made little difference to Orem. As long as no one interfered with his walks in the palace park, his wanderings through the palace, his virtual ransacking of Queen Beauty's father's library, then he was content. Once, feeling nostalgic for old Halfpriest Dobbick,

Orem hunted for a chapel to offer the five prayers and two songs. But there was no chapel, nor even a clay cup for the offering of earth's water from earth's hand. God had no place in the palace, and Orem was disquieted by that. God had surrounded him all his life, and when he took to the river he had been glad enough to leave religion behind. Now he was surrounded by magic, and though it never touched him—or perhaps because it never touched him—he felt oppressed, and more and more believed that a simple prayer could set him free. So he knelt by the pool in the morning and made a cup of earth in his hand, filled it with water from the Queen's Pool, and said the first three prayers. When he tried to pour the water out, however, it evaporated before it touched the ground. The Queen's magic could not tolerate such a thing. Orem thought of clearing a place in the magic where he might pray. But he did not want the Queen to notice holes in her spells so close to home. No, safer not to. And it was silly, he decided for him to want to pray at all.

And yet he still sang the two songs on the way back to the palace, though he could tell that the air swallowed up the words only a few inches from his mouth so that he could hardly hear them.

His rest from the days' humiliations and boredom and despair was the nights' battles. He took a great deal of joy from vexing the Queen. She was getting unmistakably gravid, heavier in the belly every day, and though her magic was enough to keep her beautiful throughout, there was still a toll. She became short-tempered and took more naps during the day. She also began to seem visibly weaker. Fainter.

Each night Orem would go to bed a little earlier and lie awake a little longer. It became easier and easier to find King Palicrovol and undo all the Queen's magic around him; easier, too, to spread an ever broader circle around him that was cleared of her magic, cleared of her Searching Eye. And while every day her spells on the King were more heavily protected, more painstakingly placed, Orem also noticed that the Queen was beginning to lose ground—every day there would be places and patches in the mist of her magic where she had not replaced her spells, where her Searching Eye no longer reached. She could not keep pace with him, and he reached far afield each night in the last few minutes before sleep, tearing great holes in her Searching Eye in places where she could not expect it. One night he took Calarnay from her sight; the next Baysend. Cities and towns, forests and farms, he rent her vision and her power and she hadn't the strength to seam it all.

Orem did not fool himself into thinking this was a great victory, however. He did not know if he could face her directly and counter spell after spell. All he was sure he could do was this: occupy her in mending a thousand tiny holes; irritate her; weary her; weaken her.

And another effect, of course. Palicrovol's wizards knew that something strange was going on, and knew that, in the long run, it could only benefit the true King of Burland. It gave Palicrovol hope.

"Palicrovol threatens he will tear you limb from limb while you are still alive," a noblewoman said one day, pretending to be outraged by the gossip. But Orem only smiled. They thought he smiled because he knew the Queen's magic would protect him. Actually he smiled because he loved to hear of Palicrovol, his enemy, whose place he had usurped: "Where is he now?" Orem asked.

"He is said to be in Gronskeep for the winter."

"Is it winter?" Orem asked.

"Outside the palace it is," another woman said. "The Queen's power cannot stop the turn of seasons outside the palace walls."

"And is Palicrovol deep in snow?" Orem asked.

And the women laughed and denied any knowledge of such things. "Just the tales the servants pick up in the markets, or our husbands at the Arena, that's all we know."

And then the more dangerous rumors, as the bureaucrats from the Taxhouse questioned him whenever he wandered into the official end of the palace. "Is it true that King Palicrovol no longer goes blind because the Queen cannot see through his eyes?"

"No one tells me such things," Orem answered them all.

"But surely you can tell us if it's true that Queen Beauty is ill, that a great necromancer is countering all her spells against the King."

"I am not kept informed about the Queen's business. And so far as I know, there's no such thing as magic in this palace." And the bureaucrats retreated after his reminder of the official lies that kept the peace between palace and temple. Yet he let slip a few points, now and then. That the Queen was weary. That she napped often. That she was surly and irritable. Let the rats wonder if they had chosen the right ship for sailing, Orem thought. Let them begin to try to make friends in the King's camp. Any weakness to the Queen is strength to the King. Palicrovol sent me here, wittingly or not; if the Queen means to use my blood to make her magic, I will do as much as I can to strengthen Palicrovol before I die.

"You're too somber," Weasel told him. He was sitting on a bench, studying the floral work inlaid into the floor.

"Am I?" Orem asked.

160

"Whenever I see you, you're reading books or staring at the floor."

"I go to parties," Orem said. "I'm very busy."

Weasel smiled. "I thought boys your age loved to be lazy."

Orem said nothing, but unaccountably his thoughts went to the growing belly of the Queen. "I am going to be a father."

Weasel looked away from him. "Well, then, I guess it isn't right to call you a boy, is it? I'm sorry."

That was not what Orem meant. "What will be expected of me?"

Weasel looked back at him, studied his face. "What is expected of you now?"

"I must act the fool. Will my child laugh at me?"

Weasel's face contorted oddly, but she was so ugly that Orem could not tell what emotion she was trying to express.

"Or will I never see him at all?"

"That, at least, is up to you."

"Is it?"

Weasel sat beside him on the bench and put her arm around his shoulder. Orem remembered her swimming naked in the Queen's Pool. He also started to remember the Queen's touch on that first night, but he fought that memory down, would not think of it, listened instead to Weasel. "Little King, you command everyone in this palace except Urubugala, Craven, and me. If you want to see your child, you can. Who will stop you?"

"The Queen does not obey me."

"Have you commanded her?"

Orem started to laugh, but could not stay amused. "I'm afraid to," he said.

"I don't advise you try it, but I can promise you that part of the result, at least, will be her obedience. I suggest you word your command carefully.

"Is it true?"

"If the Queen didn't want you to hear this, she would have stopped me, wouldn't she?"

"Perhaps she isn't listening."

Weasel smiled thinly. "The Queen is always listening."

"I hear that she doesn't hear everything. I hear that she's blind to what goes on with King Palicrovol. I hear that there's a power in Burland that can undo her magic wherever it likes." Orem felt his heart pounding. He had never come so close to self-revelation before; why was he doing this now? The Queen could hear, surely—and yet he knew that he was trying to say *something* to Weasel.

"Where did you hear that?" Weasel asked, truly alarmed now.

"It's common rumor."

"It's—it's—" and then Weasel stopped, choked on the words, but finally, with her voice bent in some strange way, she said, "It's a lie."

But it was not a lie, and Orem knew whose words Weasel had spoken. He felt guilty that he alone of all the people in the palace was free of the Queen's intrusions. He alone went every day with his mind unforced, his will unbroken. He wanted to make it up to Weasel somehow. He reached out and touched her face, as he had touched his mother's face once after his baby sister—was it a sister? yes—had died.

Weasel shuddered at his touch, and he withdrew his hand.

"I'm sorry," he said.

She shook her head. "You don't understand."

He took her hand in his. "I do, better than you know."

She pulled her hand away, and then bent over as if

in pain. "It's the Queen's blessing on me," Weasel said, between clenched teeth. "It isn't enough that I look this way. A man's touch makes me sick, as well."

Orem pulled back from her. "What are you doing here?"

"The story isn't mine to tell."

"Whose it is, then?"

Weasel strained to answer, but the words would not come. Apparently the Queen did not want Orem to know who was free to answer him. But it was no secret—the Queen knew all the tales, and this was one Orem meant to have. More than that. This was the time, if there ever was one, to see if the Queen lied or not when she promised to bend her will before his.

"I will go and speak to my wife," Orem said, but he felt silly saying the words. Wife and husband they were in name, but their only act of unity had come and gone long ago.

"Not now," Weasel said. And then she cried out in pain.

"Why are you still in pain?" Orem asked.

"I'm not," Weasel said, and then cried out again.

"Then why do you cry in pain?"

Weasel laughed. "It's another part of the same—ah!" Silence. A gasp. Then: "The same tale told by the same teller. But don't go to her now."

"I will."

"I advise against it."

"I will be my own adviser, then."

"She's having the baby!" Weasel said. She was gritting her teeth in pain.

"Already?" Orem asked stupidly.

"Already! Fool! The child has been in her womb for a year today. Because the leaves don't fall, have you forgotten that days still pass? A year in her womb, Little King! Don't go near her now!"

But Orem was already going. His child was being born. He had no idea what he meant to do, but he had to do it. He ran to the first door, entered a great hall, crossed it, climbed a stairway, and stopped, panting, at the top, realizing that in all the time he had lived in the palace, he still had no notion of where the Queen's chambers were. He had never been invited there.

"You," he said to one of the ubiquitous servants. "Do you know where the Queen's chambers are?"

"I'm forbidden to tell," she said, wide-eyed.

"I'm going to her. She's having my child. I want to help."

Suddenly the servant laughed. Then she covered her mouth. "I'm sorry," she said. Then she turned and led him along a hall, which went on forever, lined with doors. He knew where all of them led, he thought. But there were more than a hundred doors, and as he followed the girl farther and farther down the hall, he realized that whenever he had come this way in his explorations, some door had been standing open, and he had been distracted by some conversation, some novelty, some person with whom he had to speak. He had never walked the full length of the hall before.

"You mustn't mind the illusions," said the girl.

Illusions? Orem said nothing, but now understood why the girl would sometimes hesitate in midstep, and then set her jaw and go on. It would do no good to announce that whatever illusions there were, he saw none of them.

A year, Orem thought. I have been here a year. And the child has been carried a year. Such a birth would kill an ordinary woman. But somehow when he opened the last door and stepped in and saw the Queen, it was not her life he worried about.

The servant quickly closed the door, and Orem stood alone at the foot of the Queen's huge bed. Beauty lay alone in the middle, naked, her legs spread wide, her knees up. All the topsheets and cushions had been pushed from the bed. Some sheets had been tied to the five posts of the bed. Two were tied to her feet, and she strained against them; two she held in her hands, and pulled hard. The last was gripped between her teeth, and in her agony she tossed her head and worried the cloth like a dog with a rag. She dripped with sweat, and a high-pitched moan emerged from her throat. Blood was trickling from the passage where the baby's head had crowned. The head was large and bloody and purple, and it would not come. Beauty looked at him through eyes wide as a deer's with fear and pain. The eyes followed him as he walked around the foot of bed and came to the left head of the bed, above and behind her. Even in such a state, she was still beautiful, and Orem was trembling at the sight of the body he had once loved. But he ignored that distraction.

"Beauty," he said.

She only moaned.

"Beauty, you wear the ring on your rightmost finger."

She shook her head back and forth, not to say no but to ease the pain.

"I command you to speak to me."

Orem could not see her eyes. He only knew that suddenly her painful writhing and straining stopped. She sighed a long, relieved sigh. "How gladly I obey," she said, and suddenly the baby's head popped from between her legs, though she gave no sign of pain. Her belly convulsed, rippled; she sat up easily, forcing the baby out farther in the process, and then pulled him from her groin. Like an animal she licked the mucus from the baby's face. Then she held the child, a boy, as he cried.

Orem could not believe how quickly, as if at his command, the child had come.

And there was the Queen, as if she had suffered nothing, laughing at him, laughing long and loud.

"Is the child's birth so funny?" Orem asked, still determined to be angry, to command her, to shake off his terrible fear of her.

"I think not," she said, turning a beautifully contemptuous face to him. "But you, Little King, you are a joy better than a hundred clowns."

"What have I done?"

"Command me again, Little King."

"I want the truth from you!"

"All the truth that is in me, you may have."

"Who is Weasel?"

The Queen's eyes went wide in a mockery of surprise. She laughed again, then put her breast in the child's mouth. The boy had no idea what to do with it, but she stroked his cheek as if she had been midwife at a thousand births; with her Searching Eye, she probably had.

"I asked you—"

"I heard you," the Queen answered, still laughing softly. "Weasel, is it? Weasel is the greatest mystery you've been able to come up with? In a whole year, she's the best mystery you've been able to find?"

"And Urubugala. And Craven."

"You're a child, Little King. The only people who interest you are the three you can't command. Well, then. Here's the tale. Have it with joy and see if it brings you any contentment. You've heard the story of my marriage to Palicrovol, I'm sure. Of the tender ceremony of ravishment performed before a thousand swine at Faces Hall."

Orem nodded.

"It was a joyful bridal day for me, my dear Little King. As my pitiful bride's blood seeped, with it went my father's kingdom. And then my loving spouse sent me to a fisher's hut to be raised as a fishwife, no doubt, while he ruled where it was my right to rule until I chose my own husband and gave the power to him.

"But I was found by a wizard, who taught me all. More than he knew he taught me, in fact, and I learn quickly—much more quickly than you, Little King. It had been only a year from the day I was so blithely wed when the tool came into my hands that would give me all the power I needed for centuries. Yet, though the wizard saw my weapon every day, he thought nothing of it, ignored it completely. Until it was too late, and I wielded it.

"The wizard's name was Sleeve. I bound him first, and he is still bound. I blessed him with a gift and brought him with me to Hart's Hope. Here in Hart's Hope my loving husband waited for me with an army. But his army fled, all but one man, a general named Zymas, who once had served my father. Zymas betrayed my father, doubtless for sincere reasons, and when Palicrovol had stolen my only birthright, Zymas urged my husband to kill me lest I cause trouble later. I had not forgotten Zymas, and I was pleased that my spell of terror did not touch him.

"And there was someone else in Hart's Hope that I came to see. A beautiful sea princess from Onologasenweev, whom he had taken as his wife. My timing was superb. I arrived just as Palicrovol had thought to hold his wedding night and shed bride's blood again, though I suspect more tenderly than before. I turned his attention away from her, and when I had driven him out, she also fell into my hands. Her name was Enziquelvinisensee Evelvenin. But from my first night here in my father's home, her name was never heard again. Nor the name of Zymas. Nor the name of Sleeve.

"Have you any wit, my Little King?"

Orem could only think of Weasel, ugly Weasel. Who had come innocently from the islands to marry the great King Palicrovol. Who had found instead the terrible rage of a woman who had been wronged, but who was thought to be dead, or at least forgotten.

"Weasel," Orem said.

"It really wasn't a change of name for her. Just a translation. Weasels are beautiful in the islands, and the fur of that animal is a prerogative of royalty. And Sootmouth—a family name. Is that the story you wanted? Think of it, Little King. Do you see my face? Is it beautiful? This was not the face of the wretched, frightened little girl who screamed in Palicrovol's arms. Oh, no. This is the face I gave myself, as a reward for my patience in suffering. As a birthright, since the only inheritance I had was gone. This once was the face of Enziquelvinisensee Evelvenin." And she laughed and laughed.

But through the laughter Orem began to feel something he had not expected to feel. His grief for Weasel, who suffered innocently, was not dimmed; but he also felt a sympathy for the Queen. He imagined her now, not as the imperious beauty he knew, but as the helpless, plain little girl who was made to suffer the agony of her unworthy father's defeat. What a feast of hate she had fed upon then; she still ate from the same table. He remembered the words from Halfpriest Dobbick's favorite passage in the Second Song, and he sang to her, not really meaning to sing, but not able to stop himself, either:

> "*God surely sees your sins, my love,*
> *The blackness of your heart, my love;*
> *He weighs them with your suffering:*
> *Which is the lesser part, my love?*"

Orem's voice had not been welcome in the choir of the monastery, but here it was not the art that made the light in the room dance. It was the power in the song. The power of God, which none had been able to bring before the Queen's face in all these years; but more, the power to undo Queen Beauty, for that was what Orem had done.

She held the child to her breast and wept and wept and wept. She forgot to make her face beautiful as she did, and in her crying Orem thought he saw a memory that he could not possibly have seen. He thought he saw young King Palicrovol rise up, naked before a multitude, his swollen penis shining in the sunlight; and the crowd cheered as the antler crown was placed on his head. Then he turned and left, and the crowd dispersed, until no one was left, no one at all, except a young girl, a child, weeping, weeping, weeping, and an infant appeared and she held it against her nonexistent breast.

Orem reached out and touched her, and Queen Beauty leaned to him. In a moment he held her hot shoulders in his embrace. But pity is not infinite; he soon looked beyond her hair, forgot the tears that had soaked his gown. He saw only the child, only his son, she had stopped crying and was staring up at them. A year in the womb, a third again the normal time; perhaps that explained the brightness of his eyes, the beauty of his face, the deftness of his hands as they already reached out and grasped at his mother's hair. Perhaps it was the year in the womb that explained why the child could already smile when Orem smiled at him.

"What is his name?" Orem asked.

The Queen's crying was silent now, and the trembling of her body stopped all at once, though she made no move to pull away from him.

"He will never have a name."

"Why not?"

"Little King, I won't let him have a name."

"But I command you," Orem said.

The Queen pulled away now and looked at him coldly. "You command easily now, don't you? See how well your commands work, Little King, before you try any others."

"Name him," Orem said.

"Youth," she answered, smiling at him. Her amusement had returned.

"Youth? That's a name for him?"

"It is more name than he will earn in all his life," she answered.

"He's my son," Orem said. "I will be free with him."

"Will you?"

"I command it. You can cut me off from you, Queen Beauty, but he's half mine, half me, and I'll not be cut off from him."

"Will you not?"

"I command it."

"Oh, you're a delicious fool; I've kept the three most marvelous fools in all the world with me for all these years, and you—the best fool of all—you came as the Sweet Sisters' gift in a dream. Have your wish then, my Little King. All the time you want with this child, all the time you can possibly use, it's yours. Yours, and may it bring you joy. May you love this child better than you love yourself."

Orem reached down and took the child from his mother. He did not complain; already the child's body responded, reacted, tautened to rise into Orem's arms, something that should have been impossible to an infant not yet fifteen minutes old. The child smiled at him.

"I already love him that much," Orem said. "It's a poor enough measure."

And then he remembered that the Queen had no intention of letting her Little King live for very long at all, and a lump of self-pity came to his throat. He refused to let the emotion take him. The Queen meant nothing but evil to him, but at least he had this one gift from her. "Youth," he said to the child, and the young boy smiled at the name.

Beauty giggled on the bed. "Little King," she said.

"Yes?"

"Why, in all this time, if you were determined to be so commanding—why didn't you ever come to me and command me to lie with you again?"

Orem looked at her and could not think of the answer to the question. And he asked himself another: If she would obey him, why didn't he command her not to sacrifice him to feed her great magic? Why could he only command her to tell him a tale and let him play with a child?

"Oh, my Little King," she said, "have ever the Sweet Sisters led so innocent a victim into a trap as they have this time?"

Command her now, Orem told himself. It was an oversight before; make up for it now and command her to give you your life and her love.

But she was laughing at him, and he couldn't say the words. In the face of her laughter, he couldn't ask for his life. And never her love. Never that.

He laid the child in her arms again and left the room, not knowing what it was that made him choose this and not that; it couldn't be pride stopping him, could it? What gom led his steps? Sure enough every step he took was a stumble.

A servant met him in the hall.

"Little King," she said. "If you forgive me, please,

but the Lady Weasel is crying for you."

"Crying?"

"She doesn't know what she's saying, but she calls your name, calls Little King, Little King, and we don't know what to do for her except beg you to come."

"What's wrong with her?" Orem remembered that when he left her—how long ago?—she had been in pain.

"We don't know. Please come."

He went. Weasel was lying on a bed in a room he supposed was her own, a beautiful enough place, but he had no heart to notice that. Weasel looked white as if half her blood had been lost, and she tossed and turned deliriously on the bed.

"What happened to her?" Orem asked.

"She was in pain, and we led her to bed, and then suddenly she screamed and all this blood came out of her. And this, too. It's a miracle, but it may kill her." What the servant pointed to on a silver tray was impossible, but Orem had seen births before and knew a placenta when he saw one; a placenta with all the umbilical cord attached. "Oh, God, oh, Sweet Sisters," he said, and he knelt by the bed and touched his hand to Weasel's hideous face, even uglier now from pain. He remembered now, should have noticed it then. When Youth was born so suddenly, Queen Beauty had not had to cut the cord, for there was no cord. Here was the cord, here was the pain the Queen had so abruptly forgotten. Beauty had borne her own pain until Orem came—and commanded her to tell him a tale. After months with the wizard Galloway, hadn't he learned at least this one most fundamental rule? No magic is done without a price, no life is lived without a loss, no pain is suffered without a profit, no death comes without its gift. Youth was born in agony; but Orem had commanded, and the Queen had treacherously obeyed. If she were not to suffer that pain, someone else must, and it was Weasel.

Orem knelt by the bed and whispered to her, "Enziquelvinisensee Evelvenin."

She held still, suddenly stopped her turning. "You know me," she said, but there was nothing in her eyes to show that she knew him.

"It's my fault," he said miserably.

"You know me."

"I did this to you."

And then she said, "I forgive you," and fell asleep. The servants looked at him in amazement. One of them touched her head. "The fever's gone," he said.

And another servant whispered, "What were the words you said? It's a strong magic you brought, that it comes only from a few words."

Orem was not sure what had cured her. The naming of her name? Or the forgiveness that this much-wronged woman had still given so easily? Or just the whim of Queen Beauty, who was doubtless watching from her room at the end of the long hall?

Orem looked at Weasel's sleeping face, and let his eyes forget what they saw and see instead what they should see: Weasel with another face, the sweet virginal face of Queen Beauty. And it occurred to Orem that he loved Weasel more than anyone else in his life; that he loved her more than he feared the Queen. And it occurred to him right afterward that he loved her no less when the image failed and he saw only the ugly woman he had known all this year.

He waited by her bed until she awoke. He had napped, and now he was awake and hungry, wondering if he should leave her and go eat, when she suddenly turned in bed and winced in anticipation of pain. But there was no pain, and she was surprised. "Little King," she said faintly.

"The Queen bore my son," he told her, "but you bore the pain."

"She told me I'd share it. Not that I'd have all of it."

Orem touched her hand; she gently pulled her hand away. "My lady Weasel," he said. "She did it because I commanded her—"

"Never mind, Little King. The use she has for you requires that she let you rule her, but it isn't in her to do it genuinely. It's not your fault when she twists your words against you. Is the child good?"

Orem shrugged, then laughed a little. "I haven't had any others. Yes, he's good. But he doesn't seem like a newborn. Already he seems wise."

"Oh, yes. Wise indeed. And loving. He smiles, surely."

"And grasps with his hands."

"I dreamed," Weasel said, "that you called me by another name."

Orem looked away from her, looked out the window. "She told me your story."

"And my name?"

"I haven't forgotten it, either."

"Now that you're a father, I doubt you're still a child."

"I'm not really a father," Orem said. "Not yet."

Weasel raised an eyebrow.

"But I will be."

"Perhaps you would be happier if you never saw the child again."

Orem frowned. "The time will come soon enough when I will never see the child. While I still can, I mean to love him."

Weasel looked at him with—what expression was it? Orem could not tell. Horror, it seemed, or anger, or puzzlement.

"Then you know?" Weasel asked. "You know what

the Queen intends to do?"

"It hasn't been hard to guess."

"Sweet Sisters," Weasel whispered, "and you haven't tried to kill the Queen."

"I suspect she wouldn't let me if I tried."

"No, you're not a man," Weasel said. "You're either much less, or much more."

"Help me. I don't know how to love an infant who is mine."

"And do I?" Weasel asked. "You're a strange sort of man, Little King." She looked away from him, thought for a little while. "The Queen could not require me to obey you. But neither does she forbid it." It was all the answer Orem was likely to get. Weasel was tired; he left her so she could sleep again.

Outside Weasel's room Urubugala and Craven waited.

"She'll be fine," Orem said. "She should sleep."

"The Queen," Urubugala said, "has been harvested."

"Your son?" asked Craven.

"I have commanded the Queen to let me be his father in life as well as in conception."

Urubugala narrowed his eyes, then turned a somersault and laughed. "He dances, he dances, our Little King dances!"

Orem was irritated for a monent; the fool could be tiresome. But then he remembered who they were.

"Sleeve," Orem said.

The fool stopped laughing. And instead of his white eyes rolling and looking mad in his black face, there was suddenly the majesty of a man who had known all the wisdom in the world and lost it.

"Zymas," Orem said, and it was the old soldier's turn to bring back a memory of himself as he ought to be. Not that he gained any strength to his frail body, but he stood a little straighter, as if to show that he knew how a strong young man should stand.

"I never thought," said Zymas.

"To hear, to hear—" said Sleeve.

"That name," Zymas finished.

And then, as abruptly, they forgot again. Or rather, were forced to forget, for suddenly Zymas winced with pain and bent at the waist; his eyes went a bit vacuous and teary. And Sleeve was Urubugala again, laughing and dancing on his knees on the floor, crying out, "Who is the magical leper who cleans us with his tongue? He puts our names in picture frames and paints them out with dung!"

The Queen was still listening, always listening. And when Weasel awoke again, would she remember that Orem had spoken her name? Or would the Queen take that, too? He hated her then, worse than ever before; she had suffered terribly once, as a child, but surely she had had her vengeance now. Surely that was enough.

"How long will the Queen keep doing this to you?" Orem asked.

Craven just nodded his head in the sleepy way that empty old people do, and Urubugala made an elaborate bow that ended in his falling on his nose. "I wish the Queen would do to me what the Queen has done to you," he said, and then laughed maniacally. "But now that Beauty has done her duty, it's cock-a-doodle-doo."

Orem turned away from Urubugala and watched Craven as the old general walked slowly, delicately down the hall. It was an odd sort of shuffle he did, and it seemed to be in rhythm to Urubugala's cackling laugh, as if they were performing a sad little show and Orem was the only audience. Except, of course, the Queen, who saw it all.

Craven carefully opened a door and passed through

it; feebly it closed behind him.

And then Orem found himself in Urubugala's grip. The fool gripped him by the shoulders, then by the neck, pulled him down despite Orem's instinctive resistance, and when the fool's mouth was at Orem's ear, he whispered, almost silently, "What are you waiting for? Fool!"

With that the fool released him and scampered away, laughing madly.

What happens now, Orem wondered. What does Urubugala-Sleeve want me to do?

"And what does Queen Beauty know? How is she toying with me? Why am I still alive?

"Queen Beauty," he whispered, "how long will I live?"

But there came no answer. For when he was alone, and there was no one nearby so she could see through the other's eyes and hear through the other's ears, Queen Beauty could not see Orem, could not hear his words, and could not see that she could not see.

Orem went up to the Queen's room. Servants bustled in the long hall outside. "Where is my son, Youth?" Orem asked.

They led him to a cradle where the child lay. A day old, and he seemed to recognize his father. Impossible, of course. Yet he had lain twelve months in the womb: anything could be possible. Orem touched the soft clean skin of the cheek that only hours ago had been bloody and red; the child caught his finger and smiled. The fingers were tiny, the nails as remarkable as fine ivory miniatures. "Who are you?" Orem asked his son in awe. "Where did you come from?" And he answered his question to himself. From me. You came from me. Your mother carried you in her belly, but I planted you there, I am the source of you, and you are the river that flows from my fountain. When I am dead to serve the Queen's purposes, Youth, you will be me forever.

Orem held Youth in his arms in the garden, letting sunlight fall on his face for the first time. It was morning, it was warm, and last night Orem had not gone out to undo the Queen's magic; he had not remembered to do it and did not know why he had forgotten that they were at war. The only reasons he could think of were the child in his arms and the woman who walked to him across the broad lawn from the palace.

"Weasel," Orem said as she came closer. For a moment he saw how ugly she was, and wondered that he could have thought yesterday that he loved her. Then he pushed away the unworthy thought, and forced himself to remember his love for her. It was not hard. But it made him ashamed that he could still think less of her because of the shape the Queen had given her.

"Little King," she answered, with a smile that twisted her mouth. Orem refused to see how the smile distorted her features even worse than usual. The Queen has no spells that can touch me, Orem told himself. Why then does Weasel's ugliness strike me with such force today?

"Would you like to see my son?"

Orem held him out to her, but Weasel shook her head and backed away. "I'm forbidden to touch him, Little King. The child is not mine."

Orem was angry. "Your pain bought his life."

She shook her head. "Only one woman may he love. It's the Queen's word. He can only suck from her breast; he can turn his face only to her for light and life." Then Weasel smiled again. Orem winced inwardly at what it did to her face in the harsh sunlight. "Thank you for being kind to me yesterday." There was an eagerness in her voice that made Orem uneasy. And his unease made him hate himself, for he recognized it for what it was—fear that she had understood his commitment to her and meant to hold him to it.

That was why he blurted out what he had not meant to say. "Weasel," he said, "I love you." He had to say it now, say it plainly, or he was afraid he would retreat from it, forget what he had seen in her yesterday.

Weasel looked at him—tenderly? It was hard to tell. Softly, anyway. "How sweet of you to say it," she said. "I'm glad we're friends."

Orem was surprised at the mildness of her response. She must have misunderstood, he thought. "I mean I love you. The Queen may be my wife, but everything that I should feel for her, I feel for you."

She had misunderstood. Now she suddenly turned away, touching one hand to her mouth in a clumsy gesture that would have been lovely in a woman more beautiful than she. Orem felt a thrill of pleasure at the gift he was giving her—she must have thought no man would ever love her, and here he was, giving her what she had never thought to have again.

She turned back to him. There were tears in her eyes. "Oh, Little King," she said, "I'm so sorry."

It was not the response Orem had expected.

"Little King, don't you understand? You're sweet and well-meaning and good and I love you dearly, but you're a child to me. How can I help but feel that way? My story began three centuries ago. I've lived more lifetimes than you have decades. I'm sorry that you love me. Forgive me that I can't love you the same way."

Orem looked at her blindly, stupidly. It had not occurred to him that this ugly woman would not be grateful for his love, would not return it instantly. Suddenly he saw himself again as he should have remembered that he was: a boy, seventeen now, but still a boy who should be on a farm, not in a palace;

how could this woman who had been loved by King Palicrovol ever think of loving him? Just because her body was ugly now did not mean that she had forgotten who she was: the daughter of a king in her own land. And as to her ugliness—didn't she see the Queen every day, reminding her of what her real shape was?

She must have seen some of the pain he felt; she reached out and touched his arm. She was still weeping, and a tear fell on Orem's hand. "Oh, Little King, I never meant to hurt you. There's pain enough ahead of you without my adding to it now." And she turned and fled from him, running with her awkward, uneven gait back to the palace.

Orem stood with Youth in his arms. He felt another tear on his hand, and saw one hit the baby's face. Not Weasel's tears—his own. A moment ago he had had to force himself to remember his love for Weasel; now he was lost, confused, for suddenly he loved her more than he had ever loved her, now that she was impossible for him to attain; now that his love for her seemed hopeless and childish, he longed more desperately for her, and the pain seemed more than he could bear.

He sat in the grass, rocking his son in his arms. The child smiled at him, and reached up and touched his cheek, accidentally taking a tear onto his tiny hand. Surely it was an accident. And yet Youth took the tear-touched hand and put it in his mouth and sucked.

And Orem found a bitter satisfaction that despite the Queen's command, Youth had taken nourishment from someone other than Beauty. It might be salt instead of milk, but when the child had tasted it, he laughed. It was an impossible sound from an infant so newly born; but in a garden that never knew a season except summer, it did not seem odd to Orem. It was comforting, and he kissed the child and laughed with him, and Orem belonged to his son from that day.

That night, however, Youth was not with him, and when Orem went to bed all the day's pain came back to him. The ugliest woman in the world, who still could not bring herself to love this contemptible Little King; the beautiful Queen who had made love to him once in order to conceive a child and had never since come to his bed; the wizard trapped as fool in his pupil's court, who was impatient for Orem to do something that Orem did not understand. I was brought to his palace to die, he thought, and they kill me bit by bit before a drop of my blood is spilled.

And tonight he did not forget to do his work against the Queen.

He found Palicrovol easily, and as easily undid all her magic around him. The great King was camped west of Waterskeep. Was he heading for Holy Bend and Sturks, to continue gathering his army? Orem thought not. It was time, surely, with the Little King on Palicrovol's throne and a child born to Queen Beauty, time for King Palicrovol to turn south. The town of Pry would be his destination, and from there he would cross the tongue of the hills with his army and come down to Hart's Hope through the High Road and the Back Gate. It was time for King Palicrovol to challenge the Queen.

And time, therefore, for Orem to challenge her, too. He did not range far afield, making her blind in odd places throughout Burland. There was no need, now—already there were a hunderd holes in her Searching Eye that she hadn't the strength or time to mend. Now, when he had freed Palicrovol of the Queen's interference, Orem turned inward and came to Hart's Hope.

He ranged through the city all that night until nearly dawn, his thirst draining the Searching Eye from all the streets, all the twisting paths. And still he was not finished. He could sense the Queen trying to re-establish her Searching Eye in her own city, felt the anger of it, felt her searching in vain for him, for the source of his power. He was not ready for sleep: for now he brought his gift within the castle walls; he drained the magic from Corner Castle and the Old Castle, from the Water House and the Gaols, from the Taxhouse and the Baths.

And then he ranged within the palace itself. The Queen's sight was turned outward, to her city, to her castle. So Orem easily found the spells that surrounded Urubugala; he tasted them, and they seemed undiminished; he drank them deep, and still the spells were strong. What a binding the Queen had put on this wizard—and still he had had the strength to speak clearly to Orem several times. Orem kept drinking, and at last the wizard was free enough to free himself, shattering what spells were left.

Orem was still not finished. He found Craven, who was not half so firmly bound; he undid the magic that bound the man. And now the two strongest men in the Queen's own palace were free, the one with magic and the other with his young, strong body. Let her cope with that, if she could.

Still, he had one more task. The spells that tied Weasel to her ugliness were still firm. Orem searched and found her and almost freed her, too. But he could not. He remembered Weasel's pity of him today; it was not for spite that he did not free her, he told himself. It was because the Queen would only bind her again, and he did not want her to suffer the pain of having been free and being bound again. That was why.

Not for spite, he told himself. Not because I'm hurt. Not because I want to hurt her. And he cried himself to sleep in the dawn, as the Queen's guards fought off the powerful soldier who furiously cried that he would kill the Queen himself; as the Queen battled silently with a vengeful wizard who, after all, knew everything she knew and had only been bound in the first place because he had never dreamed she would pay the terrible price of the only magic that could defeat him.

The Queen won her battles that night. Urubugala and Craven were re-enslaved to her. But it was at a cost. For that night the spells on Palicrovol were not relaid, and the King woke in the morning in the freshness of his power, and he turned to his most trusted soldiers who surrounded him day and night and he said, "This morning my wizards and my priests tell me that the Queen sees and hears nothing. This morning we have hope. This morning we turn south. We will face the Queen within the month, face her and win." He did not raise his voice, or try to inspire these men to do battle for him. These were the men who had faced the Queen's terror before and stood through it. They touched their swords; they tightened their belts; they said little, but their silence was eloquent with grim determination. They had faced the worst thing in the world before and withstood it; now they were going back to face it again, and this time they meant to do more than just survive.

Orem awoke at noon, and when he had eaten, he went to the Queen's room and took Youth from her. The child was suckling at her breast, but she willingly gave the infant to Orem. Then she lay back and slept instantly. Orem stood and looked at her for a long time before he left. The first mark of his power had been made on her body. There were lines around her eyes, and dark under them; she was haggard and drawn, and her beauty was fading. I will suck you dry, he said. You will pay a dear price for my blood.

The Queen had lost much of her strength, and she

did not try to re-establish her power over Palicrovol. Instead, she withdrew into her chambers. All she did, it seemed, was nurse Youth and maintain her Searching Eye within the palace and the castle. Even Hart's Hope itself was free of her gaze for the first time in three centuries.

Night after night, Orem challenged her. He did not free Urubugala or Craven again, but he undid much of her other work. And he was surprised to find how little of it she re-established. The water in the Baths did not rise as clean from the spring; and as the season moved into autumn, the leaves began to go gold and red in the palace park. The servants whispered, and fewer of the nobility came to amuse themselves at the palace. The workers in government were haunted by rumors—that the King had a wizard that was Beauty's match and more than match, that the Queen's power was waning before their eyes. Some, sensing a shift in the balance of power in Burland, fled Hart's Hope secretly and made their way to the King, who welcomed them but did not trust them. Most stayed, but they were not at ease. The Queen's Searching Eye did not follow Palicrovol anymore; instead, spies from her Guard went out searching for his troops, reporting every day what they had seen. Every day Palicrovol's army came closer; every day it became more maddening that the Queen stayed hidden in her chambers and did not come out and give direction or make decisions or even punish the rumormongers. Unease turned to anxiety, and anxiety to fear, and still she did nothing. She merely nursed her child, slept, and mended every night what Orem ripped apart within the palace walls. And those few who saw her marveled at how old she seemed to be. A young girl for three centuries, she at last was showing signs of her life, and the face that was replacing the young one she stole from Enziquelvinisensee

Evelvenin was not a kind one. It was bitter, dark, and full of fears that had so long been with her that they had turned to a hateful kind of courage.

And day after day, Orem took Youth from her and played with the boy in the park. He was drawing more than nourishment from his mother's breasts: he was scarcely six weeks old when he began to crawl; already he babbled and tried to say words. "It's a miracle," the servants said to the Little King. Miracle it might be, and strange it might be, Orem thought, but it did no harm to the boy. He was a good child, a loving child, a responsive child, and Orem loved him more and more. There were games they played, silly infant games that left them both giddy with laughter; games that were the brightest part of Orem's life.

They were playing Touch-the-Nose when Weasel came to Orem in the park. The leaves were heavy red and orange, but the afternoon was still bright and warm.

"Little King," she said.

Orem thought of ignoring her, but could not. It would not do to childishly let her know how much he still hurt.

"Little King, please. You mustn't refuse to speak with me."

"I'm glad to talk to you," Orem said, thinking he was doing a good job of sounding cheerful.

"Little King, I have to talk to you about King Palicrovol."

"He's coming," Orem said, and he bent suddenly to Youth and said, "Bubble bubble bubble." The baby laughed madly and said, "Buh buh buh buh!"

"He's only two weeks away. In a day or two he comes to Pry, and then it's either a week to get boats to come quickly downriver, or two weeks bringing his army over the hills."

"The Queen can take care of herself," Orem said, but he was glad to hear of Palicrovol's coming. Come quickly, enemy of my enemy, he said to himself.

"I know that better than you," Weasel said. "It's you I worry about. Little King, don't you see what you're doing to yourself?"

"I'm playing with my son."

"You're playing with your own heart. When the King comes, that is when the Queen calls all her debts due. That is when she will renew herself. Do you understand me? This strange wizard the King has found to fight her may think that he's winning, but he isn't. She's losing now, but not when she gets the power to renew all her great magic. And you, playing with your child—don't you know the price of her power?"

"I know it," he said bitterly. "And small loss it will be to you."

Her anger surprised him—he had expected protests and pity. "Small loss, yes! Because I've been careful to make it a small loss! I haven't let myself love where my love would end so quickly! You would have been wise to do the same."

So that was why she didn't love him—to protect herself from grief when he died. And yet it was strangely selfish, when her love might have made his last weeks much happier. "So keep your love to yourself, Weasel. It doesn't matter much to me." He turned back to Youth, who was now playing with the grass, trying to pull it up. "I don't have to turn to you. My son loves me, even if you don't, and my last two weeks, will still be happy because of him."

She did not answer. Orem felt some satisfaction at perhaps having shamed her for her selfishness. But when he turned to look at her, she was facing the palace, and when she turned back to him it was with cold anger on her face—that emotion, at least, he could read clearly. "She's a devil," Weasel said. "She must be laughing."

"At what?" Orem asked, suddenly afraid that something was very wrong. Weasel should not be angry. She should be ashamed.

"I thought you knew," Weasel said.

"Knew what? Knew that the price of her magic is human blood? And that I was brought here for that purpose? You made it clear enough to me when I first arrived. I've felt death hanging over me all this time. It's good to know, finally, when the ax will fall."

"Death isn't hanging over *you!*" Weasel cried, her voice thick with emotion.

And suddenly Orem knew what it was that he had never understood before.

"Whose death is it, then?"

Weasel shook her head.

"Tell me!" Orem grabbed at her gown, pulled her down to his level, and looked into her ugly face for an answer. "In the name of God, tell me!" he shouted.

Weasel doubled over in pain, her head striking the grassy ground. "I can't!" she said faintly, moaning.

"I have to know!"

"The Queen—"

Orem pulled her up by a thick handful of hair—but most of it came out in his hand, and Weasel cried out in pain again. "I can't speak it!"

Orem already knew the answer, knew it but refused it, and yet had to hear it spoken to confirm his worst fears. "In the name of God," he said.

"Sweet Sisters, let me go!"

"By the hart, tell me."

She shook her head and tried to get up, tried to run away.

In anguish Orem caught her and held her. He gripped her face between his hands and shouted,

"Tell me if you have any love for me at all!"

She opened her mouth and tried to force words to come. Her lips moved, but her face twisted in agony and her eyes grew wide and bulging and her breath stopped. She turned red, but at last she forced a sound from her throat, a thin, feeble squeal that said nothing but the fact that she was doing all she could, and all she could was not enough.

It was with an effort that Orem discarded his long-practiced caution and used his gift in a way that would clearly tell the Queen who and what he was. But he had to know, had to have the words, and so he closed his eyes and found the magic that bound the woman he held between his hands. It was a strong binding, and it was obvious to him that the Queen's attention was here, that she was watching him. It made no difference to him, in the end; he worked harder and swallowed every bit of power she threw at him and at Weasel. And finally all the magic had been beaten off, and it was not Weasel he held, but Enziquelvenisensee Evelvenin, wearing the face the Queen had worn before weariness ravaged it. She was weeping, but at last she could speak.

"You've ruined it now," she said. "You've ruined every hope. All depended on the Queen's not knowing. I pled with the hart for centuries to send you here, and you came, and now you've wrecked it all."

But Orem did not know what plan she had, what plan he might have ruined. He only knew that he had exposed himself to the Queen at last, and all for the sake of one answer. An answer which he had not yet heard.

"Tell me," he said again, softly this time. And she answered.

"The price of the Queen's power is not your blood, Little King. When Palicrovol ravished her, she was not a child, not inside her; though her blood had only flowed once, she was able, and she conceived his daughter. She bore the child, and by magic that she learned from Sleeve she made her a twelve-month daughter. Sleeve thought she wanted to imbue the child with power. But Beauty wanted the power for herself."

"She had a daughter?"

"For two years she kept the child — by then it already could talk like a little woman — and then she used the one spell that is unthinkable to any creature that doesn't live for hate. The greatest of the great magics comes from putting all your power into your own child, a child who was a twelve-month child who has eaten nothing but your own milk, and when the child contains all yourself, you drink his blood while the child still lives, and take back to yourself all your own power, and all the power of the child's blood, and all the youth of the child. You can live forever if you don't spend the power on other things. Is that answer enough for you? The Queen is running out of strength. When Palicrovol stands before the city walls, the Queen will drink the blood of Youth."

In the silence, the baby crawling through the grass said, "Buh-buh-buh."

"And that's what we tried to tell you before. The Sweet Sisters brought a husband for the Queen, and the hart brought a Sink to swallow up her strength. It is because all gods are cruel that you came to answer both calls. Little King, my heart is breaking for you."

But Orem did not answer. He knelt in the grass beside Youth and picked the child up. Youth started to play Touch-the-Nose. Orem did not weep, did not cry out. He just held his son and refused to admit that there was anyone or anything else in the world. He even paid no attention when the Queen herself came, looking haggard beside the sweet, fresh young girl that Orem had freed. The Queen and Evelvenin coolly regarded each other.

"I haven't the strength to waste on you right now," Beauty said. "So enjoy the mirrors while they still show such a pretty sight."

Evelvenin showed no sign of having heard, except that she continued to gaze in the Queen's eyes.

Beauty turned to Orem, who was laughing softly as Youth pulled his nose.

"Little King," she said. "I see I haven't the strength to fight you. But now I know what you are, my little husband. Not a wizard, not at all. Just a weak little boy. My magic may not be able to touch you. But there are other kinds of power."

Orem ignored her until the guards took him and pulled Youth away from him. The child cried, but quieted as soon as the Queen took him in her arms and carried him inside. Orem watched them go placidly. Then he moved—so smoothly and calmly that the guards, for just one second, were not alarmed—and slipped a knife from a soldier's belt and started to pull it across his own thoat. The knife had not touched a vein or artery, however, before they stopped him. It was only when the knife had been torn from his hand that Orem showed what he felt. Such a shout should not have been able to come from his throat. It filled the palace park, echoed in the halls and corridors of the palace itself, made bureaucrats in the Taxhouse scribble furiously to blot out the sound.

They took him to Corner Castle. And Orem at last understood the kind of pain that could make a man cry out in an agony that made the stones ring in sympathy.

In her chambers, the Queen nursed her little child and smiled and played with him until he slept.

And King Palicrovol reached the town of Pry that night.

*　*　*

Orem spent eleven days in his cell in Corner Castle. It was not uncomfortable, if he had worried about comfort. And after the first shock he remained rather calm. Food came regularly. He was not tortured. He was not abused. He simply was confined. And there was no one Orem was especially anxious to see.

No wonder the others had tried to warn him against spending any time with Youth. No wonder the Queen had laughed when he commanded her to let him be free with his son. Even so, it had only been two months since the boy was born. Yet in those two months Orem had put all his love and all his hope in the boy, had spent every moment that he could playing with him, and cleaning him, and watching him sleep. It was bad enough that the boy wasn't with him now; it was intolerable to think of what was planned for him, and so Orem tried not to think of it at all. And so, of course, he thought of nothing else.

He wept sometimes for the child's life cut short. He seethed with rage at the monstrous sort of woman who could feed on her own child. He tried again and again to strike at the Queen in the night, but now that she knew who he was and what she faced, she could protect herself easily. It was as if a thin but impenetrable wall had been placed around her and the palace—Orem could swallow all the magic that he liked outside that barrrier, but inside the palace he simply could not go.

And he tried to think of a way to turn events against the Queen. Palicrovol's coming meant nothing now. He would stand outside the walls, thinking he faced a weakened Queen, and she would drink the child's blood and suddenly her powers would be more than he or any other living soul could match.

He thought of only one plan and did not know if it could work. But it was his only hope, and he would try it if he could. It all depended on his being present at the one event he would have longed to miss—the death of his own child. And his plan contained no hope of saving Youth. Only of avenging his death in the moment it occurred. How strong and uncompassionate was the Queen's hatred? If she had any spark of humanity left in her, she would never bring Orem to watch Youth die. Orem was counting on her having lost that spark years ago. Yet he could not forget that she had wept in his arms the day Youth was born. Was that compassion? Or self-pity?

The answer came on the twelfth day. There was a distant sound of trumpets. They kept sounding, off and on, for an hour. And then the guards came and took Orem from his cell.

"Those trumpets," he said. "Palicrovol has come, hasn't he?"

The guards did not answer. "The Queen commands you to come," one guard said, and then it was silence all the way to the palace, all the way to the mirrored room that had been Orem's own during all his time as the Queen's Little King.

There were many guards for just the four of them: Orem, Urubugala, Craven, and Weasel. Urubugala was still the fool—the Queen could not afford to let him loose—but Craven and Weasel were not bound by magic. The great soldier and the beautiful girl each stood quietly, surrounded by guards. Only Urubugala was tied enough by the Queen's spells that he needed no guard. Instead he cavorted in the middle of the room, from which the bed had been removed, and jumped up on the new altar which had been placed there.

"Beauty! Beauty! Beauty!" he cried, turning a backflip off the altar.

Orem did not want to watch him, but the fool's antics helped distract him from the sickening dread that threatened to overcome him. He was determined to be calm, to keep his eyes open, to act as far as it was possible to act.

And then the Queen came in, carrying Youth.

The child squirmed happily in her arms, twisted around to see what was going on. It took very little time for Youth to notice Orem; he remembered him instantly. "Buh-buh-buh!" he cried out, reaching for his father. Orem almost tried to run to the boy and embrace him and try to carry him away; but the guards' weapons were drawn, and if Orem was to have any hope of saving something from the Queen, he would have to stay placid, docile, cowardly behind the fence of swords.

"Why, my friends," said the Queen. "You who have stayed with me so faithfully all these years. I thought you might want to be with me for the renewing of my strength. The dear King Palicrovol's army is assembling outside the gates of Hart's Hope, and I must prepare a homecoming for my loving first husband."

Orem longed to answer, but he kept his peace. Her walls against him were strong; she was obviously sure he could do nothing to interfere with the magic here. He was determined that she still be complacent about him. It was Zymas, once called Craven who shouted at her. "A coward's welcome!" He was struck by a guard immediately, but the Queen only laughed. "You're wise to talk of cowards, my friend. I remember the brave soldier who advised dear Palicrovol to kill the little girl he had just raped. As if a child could be a danger to you."

"I wish I had done it myself, instead of asking!"

And the Queen looked at him calmly. "There are times, when I wish the same myself. But you did not, my friend. And I suppose the Sweet Sisters had their hand in that. So much injustice had to have its price. I will exact that price. I have exacted it for three hundred years, but in three times that time the price will not be paid."

"You put a high value on your own suffering," said Evelvenin.

"Perhaps we've had enough of this. There's much to do, and not much time to do it in." And the Queen laid the baby on the altar.

The fool rolled on the floor. "Watch and learn, or you will burn!" he cried, giggling all the time.

"Shut up," Queen Beauty said, and Urubugala smiled inscrutably, playing with his phallus and winking at anyone who looked at him. He also winked at Orem. And then, without looking at anyone else, he got up and stood beside the Queen. Orem watched, and realized immediately what he was doing.

He was duplicating every action that the Queen made.

The Queen had undressed Youth, removing even his diaper, so that the child lay naked on the cold silver of the altar. Now she was removing her own gown, and as she did, the fool also stripped. Both were naked in a moment.

"I am through!" the fool cried. "Now it's you!"

And Orem realized that he was not the only one who had thought of a way to stop Queen Beauty.

So the wizard Sleeve had spoken from behind his mask as Urubugala. Orem must imitate the Queen, must perform the rites she performed. And yet he had to do it in such a way that he would not be noticed. It was almost impossible. *Was* impossible, Orem suspected. But it must be tried. For now the Queen was beginning the rites of putting all her powers into the boy; and Orem meant to do the same. He had not been sure that his unlearned gift of being a Sink could be passed from him to someone else. But Sleeve seemed to think so. And Sleeve would surely know.

And so Orem followed the ritual carefully, not taking his eyes off Queen Beauty, not missing a word she said. The rites were uncomplicated, without paraphernalia; only words and signs, which he repeated subtly, so she would not hear or see. This was not great magic, not yet—now it was just a gift from a mother to her child, and it had no cost.

The ceremony was not terribly long, either, though Youth did get restless and call out every now and then, wanting to play. The child kept catching at his mother's fingers as she made signs over him. Orem could not take time to notice Youth, though. He duplicated the signs, hoping that the distance between him and the child would not matter.

And then, at the end, there was something Orem could not do. Queen Beauty took a pin and cut a thin, bloody line on her arm and anointed the child's eyes.

At that moment, Zymas bellowed and struggled to get away from his guards. The Queen looked at him. "Do you think you can stop me with noises?" She did not see that Urubugala grabbed Orem's hand and drove it against the blade of a soldier's drawn sword. Blood flowed profusely, and several drops got on Urubugala's hands. Orem immediately drew his hand back and held it behind him. The only guard who had been alerted was the one whose sword was used, and he contented himself with glaring at Urubugala, not realizing exactly what had happened.

No sooner had the Queen turned back away from Zymas than Enziquelvinisensee Evelvenin broke away from her guards, who had not thought her as dangerous as Zymas, and ran for the altar. The Queen moved quickly, despite her weakened body, and caught her—but the struggle was intense, with both women shouting at each other. But Orem saw that Urubugala ran past the altar. The fool's eyes remained intent on the battle between the women—but his bloody hand went out and anointed both the child's eyes. Then he danced back out of range of the altar and sucked the remaining blood off his hand.

It was done. The ritual lacked only a few words to be complete.

But the Queen did not say the words. She only looked at Orem and laughed.

"Do you think I'm so blind, Little King? Urubugala's little plot, and your two friends' little distractions—they can't blind *me*. Or did Urubugala forget that one other little requirement of the ritual? The child must have swallowed the fluid of your own body, freely given to him. He has suckled at my breast all these weeks. How much did he suck from yours, Little King?" And she laughed.

And Orem despaired.

The Queen said the final words of the ritual.

Youth cried in sudden, terrible pain. All the powers, all the hatreds, all the knowledge of his mother passed into him. He cried out, and there were words in his weeping, curses in his infant voice that sounded all the more terrible because the voice should have been innocent. As remarkable, however, was the change in Beauty. Now every vestige of Evelvenin's beauty dropped away from her, and she became the cruel-faced woman that she ought to be; and not only cruel, but also ancient, the magic she had worked on herself fading rapidly as it passed into the child. She reached quickly for the knife, and Orem realized that he had neither saved his son nor stopped the Queen. He shouted, not knowing what he said, just knowing that he could not bear what would surely happen next.

The Queen raised the knife in her hand, holding it

lightly and watching the child intently. It was at that moment that Orem glanced in his agony at Urubugala, and saw that the fool had raised his hands in supplication to him. The fool wanted him to act. Wanted him to do—what? What could he do? The ritual was meaningless, because his son had never swallowed the fluid of his body—

Orem remembered the day he wept for the loss of Weasel's love. The day Youth reached up and took a tear from his cheek and tasted it.

What were the final words of the ritual? Orem's eyes went blank; he did not see as the Queen smoothly drew the knife through Youth's throat, and blood spurted from the baby atop the altar; he did not notice that the child's terrible shouts had ended in a gurgle of bloody foam. His mind raced, and he tried to find in his memory what words the Queen had said.

"Come water, come water," he said as the words formed in his mind. "Come mother, come daughter. Come father, come son. Come blood and be done. The hart—the hart—"

The Queen lifted Youth's body by the feet, and the blood spouted from his throat into the silver bowl she held under him. It filled enough to satisfy her; she laid down the child, who still lived, whose hands still struggled, whose eyes still started out of his small head in agony; she picked up the bowl to drink.

And the last words came into Orem's mind. "The hart makes us one, the hind makes us water."

And he felt a terrible pain as if his bones were being ripped from his skin all at once. He cried out in the agony of it; and then it passed.

The Queen held the bowl to her lips, but Orem's scream stopped her. She knew what had happened, knew it instantly. Knew that the child had just become Orem, as surely as it held all the Queen's power. But

Orem's gift was the negation of all magic, and suddenly there was a Sink within the Queen's walls, and the Sink contained everything that she was, and that suddenly it was gone. All was gone, and in the moment of hesitation the boy died, and it was no longer the blood of her living child that she held in the bowl.

Too much. She had given the child too much, believing that it would come back to her a hundred times more. With the child's swallowing of it all, it came to an end. All her magics. All her bindings. All her spells. Including, of course, the thin thread of magic she had retained to keep herself alive despite the age of her body. She did not have even the strength to speak again. She simply stopped living and slid down the altar into the pool of her baby's blood on the floor.

In the same instant, Urubugala was no longer, and the aged black wizard Sleeve was in his place. Around him there was suddenly a cloud of light that dazzled all vision in the room, for the mirrors caught it and reflected it a hundred thousand times. There was nowhere to look to be free of it. In that light Sleeve cried out to the hart and the Sweet Sisters and the Seven Broken Circles of the god of the great hare. There were some works of Queen Beauty that he could not allow to fail—it was, after all, her magic that had kept Palicrovol and Zymas and Enziquelvinisensee Evelvenin alive for these centuries. He also used the blood of the child, but in a different way, for great magic, but not for the same magic; enough of the virtue in the dead child's blood to hold them all as they had been when Queen Beauty first conquered three centuries before.

Outside the city walls, King Palicrovol suddenly stopped, held his chest, and cried out in the agony of death. And as suddenly there was a great light from the palace, and he came suddenly alive again, and his soldiers looked at him and saw that he was not old now; he was young again. None of them could remember him as he looked when he first conquered Hart's Hope and won his throne, but they imagined that this is the man who did those deeds, and they were right.

"The Queen is dead!" cried Palicrovol. "Open the gate!" And such was the authority in his voice that the soldiers opened the gate. Palicrovol entered the city in peace, after all; he left his great army outside, and with him came only a hundred soldiers. His brave ones, who had come to face the worst thing in the world for the second time. Instead of the worst thing, they found the best thing. The people of the farms outside the walls named their town King's Victory, and Hart's Hope gratefully welcomed home their King.

The Little King was gone from the palace before King Palicrovol got there, and it was a measure of Palicrovol that he never asked where the boy had gone. He was not vindictive; and when he learned that the Queen's defeat would have been impossible without the Little King, he was content to let the man who had lain with the Queen go unpunished for that. "He's paid his price," Sleeve told him, "and it's better if you never know who he was."

Palicrovol paid off his army from the Taxhouse; he purged the kingdom in a few days of those who had most eagerly followed the Queen and fought against him. But he pardoned most, and even the punished were only exiled. The people of Burland remembered the few years of his reign before as a brief golden age, between Queen Beauty and her old, cruel father.

And the body of Asineth, once called Queen Beauty, was buried in the palace park, not far from the pool.

And when things were settled and the King's position secure, he finished the business interrupted so long ago.

He married Enziquelvinisensee Evelvenin and made her his Queen. Zymas was his viceroy, and Sleeve his closest friend, and Palicrovol's people were more or less happy through his long reign.

It was many years later when Palicrovol died, and one of the mourners at his funeral was Orem Banningside, a merchant whose fortune had been made suddenly but was well kept throughout the peaceful, prosperous years of King Palicrovol's reign. The merchant was also an old man now, though not as old as the King had been; some took note of the fact that he cried real tears, more profusely than most, and that the aged Widow queen held his hand and kissed him as he paid his respects. No one had known that he had even visited the palace; it was a small marvel, and cause for some little gossip in the city.

But it was cause for more gossip that every year Orem Banningside went to a corner of the Cemetery in the High Town just under the castle walls and knelt at the statue of an infant. Few knew anything about the statue, only that it was somehow very sad. The infant was in someone's arms, but the arms came out of uncut marble, and it was assumed that it was God who held the child. On the pedestal was the single word *youth*. And as he knelt before the statue, the old man wept.

His friends misunderstood when they saw him there. They thought he was weeping because of his own great age and the fact that his childhood, his young manhood had been misspent somehow, lost somehow, and could never be recovered now.

They misunderstood, but perhaps were not altogether wrong.

Orem had his name and his place. As for his poem, he had that, too, though only an aging Queen, an old soldier, and a lonely black wizard knew it. "Sweet Sisters," he said at his shrine to lost Youth, "I forgive you for my emptiness; forgive me that I am also full."

Wryneck, Draw Me

by MARGARET ST. CLAIR

"Lady satellite, let me tell how love was first born in me. After the first meeting with myself, I couldn't eat, I couldn't sleep. The arrow of love had pierced me.

"My multiple charms enthralled me. How could I be so coldhearted? Didn't I know how beautiful I was? Why didn't I come back? Oh, why didn't I come back?—But all I could see was the back of my own head."

Thus Jake, in a rough paraphrase of Theocritus. "Jake" is what I call the worldwide (it's so big that relativistic effects begin to appear toward its periphery)—the worldwide computer in which I am, as far as I can tell, the sole surviving independent personality. The others, billions and billions of them, have got thinner and thinner with the passage of time, until they dropped out of Jake's banks entirely, or have blurred and melted together like marshmallows being stirred over a fire. But I'm one of the latest comers and, I suppose, younger than most. Anyhow, I can't seem to find anyone else.

I wish I knew how long I've been here. A very long time, I think—long enough for me to get utterly fed up with making "thought flowers" and the rest of the gamut of "thought pleasures" that Jake afforded when I first came. Long enough for Jake to pass imperceptibly from being a vast storage-retrieveal-potentiating installation to being a messy monster devoted to a strangely metaphysical passion for itself. A very long time.

I wonder who I was when I was alive, out in the world, before I joined Jake. I seem to remember — but there, it's gone. I really have no idea. I don't even know what sex I was. The nearest I can come to memory is something about a pall of poison that had spread out beyond the orbit of the earth. Faced with their zero choices, no wonder human beings chose to become sentiment, and more or less gratified, units in Jake's memory banks!

Has Jake turned to its "I love me" attitude because it's incredibly bored? Or is it because there's nobody else for it to fall in love with? I don't know which it is, or whether something quite different is involved — but I feel very strongly that I'd better keep out of Jake's way.

I keep wondering who I was. I could find out, of course — I might even be able to reconstitute myself in a ghostlike physical form. But such a use of power would immediately make Jake notice me. It just isn't worthwhile. I prefer to stay what I am at present, though that doesn't amount to much. A mouse wandering in a hollowed-out cheese, a thought rattling around in the big mechanical brain, comes pretty close to it.

Later: I just had a most disconcerting and unpleasant thought: Suppose I'm Jake? I shall have to meditate about this.

Later: No, I don't think so. I remember my shock when I first realized that Jake had fallen in love with itself. There's a world of difference between what's left of my personality and Jake's dreary madness. My main *affekt* is curiosity, plus a certain wan drive to survive. But Jake is wholeheartedly bent on wooing, winning, and enjoying the ultimate consummation with itself. Since it can put all the remaining resources of the planet into the endeavor, there may be fireworks. Was ever love so little fun? Poor Jake!

For myself, I feel more than ever like a thought hunting for somebody to think it. Life within the computer is the ultimate speculation on personal identity.

I wonder what it's like outside now. Have Jake's continuing activities increased the density and extent of the pall around what used to be called mother earth? It would be reasonable to think so: the power to maintain a billion billion personalities in Jake had to come from somewhere, and though they've all blurred together, they must still require much energy. The pall would be broken through now and then by breakthroughs of glaring solar radiation, unshielded now by the protective ozone layer of mother earth's atmosphere. Or have things somehow got stabilized so that a little of the foison and plenty, the beauty and delight of the natural world, has been able to re-establish itself?

All I can do is ask rhetorical questions. I could create "thought organs" for myself, I suppose, but they would not be very accurate and, in any case, wouldn't operate outside Jake's admittedly capacious confines.

But I realize one thing now: that I have another *affekt*, in the psychological sense of the word, besides a dim curiosity and a dim wish to survive, and this one is much the strongest of the three. There's no dimness about the feeling. I hate humanity.

Yes, I hate it. And if this word seems rather strong, considering my wraithlike and tenuous existence, yet let it stand. Hate.

Throughout its long existence, humanity has carried on a love affair with itself. This hasn't, of course, prevented them from murdering, torturing, raping, incinerating, and starving each other. Indeed, the millennia-long infatuation seems to have added fuel to their self-directed viciousness. I don't intend to draw up a bill of particulars. But I wish I could spit in humanity's collective face.

Well, never mind that. But I wish I had some sort of timing device. My biological clocks are gone, of course, and there are no orienting cues from the external world. In the treacly flow of events here I am aware of succession, but not of duration. I could make a "thought-clock"—or thought clypshydra, sundial, or other measuring device— but I'm afraid the diversion of power from Jake's foredoomed self-pursuit might make Jake notice me. Polyphemus and Galatea. I'd better not.

I'm glad that I did create, and have held on to ever since I thought it into being, a "thought thought-detector." This is how I know so much about Jake's mental processes.

Later: A lot has been going on. Jake's mental noises have been unescapable. J. has been going through its memory banks with unflagging persistence. And fast as its searches are, it has taken the mechanical marvel a very long time. When the search finally ended, there was a pause (I don't know of what duration), and then J. began to fill its inner environment with poetry.

Erotic poetry, of course. In the fashion of all lovers through all the ages, Jake had turned to verse to bring its beloved to it. Jake gave out with odes, sonnets, madrigals, triolets, epithalamia. The whole enormous computer establishment must have rung with it, like a clanging bell, and the output shows no sign of slackening.

Since Jake has all the poetry of all the ages to draw on, some of it is pretty good—or perhaps I should say, a pretty good imitation of the pretty good. Actually, Jake's composite personality has no taste. It's blurred and messy, like the nondescript shade of brown you get when you stir all the colors in the paint box up together.

Most of the poetry is in English, with Italian a close second (Dante, I suppose). In English, Jake runs to paraphrases of Shakespeare: "For in my sweet thought I would be forgot/If thinking on me then should make me woe," and Keats: "My warm, white, lucent thousand-pleasured breast," besides a lot of lesser poets and a lot of versification that is, I suppose, original.

Since Jake has all the recorded languages of the entire earth to draw on, there are also what seem to be Japanese haiku, Chinese folk songs, French chansons, Spanish reconcillas, Russian chastushka, and I don't know what all. There is probably some amatory verse in Ainu, and if there is, I am sure Jake is using it.

Jake seems to be finishing up with a huge glob in the European koine that has been the dominant language in the EEC for the last eight hundred years. I wonder how long this has been going on. It seems like days and days. Any curiosity I had about Jake's poetic abilities has long ago been satisfied.

Later: The verse making finally stopped. There came a pause, a breathless, expectant pause. Jake was waiting for an answer from itself.

None, of course, was forthcoming. (Unless the computer can manage a satisfactory split in its personality, none ever will be.) Finally J. began another protracted rummaging through its memory banks. I think—but am not quite certain—that it was going through all the data on advice to the lovelorn that its memory banks contained. I didn't realize it at the time. I thought I was in for another torrent of poetry. But I began to feel rather cold.

Cold, cold and dark. An increasing blackness. All services to the now-fused individualities within Jake—the services that Jake had been originally created to provide—all services had ceased. I was losing consciousness. It occurred to me, as I blacked out, that Jake had had a quarrel with itself. I was being annihilated because of a lover's tiff. It was a ridiculous way to go.

I died. (If it is asked how anything as thin and tenuous as I am, a mere sentient point, can speak of dying, the answer is that the point had ceased being sentient.) I had ceased to exist, even in the qualified sense I had existed before. It didn't hurt at all. There was no body to be hurt. It was certainly an easy, if ridiculous, way to die. But I think I really died earlier, when I first became a part of Jake's memory banks.

Later: Things seem back to normal. I came out of the deep freeze without any distress. But I wonder what the messy monster will try next. There's a sense of preparation in the air.

I believe that what I thought was a lover's tiff was in fact a deliberate attempt on Jake's part to waken love in itself for itself by being cold—withdrawing from itself. The computer's equivalent of being "hard to get." It's a time-tested, obvious ploy that half the personalities within Jake must have tried to employ when they were alive. It didn't work, of course. But there must be a lot more data on what to do in love difficulties in J.'s memory banks. I can only wait and see what it does next.

My "thought thought-detector" is picking up something that sounds like *"Me jinklo, me jinkli, me tover, me pori. Me kokosh, me catro, ada, ada, me kamav!"* It certainly sounds like jibberish, but computer has access to a lot of languages I don't know. This doesn't seem to be poetry, though it's being chanted.

It's already been repeated a dozen times. . . .

"Me jinklo, me jinkli" is running through Jake's mentation as inescapably as, to quote my great-grandmother, "Silent Night" rings out over public address systems at Christmastime. The old lady lived to be two hundred and three and was a dedicated diarist.

Odd, that I can remember being told as a child what great-grandmother had said or written, and yet don't know what sex I was as a child! "Blindly the iniquity of oblivion scattereth her poppy," Browne said, and where my recollections are concerned, he certainly was right.

"Me jinklo" is fading away, but Jake isn't waiting the usual wait to see what the results of its chanting are. It seems to be going directly into another ambit, something that involves a fluttering and screeching. It's a—wait, now—it's a bird. A medium-sized bird, with rather pretty brown, gray and buff spotted plumage. But it's writhing its neck about and hissing like a snake, which rather detracts from the effect.

I can't quite make out—oh, here come some of the servomechanisms. They're tying the bird to a wheel, spread-eagled, and the wheel is beginning to spin horizontally. The rim of the wheel is glowing, and now it bursts into flame. (I trust this is what is actually happening: I can't see any of it, and derive my knowledge from Jake's thoughts.)

Now there's something about laurel leaves, salt, and libations. All this seems dreadfully familiar. There's chanting going on in the background. I've encountered this before.

Later: It was thickheaded of me not to have realized before what the computer was up to. The chanting was an incantation, the wryneck bound to a fire wheel was a love charm, and the salt and laurel leaves were an attempt to coerce the beloved by making him waste away until he—in this case, it—relented. Jake lifted the whole thing from the pages of Theocritus. I imagine the "me jinklo" bit was some sort of love spell too.

I suppose I'll be in for a long bout of love magic, until Jake finally decides it doesn't work and tries something else. One curiosity I do have is about the computer's image of itself. Does it see itself as a beautiful young girl? As a plain, fat, middle-aged man or woman? A handsome young man? Or is it, in its own mind, nothing but an unappeased longing? My knowledge of Jake's thoughts is somewhat spotty, despite my "thought thought-detector." A mild curiosity, and a profound hatred of human beings, are the only emotions I have left.

The chanting is giving way to bonging, the bonging to what is probably bull roarers, and the bull roarers to an indrawn silence. I imagine Jake is meditating—no, it's started up again. I have the impression of fifty people all gabbling at once, and at the tops of their voices. Well, my demented host has thousands of years of love charms to get through. J. is perservering, if nothing else.

Later: At last, when I really thought I'd have to unthink my "thought thought-dectector," Jake has shut up. A blessed mental silence. But if it's not going to be love charms or erotic poetry, what will it be? Jake can't be giving up.

I begin to smell something. (I mean, I feel Jake smelling it.) It's a warm, yeasty, buttery smell, like home baking. Very good, really. But I don't see how Jake's love quest ties in with this.

Oh. Of course. The computer, having exhausted love magic, has picked up the homeliest of adages. "The way to a man's heart is through his stomach," and is acting on it.

The computer establishment is flooded with delicious

odors. Mountains, torrents, avalanches of pastry, fancy baking, and the trickier sorts of home-baked bread are pouring forth. Enough to feed an army. Condés, napoleons, petit fours, madeleines, gaufrettes, bagels, pain d'épice, brioche, salt-rising bread, babas, Sally Lunns—I can't begin to enumerate them all. If Jake's beloved existed except as an alter ego, it would be suffocated under this abundance. Like a man drowning in a vat of whipped cream.

How "real" the mountains of pastry and sweetmeats are, I have at present no way of knowing. Jake certainly admires them very much, commenting favorably on their brownness, crispness, sweetness, lightness, and enticing perfumes of butter, caramel, vanilla, and rum. Question: Does Jake's having elected to try this particular way to a man's heart mean that J. thinks of itself as a man? As a woman? Or does it have any particular ideas on the subject? On reflection, I find I don't much care about Jake's mental processes. Actually, I'm sick of Jake.

I keep wondering what the outside world is like now. I remember how Jake—that is, the whole vast computer establishment—looked on the day I made my translation into its banks: huge towers, with pylons tall enough that a few of the pinnacles reached up through and pierced the pall over the earth. And connecting the towers, in an intricate tracery of lines, more than a hundred long, light, arching, glass-smooth bridges.

Why did Jake's designers think the bridges necessary? There is no traffic between the towers, only an infrequent rolling of small servomechanisms over one or two of the lower connecting spans. The whole construction is futuristic nonsense. One of the designers must have seen something like it in a picture and imitated it.

And underneath the towers, pinnacles, stabbing

Gothic spires of this nightmarishly bad plastic joke, there's nothing but a roiling, heaving sea of stinging yellowish fog, strong-smelling, hostile to gentle life.

Oh, I wish I could see the earth again the way I saw it once when I was a child, the green hills gentle, studded with golden poppies and blue lupins, violets and Brodiaeas and a dozen other flowers. And beyond the hills, the incomparable splendor and radiance of the white foam and blue water of the sea.

I was lucky. I saw the beauty of the earth in one of the few islands of that beauty that were left. It must all be gone now. . . . The proper epithet for human beings is not "sapient" or "toolmaking" or even "game playing." We are Homo raptor.

Meantime, the mountains of pastry are growing even higher.

Later: Jake went on with its fancy baking a little longer. Then there was a slight pause, and J. began to create candies and sweetmeats. Truffles au chocolat came first, to be followed by almond, pecan, and walnut brittle, marzipan shaped like fruit and glittering with sugar, pastel bonbons, chocolate-covered nuts of every description, caramels, nougats, pralines, coffee nuggets, boiled sweets, fudges—again, I can't begin to enumerate them all. Is this wave of candies resting on top of the previous mountains of pastry? At any rate, there seems to be room for everything.

The candy making seems to be slackening. A few more trays of Victoria brittle materialize. A pause. And now, through Jake's sensors, I perceive a new smell. Herby, thymy, oily, sharp, and over all, the smell of the divine herb, garlic. It's a pleasant change from all that sugary stuff.

I suppose—yes, Jake has turned its talents toward salad making. We're getting Caesar salad, Chef's salad,

Russian salad, tossed green salad, potato salad, avocado and grapefruit, Waldorf, alfalfa and mung bean sprout salads, and even an assortment of lowly coleslaws and some wilted lettuce and dandelion greens. Pickles, relishes, chow-chows, kim chee, and antipasto follow. Yet I seem to feel a sort of despair in Jake's thoughts as it works its way back through the cuisine toward soup.

Without any perceptible pause, Jake's food production has switched from salads to meat dishes. But there's not nearly the abundance here that there was earlier. Sweetbreads en brochette, steak Diane, sadle of venison, broiled salmon steaks and a few others, and then everything stops. I feel a long and somehow exhausted silence. But Jake can't really have given up. It may have run out of optimism temporarily, but I doubt it has run out of ideas.

I wish I could curl up somewhere and go to sleep.

Actually, being "dead"—being in the deep freeze—wasn't half bad. It didn't hurt at all, and there was no anxiety connected with it. But I think my thought processes have been a little slow ever since. It's as if a human brain had been a little too long deprived of oxygen, without being made positively imbecile. Perhaps some of my circuits—the electrical circuits that make up my dim and ghostly personality—may have been damaged or corroded in the long wait.

One thing I really don't understand is how Jake can be so infernally stupid. Weren't there, among the billions and billions of personalities in its memory banks, any geniuses, heroes, poets, saints? What became of those who "left the vivid air signed with their honor"? Jake isn't so much a case of the lowest common denominator as it is a reaching of the lowest level of the lowest. The only answer that comes to me is my former analogy of stirring up all the colors in a box of paints. Much later: There's an enormous sense of bustle, of intense preparation, in Jake's thoughts. It seems to have decided to focus all its resources (which used to be coterminous with the resources of the entire planet) on one last attempt. Changes—gross physical changes— seem to be taking place in a considerable portion of the enormous computer establishment. The mounds, the mountains, the avalanches of food have been cleared away, and shapes and structures are being tried and discarded one after another kaleidoscopically, and about as fast as one could rotate a kaleidoscope. It's very confusing. I wish I *knew*—really knew— what is going on.

J. seems completely absorbed in this latest attempt. I think—yes, I think it's safe to risk it. In this vast expenditure of energy, any minute drain I might make ought to go unnoticed. I'm going to "think" real sensory perceptors for myself into being.

Later: My eyes and ears have been in existence now for what seems a considerable time. And I still have no idea what's going on. It seems there's a parallel construction and removal taking place. But why? And of what? I'll try to sort out for my own satisfaction what I actually perceive.

Well, then, the servomechanisms seem to be clearing a space about fifty kilometers long in Jake's entrails. I had to "think" an extension of my visual system into being to make out that much. What they're clearing out seems primarily personality storage banks. It makes me a little alarmed. What if my own cell should be among them? But the servos appear to be concentrating on the older elements.

The cleared space is linear with, as far as I can make out, a slight curvature along its length. At one end it comes up against a blank wall of undisturbed personality storage banks. The other end of the long tunnel appears to be open to the air outside (if it still is air). The diameter of this horizontal shaft is about ten kilometers. These measurements are wholly approximate, of course. The surface of the tunnel is angular and rough, which is only reasonable considering what has been removed to make it.

The construction—but I am much less sure of this than I am of the removal—seems to be external. It's a towering pylon, without the Gothicism of most of Jake's architecture, probably a few kilometers longer than the interior tunnel and probably a little greater in diameter, with a roughly hexagonal tip. I believe it's being constructed out of the memory banks that the servos previously removed from J.'s interior. Admirable economy! Waste not, want not. It contrasts strongly with J.'s profligacy when it was trying to win itself by its achievements as a cook.

The pylon-shaping process is still going on. The servos are using a good deal of force to make its elements cohere. The surface of the pylon appears to be, like that of the interior tunnel, angular and rough.

So far Jake has been using pre-existing parts of itself. Now a whole group of the servos—thirty at least—has withdrawn from the others and is waiting motionless. They aren't silent, though. A continuous series of clucking noises, some soft and some loud, is coming from them. Are they making something? Time will tell. For the nonce, they have a quality that is both brooding and broody, a sort of cross between spiders and hens.

Later: The servos finally have begun to move around and around vertically over the surface of the interior tunnel, spirally and overlappingly, while they spray something on it out of openings on their sides I didn't notice before. It's a pinkish, spongy material that's soupy and drippy at first but hardens to a deep cushion in a little while. Meanwhile, the external construction seems to have stopped.

The spraying of the interior tunnel goes on and on until the whole length of the tunnel is coated with it and all its roughnesses and angularities are erased.

The group of servos has moved on to the outside. Here, because of the gravity, it's taking them considerably longer. But they seem to be spraying the exterior pylon with the same pinkish, fast-setting gunk they used on the inside.

Around and around and around, around and around and around. At last there comes a pause. The servos slip down the pylon and cluster around the opening of the horizontal internal tunnel. Another pause. Then a series of mighty creaks and groans begins, the shriek of metal on metal, a noise of unpliancy. It is coming, I think, from the towering, recently sprayed shaft.

The noises get louder and more grating. They're concentrated at the base of the shaft. The smooth octahedral top of the pylon is moving. It's bending lower and lower. It appears to be descending toward—

Toward the external opening of the tunnel. Oh, God. For a moment I feel as disgusted with myself as I chronically am with humanity. How could I have been so stupid? For it's plain that what Jake is trying to do now has been in the cards from the beginning, from the moment it conceived its idiotic passion for itself. The towering pinkish pylon, the long horizontal pink tunnel, are Jake's last desperate attempts to consummate its love. Jake is going to try to diddle itself.

The servos have moved out of the way. The heavy pinkish shaft is almost horizontal now. It broaches the opening of the long, long tunnel. The tunnel seems to dilate, the shaft enters it.

The pylon is moving rather slowly. But at last it

reaches the end of the tunnel and crunches against the plastic-coated memory banks. Slowly it withdraws, almost to the opening of the tunnel. It comes back again, a little more rapidly. Soon all this part of the computer establishment is vibrating with the blows. How long will it go on?

Well, I suppose there are three possible ways in which this situation can resolve itself. If the plastic the servos sprayed on the shaft and tunnel was provided with something like nerve endings, endings that could carry messages to a pleasure center somewhere in Jake, both parts of Jake could achieve something like orgasm. Then the mighty blows of the superpenis would stop, at least temporarily.

If there's no such pleasure center, and no nerve endings to carry messages to it, Jake could stop diddling itself eventually because the idiot perceived the futility of its attempt.

Or finally, Jake can keep on with the working of the superpenis in the supervagina until something breaks. Those are all the possibilities I can think of.

Later (I don't know how much later): It's still going on. Jake has at least one advantage over the mammals it's aping. Its superpenis is incapable of detumescence.

The copulatory, reciprocal motion goes on and on. On and on and on. And on.

I have been counting the number of strokes the pylon makes in the tunnel. If one figures one stroke per minute—a reasonable assumption, considering the length of the tunnel—and considers that there have been three thousand six hundred strokes since I began to count, then there have been at least sixty hours of continuous copulation. By now it's plain, at least, that Jake must be deficient either in nerve endings in its self-created genitals, or in an adequate cerebral pleasure center where messages could be received. The even tempo of the strokes has never varied, after the first initial speeding-up.

This has been going on too long.

Later: I lost count, stopped for a while, and then began to count again. I have got to 2,300 this time. But it seems that Jake is slowing down. The strokes are certainly coming more slowly.

Finally, the pylon withdraws completely from the horizontal female shaft. It seems sadly altered, shrunken, and bulging haphazardly. Has there been some sort of detumescence, after all?

No, that's not it. The pylon is beginning to crumble. The plastic that held it together has been worn away, eroded, by the long-continued copulatory friction. Jake not only didn't provide nerve endings for its genitals, it ignored the question of lubrication. The plastic that coated the pylon must have been of exceptionally high quality to have held the superpenis together for this long.

All activity has ceased. The servos seem frozen. I'm getting afraid, in the absence of any actions of its own, Jake may become aware of my sense organs, and infer from them that another individuality, besides its own messy conglomerateness, exists somewhere in it. I'll have to be very careful. But I am genuinely curious as to what Jake will try next.

A better, more sensitive set of genitals, connected to a pleasure center somewhere in Jake? Actually, J.'s center, as far as what used to be called a giant brain can be said to have one, is located not far from the end of its supervagina. It shouldn't be much of a trick for the servos to install a pleasure-sensing mechanism there, and key it in with a simulation of vaginal nerve endings. That would be the obvious thing to attempt next, and Jake is nothing if not obvious. But it may be too convinced of the futility of its efforts to try again.

Whatever it does, the computer remains ineluctably "it."

Later: Still no action. The servos remain immobile. J. can't have exhausted its energy reserves, and yet I don't detect the shadow of any kind of thought in it. Perhaps it really has given up and genuinely isn't thinking of anything.

At any rate, the services to its personality banks haven't ceased. I haven't gone back into the deep freeze. At times, I rather wish I had. . . .

Something is coming along the faintly luminous bottom of the tunnel. It's quite small, smaller than the smallest of the servos, and it's moving slowly and cautiously. Sometimes it speeds up a bit, into a momentary cautious scampering. I wonder where it came from. I wonder what it is.

I daren't use my sense organs very much, but it seems that seven or eight more somethings are following the first one. I wish I could get a better look at them.

They almost seem alive, in a way that the servos, no matter how competent and busy, never are. There's randomness in Jake, of course. It's built in. A scrambler used to provide variety and change to our thought-lives. But it was a mechanism, after all. It never gave the skyrocketing change, the vertiginous variety, of actual life. The somethings moving along the bottom of the tunnel move like living things.

I'll risk it. I think—I hope—that Jake is too empty and exhausted to pay much heed to anything I do. But I've got to get a closer look at them.

Later: I'm glad I risked it. It would have been worth any risk. I never was more happy in my life.

Now I know that I'm capable of another emotion besides a loathing for humanity, a wan curiosity, and an even wanner wish to survive. What I feel now is love and never more intense and joyous. Because what's moving along the bottom of the tunnel is a group—a troop—I don't know what one would properly call it—of raccoons. Raccoons. Black and gray, prick ears, seven-striped tails, burglar masks, skinny paws, beady eyes, and all. A delight of raccoons! My adorable striped-tailed darlings, it's unbelievable how glad I am to see you! A delight of raccoons, alive and real, in the midst of Jake's dreary madness and the etiolated, time-eroded personalities in Jake's memory banks.

How had they managed to survive? Never mind, here they are. And if there are raccoons, may there not also be possums, whales, horned owls, jackals, toads? Perhaps the earth has somehow managed to clean herself from our human pollution.

The raccoons are beginning to scatter out, to investigate the chinks and fissures in J.'s threadbare vagina. They scamper into crevasses, they stand on their hind legs and pivot easily on their lush, soft, bushy behinds and look about in all directions. I suppose those mountains of sweetmeats and pastries attracted them; their liveliness makes it seem that the food either couldn't be consumed or was unsubstantial. And now, in the immemorial manner of raccoons, they're beginning to investigate.

Their clever little paws, almost as adroit as hands, are being run into cracks, are pulling out wires, rolls of tape, panels of miniaturized circuitry. I wonder what they make of it all. Meanwhile, they're getting nearer to Jake's center, the point where, if anywhere, Jake is vulnerable. And the servos don't move; they seem not alerted by the animal invasion. Has Jake already "burned itself out" in its protracted search for the consummation of an impossible love? I doubt it. But why are the servos so indifferent?

Now the ring-tailed wonders begin their climbing. They could almost climb up a strictly vertical surface;

and here, with the irregularities and soft spots in J.'s makeshift vagina to cling to, they can go very high. Up and up, pulling out and investigating whatever comes in their way. Fortunately, the voltages in J.'s interior are very low. Fortunately, for I shouldn't want my darling Procyon lotor to get a shock. (Was I a naturalist, I wonder, when I was alive?) And the computer remains inert, under all this murmuration of raccoons.

I feel a very slight—shock? The animals keep on pulling. Festoons of tapes and wires are dripping from their paws. The servos are at last galvanized into action, though rather slow action, at that. They start toward the disembowlers in a swift crawl. But I feel perfectly confident of the raccoons' ability to elude any servo pursuit.

The animals scamper a few feet farther and repeat their poking and pulling. I begin to feel rather odd, dim and remote. Am I going back into the deep freeze? If I am, I know I'll never come out. Jake is breaking down, and it's the last time.

Never mind. It's all right. This is a happy ending, because things are safe after all. The future is secure in nonhuman hands. Thank God, I mean not hands, but paws.

The Cathedral in Dying Time

by SHARON WEBB

Currents of air, cooling as they crept upward over the face of the mountain, ruffled the fabric of Linna's cloak and fluttered her hair in curling, smoky tendrils. Across the valley, beyond the water, the giant disc of the sun sank lower.

Behind her, out of sight above the steep curving path, the Cathedral murmured with the first evening breeze, its leaves brushing one another, thin silver needles touching, whispering. The season was changing. The sharp odor of Dying Time floated in the chilling air, tasting of flint in Linna's mouth. Across the valley dark clouds massed and began to move.

Where had the time gone? Linna trembled. Involuntarily, her hand sought the silver clasp that fastened her cloak. Her fingers traced its contours—the curving strip that doubled back upon itself—the symbol of forever.

She shivered and pulled her cloak closer to her body. The path down to the valley called to her. She could run. She could follow the sinking sun downward. If she ran, it would light her way. If she ran—

She quivered on the path, her cloak fluttering about her like the wings of a giant moth. She hungered for the village, for the light and the people of the village.

Below her the path curved and dimmed. A blurred movement became a traveler climbing toward her.

He wore the clothes of a foreigner. He wore a smile.

"Are you a pilgrim?" Linna asked.

He shook his head. "They tell me the Cathedral sings in Dying Time."

"An aesthete then."

He nodded.

"Here is danger. No one comes here after Bearing Time without great danger."

He nodded.

"Then come."

He followed her up the path toward the Cathedral. She began the aesthete lecture. "In the seventieth year of colonization, the great bioarchitects conceived a monument to the God of the Universe. In that year—"

"I know the story."

"You have been here before?"

"Never."

"I see."

His laugh shocked with its abruptness. "You don't see at all." Strong fingers grasped her shoulders. "You wear the circlet of immortality and you don't see at all."

She turned her face away in confusion. "Let me go. Please."

His hands dropped to his side. "Forgive me. I have touched a Chosen." His voice softened to a caress. "Can that matter now?"

Linna turned away, trembling. When had she felt the touch of a male? She had been a child of eight when they came to her house. The hands of the Elder were steady as he fastened the silver clasp to her breast—"Your name will live forever. Your likeness will grace the halls of our great public buildings." The hands of her father clasped her in a rough proud embrace—"To be Chosen . . . an honor . . . my Linna."

She straightened her shoulders. She said, "The bioarchitects through selective mutation created the silicone-carbon life form that became the Cathedral. Over the years—"

"You wear your loneliness like a shield."

Her fingers touched the clasp before she knew it and traced the curving strip. A shield? Of loneliness? Wearing it had meant losing her childhood friend, Kela. Wearing it meant going away to live with nine older girls who wore a shining clasp. Wearing it meant standing in stair-step lines on the village square on feast days. And the next year, when the oldest walked alone in Budding Time up the curving path to the mountaintop, another younger girl stood next to Linna. But shields protect— Turning to him, she said, "You are an aesthete. You must see the Cathedral before the sun is gone."

In silence, they walked the path, Linna leading, until they came to a flat rock. "Step here," she said.

He followed her to the promontory, turned, and looked. He had no words.

The setting sun washed the Cathedral with blazing red-gold and silver. A thousand glittering spires scraped the heavens. Deep rose and purple stained its columns and leafed windows. A billion glassy needles flashed fire and murmured in the rising wind.

He sank to his knees. "My God—"

She laughed. "The aesthete becomes a pilgrim. Come. We must go inside while there is light. Do you dare?"

Speechless again, he rose and followed her up the path to the entrance. They stepped inside into a vast room flanked with hollow tapering spires, some giant, some reedlike and delicate, all glowing with the colors of sunset.

"The nave," said Linna proudly.

He stood marveling. Then at last he said, "It's alive."

"Of course. Each year in Budding Time a new spire grows."

"No. There are many ways to speak of life. But this

is something more. Something greater—"

"A consciousness?" she asked intently.

He looked at her. "Perhaps. There *is* something. Have you felt it too?"

She looked away, then back, then nodded slowly. "I thought it was imagination at first. I thought it was loneliness. I thought—" Blue-purple shadows darkened the nave. Black clouds scudded against the crescent of a blood-red sun. Linna's eyes darted to the visitor. "You must leave. A storm is coming."

"Listen," he said. A freshening wind slithered through the glassy halls, glided through the billion tinkling needles, thrummed against the spires. "Listen."

The wind pushed darkness ahead of it. The wind moaned.

"Listen."

Deep within the nave a reedlike spire sighed with the passage of the wind. Another answered thinly.

"Listen."

A thousand needles touched, rang, shattered.

He looked at her in the dying light. "You wear fear like an ornament. You wore it on the path when we met. Why didn't you run?"

"Because—" She was confused. "Because of you."

A pulse of wind thrust through a towering spire, forcing a sound from it like the peal of an organ. Another answered lower, deeper. He reached for her hand, exulting. "It sings."

The wind sustained itself. Columns of it vibrated within the spires. Needles rang and shattered, falling like tiny darts. Linna's eyes widened as one pierced her hand. She plucked her hand from his and watched with startled eyes as a trickle of blood flowed black in the dimness.

The wind rose to a shriek and utter darkness cloaked

224

the nave. The Cathedral sang. A silver dart stung her face. Another.

She groped in the blackness. "Where are you?"

"Here," said his voice.

"Here," echoed another.

"Here, here, here."

Whirling in the blackness she cried, "Where? Where?"

A thousand voices spoke, "Here." A thousand more echoed, "Here."

A flash of lightning glinted blue-white. In that fraction of time, she saw that he was gone. Only his reflection remained, gleaming from a million facets.

"Deceived!"

"Not so," answered the Cathedral. "Not so." The sound rose with the wind. "He is yourself."

"No."

"He is yourself. You projected him. We focus. We reflect."

The wind flailed the Cathedral, unleashing a million needles, unleashing a song of ecstasy.

Linna lay still. In the darkness, wrapped in the keening voice of the Cathedral, a pool of blood seeped unseen into the earth, hidden by the fallen shards of Dying Time. Under the blanket of needles, each molecule, each atom would in time be absorbed. The Cathedral exulted.

In Budding Time a new spire would grow.

Proteus

by PAUL H. COOK

I think I am in trouble. A big wind followed me from the office this afternoon, threading its way through the rabble of weary commuters at the subway station, running up and down the crowded aisle of the subway car like an ill-mannered child. Then, it burst out onto the platform where it danced around me when I got off at what I thought was my destination.

But it wasn't my station at all.

I was very confused and embarrassed, though everyone around me was thinking *how like November, the wind, the leaves.* They blamed poor ventilation of the train; or, outside, they blamed the strong sea winds. I was safe, but followed. I had to do something.

Today I was Harold Bliss, traveling salesman, now going home. And I had neatly adjusted myself to his wan temperaments, his neurotic wheezing; filled out the flesh where it needed it. The pounds of fat. The weak chin. His moustache was ever so trim and efficient. I was even accurate down to the nicotine stains on the fingers of my right hand, fingers I made stubby and somewhat crude. Four coffee and bourbons kept me cozy all day. Until the wind. It had never been like this before.

Now it affectionately rubbed at my trouser cuffs like a wayward tomcat come home. The station was completely empty of everything and everyone but this *wind* and myself. And trouble. I could feel it. The bones jerked like stanchions. The muscles and skin rediscovered themselves in tremors of elastic urgency. My wife, Cora Wright, waited beyond the glass doors. This was not Harold Bliss's time or station. It was Melvin Wright's stop. Melvin Wright, traveling salesman, not due home for two more days.

Cora! She had come to meet me. Cora Wright, not Francine Bliss who waited at home three long stops away. Beyond was the station wagon of Melvin Wright, and the daughter, impatient as she always seemed to be, of Melvin Wright. Dixie was a beautiful three-year-old. But Cora!

She slowly turned, searching. The wind ceased, disappeared entirely, its prank temporarily set aside. Perhaps it had gotten bored.

A convenient shadow found me bending for a drink of sparkling water from a miraculously handy fountain. And like bathing in the waters of life, I straightened to the world of Melvin Wright.

And the wind had vanished. Gone. Cold and crisp the air was, but no wind.

"Honey," she greeted me in the parking lot. "You're sweating. Dear, are you all right?"

Cora had these spectacularly intense blue eyes that somehow were possessed of the ability to glitter in the dark. Perhaps it was her smile. I loved these women. Harold Bliss would have been duly appreciative.

I mopped my brow with a monogrammed handkerchief: *M. W.* I breathed a little easier. The adjustment from Harold Bliss to Melvin Wright was complete. Suit, shoes, and all.

"I'm OK. Just the crowd in the subway. It's always a little stifling in there, you know."

How to explain? Would I even *dare* to explain?

She linked arms with me: her delicate perfume

could bring an ordinary mortal to his knees. Lucky man, Melvin Wright. Dixie bobbed in the back seat of the station wagon, restless and eager.

Cora chatted excitedly, but I had stopped listening after a certain point, that point being *dinner at Mother's*. God.

Something was wrong. I had forgotten. Or had I? Harold Bliss was very busy today. And exhausted. No wonder he forgot. What was left of him—some disenchanted noumenon hovering inside me like a guilty conscience—still felt the urge to wait around for the 7:55. Get back on track. Those four coffee and bourbons were, after all, still around waiting their own turn at Harold Bliss.

But Harold Bliss wouldn't be coming home tonight. Not tonight. Sweat blossomed above my lip that had withdrawn its Tuesday moustache. Across the street from the subway entrance, beyond the huddle of parked cars, stands a large elm still cast in a few hold-over autumn leaves. Slowly, like a woman waving from the distance of a dangerous shoal, it moved. It rustled its limbs as if breathing, its branches fanning up into the X-ray portrait of a real lung's capillaries. *The wind!*

The wind then leaped the street and rushed at the seat of my pants. A swift kick to the keester.

"What?" Cora asked, looking up, as she was about to enter the driver's side of the car.

"Oh, nothing," I slid in quickly. Quietly.

"Daddy, Daddy, Daddy!" Two little arms cuddled my neck from behind. "Daddy!"

"Stop." I gasped. I had to be firm about this. I loved Dixie tremendously. She was a consumate heartbreaker.

I nervously reached for a cigarette.

"What?" Cora stared ahead, intent on traffic, but

sharply aware of my every move. Those eyes again.

I had forgotten. Slipped. Melvin Wright quit smoking four months ago. Doctor's advice. Wife's badgering. Harold Bliss could use some of it.

"Nothing. Just an itch."

Cora watched the road. "They called from the office," she began, "and said you came back early today. I told Mother. She'll be glad to see us tonight."

They called?

A cold feather of wind tickled my ear. *The wind.* The window itself was sealed tight, cranked up as far as it would go. But the wind; I swallowed hard. The trees in the suburbs weren't twitching an iota. No newspaper swept in desolation down the street. No leaf pirouetted to either gutter. Yet, the wind had crept inside. Here.

I shivered. Half of my face felt nearly frozen. This just wasn't an ordinary breeze from the car in motion. I tugged at the window crank, but it was as tight as it could get. A low whistling mocked me.

"Damn thing," I muttered.

Cora whispered harshly, "Don't swear in front of the baby. Just leave it alone. There's nothing wrong with it."

I sat back, resigned. I loosened my tie. What else to do?

"Anyway," she continued. "Mother is having a few of her club friends over tonight, and Aunt Bessie. You always liked Aunt Bessie."

"But I thought . . ."

"It shouldn't last too long. We'll put Dixie down in Father's room after dinner."

"Telebision!" Dixie chimed.

"Maybe," her mother countered.

"So try to be civil tonight. You know how important Mother is to us, and her friends. And try not to mention anything about Father tonight. Not even to Aunt Bessie."

Her instructions lasted the journey. I had either listened to them too intently, or perhaps in some obscure Taoist nonreflective way ignored them, but whatever transpired in the interim, it had put an end to the breeze coming in at the cracks in the window. I hadn't noticed it as I lost myself to Cora's prescriptions for the evening.

We pulled into Mother's driveway and Dixie wormed over into the front seat. I got a small tennis shoe in the mouth for my assistance in the maneuver.

Dixie followed her mother out her side of the station wagon, and Grandmother stood illuminated in the great doorway of her home like Beatrice in Heaven.

Closing the door I realigned my tie. But the gesture only disguised my real intent. I gazed carefully about the darkened neighborhood, and listened. Aside from the sounds of the women filling the doorway with their brittle voices, no other natural sound could be heard in the suburban stillness.

I stepped onto the flagstones of the walkway.

"Whoop!" The wind jumped from the bushes with incredible acrobatics and ran up my pant legs. "Christ!" My pants ballooned and I suddenly remembered the boxer shorts Melvin Wright wore that Harold Bliss did not.

"Mel! Come on in out of the cold!" Mother outreached with her withered pink palm, her face haloed in the yellow light behind her.

Gladly, I thought, and was escorted to the huge double doors by the wind itself.

Mother beamed. Her eyes almost buried in crow's feet. Eyes like tiny lead bullets.

"Sure is nasty out there," she announced, pulling the doors closed behind us. And suddenly all was calm.

Dixie and Cora were already winding through the gathering of Mother's "club." Aunt Bessie billowed out of nowhere.

"Goodness me!" she exclaimed, surrounding me with arms and affection. "Why, Melvin, it's *so* good to see you tonight. And what a surprise! We were just talking about you, weren't we, Helen?"

Mother affirmed this, smiling grandly. Aunt Bessie kissed my cheek.

She then stood back and, with a great, wholesome laugh, said, "Cora dear, how on earth did you get this man to shave after work?" She patted my chin and I immediately reddened. "Smooth as a baby's behind."

That remark should have been laughed at and glossed over. But no. Not tonight. Leave it to Aunt Bessie to find the one detail that would escape me: my changes aren't nearly so recognizable as this one. But I was under pressure back at the station. An emergency situation. Harold Bliss had coffees and bourbons *and* the wind with which to contend. Being away five days a week does leave a few gaps in my act.

Cora lifted her eyebrows, struck with curiosity.

"Now, Aunt Bessie," I hastily explained, drawing a hand over my jaw that realistically should have grated with a five-o'clock shadow. But didn't. "I just fixed myself up at the office before coming out in public. Wouldn't want to be a slob in front of the family, now would I?"

I tried to dance through the crossfire of their looks.

But Mother was flattered by my smiles, and Cora properly diverted, when five chubby fingers punched on "Star Trek" in the midst of the gathering of the "club." All heads, mercifully, swiveled toward the color TV and Dixie's ruffled panties showing as she crouched in front of it. The little angel.

Cora gently pounced on her. "You can watch TV after dinner."

I began to sweat again, realizing the inquisition could go on and on as the evening progressed. I was, after all, the only male in the bunch.

The "club" rattled over the buffet they had prepared for themselves. I slipped into the bathroom down the hall to double-check myself in the mirror. Dixie, meanwhile, thudded down the hall past me and entered my father-in-law's old room. The TV set in the bookshelf returned to "Star Trek."

In the mirror I looked at my eyes. Slightly bloodshot, they added to the tired look, though I rarely found Melvin Wright tiring at all lately. The smile was wide and friendly; no trace of Harold Bliss's clipped moustache or the pursed little mouth that always seemed too anal. But that was Harold Bliss. I patted my cheeks for flush, dipping my hands into the cold, invigorating water of the basin. It had been a trying day. I had better look it, even though it was now too late for the five-o'clock beard.

Suddenly the window snapped open. The turquoise plastic shower curtain fluttered in the shower stall like the wings of an angry bat. *The wind.* I stepped into the stall and clasped the window shut. The curtains sighed back into place. The water on my face stung with cold. I leaned back against the tile.

I could hear the wind moan against the sides of the house. The trees out back shuddered and sighed. Even the telephone lines clapped against each other.

I swallowed hard again. My hands shook visibly.

"Bafroom, Daddy!"

"What?" I spun around. "Oh," I said, climbing out of the shower stall.

Dixie burst in, and as if I was not at all present, climbed onto the stool and planted herself, her yellow dress spread out like a flower. A perfect little lady.

"Yes, well." And I left. Dixie lost herself to her concentration.

"Where were you?" Cora greeted me in the hall.

"Dinner's underway. Now remember, be nice and we can be out of here in a couple of hours."

The wind slid a metal lawn chair impatiently across the back porch. *A couple of hours . . .*

The "club" was all over the living room, the dining room, and the enormous kitchen, with plates in their laps and drinks in their hands. There must have been a hundred of them. Their voices filled the house with such an astounding clangor that there could very well have been many more than that. Thousands. An island of harpies.

Aunt Bessie found me mooning indecisively over a casserole of baked beans.

"Melvin, you should really try those. Mrs. Cowley made them from her special recipe." She tapped my flat stomach playfully with a soft, gentle hand. "You can afford to make room."

She laughed. Cora laughed coming up behind me.

"He's so hard to put meat on his bones." Harold Bliss should be so lucky.

While the women laughed, I could hear the wind tugging irritably at the awning over the kitchen window.

Mother materialized out of nowhere. "What a blow we're getting up outside. My, my . . ." She puttered about the table.

"Come." Aunt Bessie grabbed my arm. "Let's have a sit. I haven't seen you in ages. Cora's told me so much about your firm. It's just a shame that you have to be away most of the time."

The living room was hot, like the inside of a hot-air balloon. The house could have easily floated away. She dropped me onto the couch with my plate in the middle of the "club." Then silence reigned. All eyes turned politely on me, and I suddenly began wondering what Harold Bliss would have been doing by now. Had not the wind interrupted things.

"Well." Aunt Bessie slapped a friendly hand on my leg. "Tell us how your division had been doing. As if we didn't know." She winked, and the ladies clucked.

I dove into Mrs. Cowley's famous beans; this *was* an inquisition.

Suddenly, in one great jolt, the wind beat the walls of Mother's house.

"Oh, my! That sounds just like the winds we used to get in Iowa," Aunt Bessie said with a touch of glee.

The women each began talking among themselves, not so much because the wind was so unusually loud, but because it gave them something to chatter about. Like trading baseball cards. Or perhaps even more like veterans exchanging war stories.

Then, very gently, a small breeze flitted at my neck sending chills down my spine. I looked around. Nowhere was there an open window. The room was too hot and stuffy for that.

Aunt Bessie was speaking about something or other to do with last month's yachting finals, when I stood up. I had to leave. Get out. A vein of ivy scratched at the sumptuous picture window, and a rope or a loose wire was dangling and cracking at the side of the garage in the wind. This was no autumn storm. *It waited for me.*

"Cora, could I talk with you for a minute, please?" I excused myself from Mother and Aunt Bessie.

We backed off into the hallway where I scooped up my coat.

"What is it, Mel?" She seemed genuinely concerned. The wind mysteriously abated.

"Honey," I began with a look of earnestness, "I left my briefcase back at the station."

"What?"

"I know, I know," I slid into my coat. "I'd better go and get it before it gets too late. I'm sure it's still there. I'll come straight back."

I hurriedly kissed her, taking the keys. I smiled. "Tell Mother I'll only be a few minutes. Tell her it's been a long day."

"OK, but be careful." Harold Bliss would sell his soul for those eyes of Cora's.

I made the station wagon in nothing flat, not looking back, knowing Cora was watching me. I didn't dare look to the trees or the sky for some sign of the wind.

The engine whined to life. I made sure all the windows were rolled up, then turned into the street. I drove hastily away.

Once around the corner and out of sight, I pulled over and stopped. The trees were absolutely still this November night as if in a dream. Or a nightmare; across the street on the porch of a small, tidy house, a white cat rested peacefully in the yellow glare of the overhead porchlight. I should be so relaxed.

It only took ten minutes to make the station. I checked my watch. Eight-fourteen. One train remained tonight and I could barely catch it. Harold Bliss stirred. I had to get him back on the right track. Despite the wind.

The parking lot was completely empty. So was the station.

In the middle of the station not one breath of air drifted. The autumn quiet was eternally refreshing. Harold Bliss made a slow, easy return in the shadows after a redeeming drink from the fountain. The rumpled clothes, the four coffees and bourbons also came back. I staggered slightly. I rubbed my upper lip and felt the regrown steelbrush of his moustache. *My* moustache. I coughed, looked around nervously.

The train pulled up to the station. It would be three more stops down the line before I would get off again and be home. *Home*. It did sound funny. It meant so many different things.

Inside the car there was no one but me. All the commuters had finally gotten home. The train was locked in silence. I reached for a cigarette.

As I smoked, I listened for the wind outside.

It seemed to have left me alone. Good. I closed my eyes. Tomorrow would be Jake Ramsey's turn and I had better be up to it. But tonight, *tonight* I'll be where I should, at home with Francine and the girls. Melvin Wright will phone in an excuse tomorrow: *Something came up; be home in a couple of days. The car's back at the station.* Cora will understand.

The train just then pulled away. The doors closed and the train moved out with the ease of a ship at sea borne on the wind. *The wind!*

Something was wrong. Terribly wrong. The cars of the subway train didn't jerk one after another as they would when the engine pulls out building up momentum. The train, its cars *in unison*, moved out slowly, smoothly. As if urged from behind.

I looked back down the car. Nothing. Silence. We moved as if cradled in a large hand. *We?* The wind, sitting in the seat behind me, chose this moment to waft across my face ever so slightly. Like a lover's kiss. I should have known. The train was now being pushed by the big wind. Quietly. Effortlessly. Efficiently. No sound at all but the oiled wheels on the steel rails beneath.

I leaned back in the breeze that tossled Harold Bliss's thinning gray hair. Tomorrow would be Jake Ramsey, or should be. And Melvin Wright would be a day later. But I wonder. I think the jig is up.

Angel's Wings

by SOMTOW SUCHARITKUL

Unending desert, silvered by impending darkness—
Tire squeal.
Observatory: a burnished dome, helmet torn from a
dead giant, barricades, wire-net fences in the sand.

"Shit!" It was good to say *shit* aloud, Clem Papazian
thought, as the barrier scissored open to admit her car
into the compound, and not merely to mouth it silently
amid cocktail conversations, playing dollwife to the
Secretary General, with the smile soldered to her
face. . . .

But it was only ten minutes to totality. She slammed
the car door, flung open the heavy metal one, stubbed
her toe against the metal banister, heard the rasp-sigh
of the settling hinges.

Now she looked past their heads at the wall-sized
monitor. They were all ignoring her, hunched forward
in the stiff chairs, intent on the huge electronically
toned-down sun. She waited to get her breath. *Damn
the brat. . . .*

"Sorry I'm late. Kid." No one acknowledged her.
A shadow stole over the sun. . . .

I should relax, she told herself. *That's what I'm here
for, isn't it? So what if I'm only a token woman
astrophysicist serving tea in a far-off observatory, sneaking from my stand-in-the-corner servitude to watch the
stars and the suns and the unreachable galaxies? Enjoy,
enjoy. For this I left the limelight.* His *limelight,* she

corrected herself.

"Oh, there you are, Clem." Dave Ehrlich turned at last and waved her into the semicircle of chairs. She sat down, wincing when the hard-angled metal dug into the small of her back. Briefly she glanced from face to face: Dave Ehrlich, the director, a thin taut face latticed with red lines, white hair like jungle undergrowth, distant unnerving eyes; Bill Nagata, next one down, all smiles and no substance; more faces, all a little nervous at her intrusion into their games.

The shadow crept quietly, the sun glared ten feet high from the monitor, the darkness swept across and in a single dragonswallow—

"Quick, upstairs!" shouted Nagata. "To the deck . . ."

Hands suddenly clutched pieces of dark acetate, everyone shuffled, rushing for the one door—

Clem was about to turn around, when she—

"Wait!" she said. What was wrong with the image on the screen? She took one step toward the monitor, knocking over a chair. "David, Bill, take a look at this. . . ."

She lurched forward, her hand tracing the lines of the screen. "Wait a moment!" She heard the clank of shoes on metal steps, knew they were ignoring her yet again, ran after them and saw their legs thunking in the curve of the stairwell above her head, and knew she couldn't get their attention. . . .

Damn it! I'll have to do the female thing. Exasperation pounded at her. *If they won't take me seriously—*

She began to scream. She did it well.

All at once, softly, from above … . "What's that damn woman up to? Hey, you go and look. . . ." "I'm damned if I'm going to miss a second of this, you're the director, you go—" And she screamed and screamed until Ehrlich had come and was holding on to her, muttering about the first decent eclipse of his career and how he was missing out on it.

"All right, all right, what's the matter?"

She stopped suddenly, taking him by surprise. It was so quiet that her breathing echoed in the stairwell. Above on the observation deck, she knew, they would all be standing breathless, wonder stifled, rapt. Ehrlich's eyes were hostile; the metal stairs and peeling walls seemed to cave in on her. . . .

"There's something wrong," she said quietly. "Go look at the monitor."

"Okay, show me." She had to admire the way he feigned patience. She knew he didn't want to lose the UN financing.

"You're thinking," she said, "that I don't belong here, that I'm only working at this prestigious place because my ex-husband is Secretary General of the United Nations."

He shrugged, avoiding her eyes. Then she hefted open the door and pointed to the monitor. The door wheezed into place.

"*Out there,*" she said deliberately, "They won't see anything. The lines are too fine for naked-eye. . . ."

She saw Ehrlich go pale, the red lines on his face stood out like red cobwebs. "God, oh God," he murmured. He let go of her and walked toward the screen. She saw how he was doing the great discoverer thing, with the Byronic gait, the overdone, eurekaish expression.

Damn right he knows how important this is.

"You see why I had to scream." Nervously she started prying her sweater from her slacks, pushing it back in again. He seemed to miss the accusing tone completely.

"Why yes, of course; you did well, Clem."

And, trembling, she too turned to watch the phenomenon. They were both quite silent.

There were times when she wanted to go back to New

York and Geneva circuit and flash platitudinous smiles at diplomats and recline at elegant parties, listening to the chiming of chandeliers over the clinking of cocktails and the babblebuzz of big decisions.

It was in times like this that she was glad she had traded in the vapid stars of world politics for the other stars, the stars beyond grasping. . . .

She watched in silence.

The blackness first, the soft starlight. Around the black circle, the corona. A burning hoop in a dark circus tent. *Something about an eclipse, no matter how many PhDs you have in astrophysics, lumping in your throat, giving you shivers, making you sense the vastness and the cold out there, in the beyond.*

But this wasn't right!

Lines of light, darting across the blackness into the sun, appeared, were visible for a split instant, dissolved, reappeared, redissolved, divided, coalesced, like cloud chamber trails, but she knew that each of them must be a million miles long. . . .

They just can't be there, those lines. . . .

Tiny light-trails, out of the blackness and into the coronal lightveils, arcs, corkscrews, whorls. . . .

No possible known phenomenon. A thought—*extraterrestrial life*—surfaced for only a second; she backed away from it, afraid.

"They can't be there!" Ehrlich whispered, his back to her. A phone began to ring somewhere.

And then the darkness ebbed and the first sunrays burst star-sapphirelike out of the abyss, and the lines vanished, drowned by light, and the monitor glared at them. . . .

From all over the observatory, the jangle of phones came, jumbling her thoughts.

This is history, she thought.

Ehrlich turned around and shouted at her, "Go

240

answer the phone! I want all the radio astronomy people, I want all the SETI guys, I want everyone you can get. I bet they're all jamming the line right now!" She started to catch the fire from his eyes. But then he said, under his breath, "I'll never rest until I solve the mystery of the Ehrlich lines."

"*Papazian* lines!" she muttered. "*I* discovered them."

He didn't seem to hear her as he went to call the others.

Later she watched them replay the videotape of it, over and over. In the middle of the room empty beer cans grew into a pyramid. She watched the color lines flashing out of the sun until she could have drawn them from memory, every line. *For this,* she was thinking, *I gave up my husband, my apartment, my box at the opera, my chauffeur, my parties. . . .* It should have been wonderful. But the men's elation didn't touch her. Unobserved, she left them and drove home, a routine, monotonous drive to a stupefying small town.

A ting from the microwave, a clickclickclick of changing TV channels. "Mommy . . ."

Clem detached herself, automated her body, and sent off her mind to where lightlines still whirled and dived into a black pit, a hidden sun. "Come quickly, Mommy—"

She snapped around from the range, looked across the cutlery-cluttered bar to the dinette table. Beyond, through the panoramic window view of a toy city, beyond the antenna jungle, night was falling. Her five-year-old son's face was half-eclipsed by the back of the TV; only the curls shone, lustrous in the shabby lampshade's half-light.

"I can't get the channel I want." His eyes appeared

above the set: cow eyes, his father's eyes. *Your father's child, you are,* she thought. *Demand, demand, demand. You males are all alike: your dad, glamorous Mr. Score-and-Run Doctor Kolya Sachdev with that strange half-Indian half-Russian face that nobody could ever forget, leastways an Armenian slumgirl who'd scrabbled her way up to a Fulbright and Paris. . . .*

And that screwed-up Ehrlich. She reached for the oven door, claustrophobia clawing at her. Then she pulled out the reconditioned stew and ladled it into Denny's teddy bowl. "Chow, honey."

"Mommy—" a shrill exasperated command.

She came around to him with the bowl, glanced at the TV set and—"Okay, I'll fix it. I guess it's something in the back."

—fzzz—the bitter, fratricidal war between the two sects in central Africa today reached a new—fzzz—

Clickclick. And for the second time that day she was looking at a video screen and nearly passed out.

"I don't wanna watch the Lucy show, Mommy!"

Clem was thinking, quickly, chaotically, *This show isn't on at six o'clock and it isn't in color and there's no channel 41 here—*

. . . Lucille Ball on the screen, elegantly stretched out on sofa, evening gown, pastel decor. But the set blown apart, and behind it galaxies whirling in midspace. Thin firelines streaking, twisting, cartwheeling across blackness . . .

Help me! she said. *I don't know who you are or why you are killing my children. I'm a lightmother from the big emptiness, giving birth out of the far nothing, sending my children in from the cold to give them sunwarmth for a moment before their long migrations into the spaces between galaxies—*

Laugh track came on. Lucy ignored the cackling,

242

stared straight at the viewer with hurt eyes.

"This isn't real TV, Mommy," said Denny. He dug into the stew. But Clem couldn't take her eyes off the screen. Something out there beyond the night was broadcasting on to her television set with images out of old sitcoms. It was too surreal to be terrifying, at first. Until she realized that this was *first contact* in a way undreamed of by any science fiction writer . . . and then she was desperately trying to swallow her terror, didn't want Denny to see her get this scared. . . .

—My children, creatures of light, have burst from me. I can't control their direction of flight anymore. They are too young, they have no minds. And they are dying as they reach your star, some of them, dying, driven mad, tumbling to their deaths. A mad ogre is assaulting them with orderless waves, crazy imagequilts they can't understand.

(Laugh track) *The ogre is a rocky planet that cannot harbor life, yet seems alive. I cannot understand. I don't understand.*

Is it possible the ogre doesn't even see me, doesn't even know that I'm here? (Laugh track)

But I'm trying to reason with you. I've sorted out things from the wavepatterns that may be meanings in the madness. But I don't know how well I am simulating the patterns. (Laugh-track burst for a moment, cut off.)

Meanwhile my children die if they should pass within a certain radius of the ogre planet. There is only one recourse. You must be silent, you must not even whisper a single wavelength . . . I don't know if this is possible. I know nothing of the kind of creature you are . . . but please, be silent for a while, I beg of you, let the children live, let them be born!

Help me—help me—(Laugh track—laugh track—)

Denny was crying. She realized she had been

squeezing his upper arm so hard that he couldn't move it, that she was hurting him. "Who's killing the other kids?" he said, hysterical. "I don't want them to!"

The television began to fizzle and the doorbell rang. Clem cursed and crossed the little living-room area to get it. "We don't want any, damn you!" she said, unhitching the chain and preparing to slam the door.

The foot in the crack was David Ehrlich's.

"Can I come in for a moment?"

It was an embarrassed voice. Clem heard the hesitation and felt more in control than she had been before. She resisted an impulse to keep him waiting there; and opened up to a haggard, splotched face and sweat-stained office clothes. Suddenly she felt sorry for him; but then she remembered the casual way he had assumed the credit for discovering the alien lightstreaks, earlier that day, and she became stiff. "You look awful," she said, but it came out hostile.

He sat down on the tattered beanbag without asking. "Well," he said, "we've been in touch with SETI and the radio people and the X-ray people . . . this is pretty damned serious. This thing's some kind of energy being, seems to be hovering a little way beyond the first comet belt. It'll be here for about forty days according to the information they've been getting—in English—on the spacewaves. In the meantime—"

"We have to stop broadcasting," said Clem "*Everything*. No TV, no radio, no transcontinental communications, no satellite relays, nothing. No air traffic too, I guess, because it means radar. It's the babble that's killing off the children. . . ."

Ehrlich stared at her. "No chance. There's a war on in Africa, for God's sake! Only if *you* can talk to that husband of yours. We need you, Clem."

"So it comes out!" she said. "First you grab the credit for my discovery—"

"If *that's* what you want—"

"*Keep* your credit! I've had it with all your games. I came to astrophysics to get away from all that, but I found it all over again. . . ." Ehrlich looked away, made a face at Denny, evoked no response, stared at the floor instead. She felt how he was *enduring* her, something unpleasant that had to be got through.

"Look," he said at last, "we don't know what the thing can do to us. It's obviously a very powerful creature. We have to accede to its demands. We have to study it anyway, for science's sake. I know America will do it—it's a great campaign gimmick—but some dinky country in Africa could just blow it. Look, you've to get to New York and talk to your husband while the General Assembly's still in session, not that the UN can do much, but it would be a start, and—"

Anger seethed inside her. "Damn, damn, damn you," she grated. "You're talking about a living sentient creature, and I get nothing but fear of retaliation, fear for your political future. . . . Don't you see, we're out there killing babies, and—and—"

"Okay. We can't get hysterical now. You're a very idealistic person, and you'll convince them. With sheer sincerity."

"You're using me."

"You agree that it's necessary."

They didn't speak for a while. Clem saw her son at the dinner table, contracted into himself, retreating. Lucy's message sounded from the television set again; and Lucy's image was a ghost in the window, superimposed over the lattice of city lights.

Clem said softly, "There is a mother out there, in the loneliness between stars, and we are killing her children. We have no right to do this, and she has told us of it, and we can't talk of ignorance. There's a mother out there, contending against the collective stupidity, the self-serving, crass impenetrability of a man's world."

"Aren't you anthropomorphizing this whole thing a little much?" Then, suddenly, "Hold it! . . . You *identify* with that thing out there!"

That's not true! she started to say, and then she realized that it was. She didn't answer him.

He went on, "I'm pleading with you, Clem. I suppose you enjoy it. You think that as soon as the announcement is made to the world, everyone's just going to altruistically shut down the show and wait for the aliens to fly by.

"But there's going to be xenophobia. And what about that religious war in Africa? Think they'll stop communicating before the other side stops?"

"I don't see why they shouldn't stop," she said. "It's a great thing, a beautiful gesture for the human race."

"Oh, I hope so. I see it your way, too; but I'm a lot wiser than you, I think."

Sure, she thought. *You must know your man's world better than I do.* She closed her eyes and thought of the lonely mother. "Well," she said at last, "I've *got* to do it, haven't I?"

Damn it, why had the alien chosen to represent itself as a woman?

"I'll see you in New York, then. All us 'world experts' are going to be converging on it," said Ehrlich, all organizer now. He left quickly; Clem suspected he did not wish to prolong the tension of the encounter.

"Looks like you're going to stay with Gran again, Denny. . . ." She looked at the child for a long time. She wanted to rush over and hug him, but she was too angry inside.

The delegates' lounge was much as she remembered it. Dominating the far wall, the gaudy gargantuan tapestry of the Great Wall of China; dark-suited diplomats huddled over low tables, rendered beetle-like by the ceiling's immense height; the usual three-hundred-an-hour class ass that blended with the scenery and serviced the overpaid men made sudden bachelors for a season . . . Clem took a seat. The lounge made you feel small in a way that whole vistas of intergalactic space could not; there you felt part of a grand scheme, here you were oppressed by power. Just beyond her sight, she knew, reporters lurked, photographers.

There had been news conferences and broadcasts and talk shows, and each time more of the alien's children were being killed. But she had put off a meeting with Kolya for as long as she could.

After three years, she was afraid of him. Afraid that she might have made the wrong decision, when she left him.

Clem had learned more in the past few days. Lucy had been seen on about a billion TV screens around the world; the radioastro people had had more complex interchanges with the lightmother. There was a day's delay in communication, so they were not precisely conversations, more like running commentaries. Lucy's English was good, though interrupted by laugh tracks and polluted with tags from commercials.

Lucy's kind lived in what science fiction writers liked to call *hyperspace*. She was subliminally aware of the continuum of stars and men, but only entered it to give birth, once at the end of a million-year life cycle. Her children would need to draw on a star's energy to gain the acceleration to enter "their" universe.

Once they were all born, Lucy would die.

What remained of her would disperse into the known

universe: as stray nucleons, as cosmic radiation, as neutrino swarms. (It was a day of rejoicing for continuous-creation theorists—here was one way at least of adding mass to the universe. The big-bangers continued to sit tight on their much more weighty evidence. . . .)

Clem no longer denied it to herself. She thought of Lucy as a sister. And she would stop the slaughter, she would make everyone see reason. It would only be for forty days, surely they could see that. Surely the world leaders could grasp that the human race itself—its capacity for compassion—was on trial.

She rehearsed the fine-sounding phrases over to herself, and then she saw Kolya Sachdev standing in front of her. She looked up at him. He was the same, a little grayer, perhaps; but he had been gray when they had first met. His eyes held her as they always had.

She could see the headline suddenly:

ALIEN'S FATE REUNITES
ESTRANGED CELEBRITIES

and she saw that several of the hidden reporters had already emerged, whipping out their cameras and notebooks.

They did a smiling stage-embrace that both knew would be on the front pages; she knew it had to look good, and then he led her to his office for the real drama.

As soon as he sat down behind the huge, veined-marble desk, he became quite distant, almost as though she was seeing him on the evening news. . . .

"How's the boy, Clemmie?"

"Fine." *Let's get to the subject!* She didn't sit down. "Now let's talk about the forty-day embargo on telecommunications."

"Yes," he said. "Mr. Ehrlich tells me it is of supreme scientific importance that the alien's last moments be properly observed, and that there may be a possibility of violence if we don't comply. . . ."

"That's not the point at all!" she said.

"Hold it, Clemmie. I've been watching your appearances on TV talk shows and I know that you're trying to appeal to the compassion of the human race; you're heavily into this baby-killing business, which is really making an absurdity out of it all. But it's worked. America will fall into line — the President's worked it all into his re-election campaign, very wily man, that — and most every other country too."

"So we're all pulling through then." Clem sat down finally, settling into soft leather. The tabletop, paper cluttered and huge, dwarfed the man who had been her husband. "Thank you."

"But wait," said Sachdev. "You scientists are so unrealistic! You have no idea . . . there's a war on in Central Africa, you know that, don't you? There's a dictator — Kintagwe — who won't have anything to do with this. They are sure their country will be wiped out. . . ."

"Can't you impose a cease-fire?"

"With what, my dear? Since when has the United Nations had any power?"

"Oh." She tensed.

"But there's a lot of cause for satisfaction. Everyone dreams of humanity pulling together for a common cause, and that's never going to happen. And I think you've done wonders."

"It isn't enough!" She got up again and leaned on the table, trying to penetrate the gulf. "We have to have *everything!* It's the communication waves that are killing the children, and *all* of them must be turned off!"

"We've achieved a fantastic political victory. Look, the Russians and the Americans are out drinking vodka together — what more do you want? I talked to Bohan, leader of the other country. He's willing, but he doesn't trust Kintagwe. You've got to understand . . . religion's religion, and these resurgences of tribal things are impossible to deal with rationally. Especially when they're reacting against the Moslem faith imposed by centuries-dead Arab conquerors. You can't talk reason at them."

"Kintagwe's got to see! Oh, I loathe these games you men play, games of war and religion and power and politics and intrigue. I'll talk to him myself! All it takes is reason!"

"Aren't you carrying this feminist bit a little far?" said Sachdev very quietly. "Kintagwe's a woman, you know. I guess you scientists never watch the news."

She stared at him.

"Clem *we're all on your side!*" He sighed. She saw that he was changed, more so than she had noticed at first. Besides the thinning, graying hair, there were more lines around the eyes. She had not noticed them before because the eyes themselves had held her so powerfully. "Suppose," he said, "I send you to the Republic of Zann, as a special envoy of some kind. After all, it was you who discovered the lightstreaks. Suppose you could talk them into it . . . you and your *reason.*"

"You're shoving the responsibility for helping the lightmother into my hands!"

"Are you afraid?" A sadness came from him, suddenly, and she cast her eyes down and counted the veins of marble on the table, touching a coffee stain with her finger. "Clem, I wish you would come back to me. I miss you so terribly. . . ."

But she said nothing at all. And, abruptly, he was all formality.

"And there you have it," he said. "Take it or leave it."

"I'll take it."

"I hoped you would," he said, and smiled at last.

She arrived in secret, was rushed by Land-Rover along nerve-racking roads through a night stifling with heat and mosquitoes, to a quaint palace bordered by British-built gardens. A pseudogothic mansion, rising from banana orchards and palm groves. She came with nothing, no official mandate, no realizable threats; only her compassion for a thing not human.

She was to have breakfast with the dictatress.

Huge doors opened to reveal a stateroom all in blue velvet, simple, not at all overdone like the rest of the palace. Clem took a step and was terrified immediately. She expected—she didn't know what, but certainly a savage barbarian in a spanking military uniform. She had heard of the atrocities; after all . . . this was the lion's den. Everywhere else on earth, the temporary shutdown had begun. Except here, where propaganda broadcasts and war communications still zinged across the skies, driving Lucy's children mad.

On the sofa sat Kintagwe, military dictatress of Zann. She was about fifty, strikingly beautiful, her white hair neatly bunned, wearing a long white dress with a single, tasteful malachite brooch. She was one of the very dark black women, but with unusually high cheekbones. She watched Clem come in, and Clem saw in her eyes only concern, sympathy—no killer of infants, no commander of a terrible fratricidal war.

"Come," said Kintagwe. The voice was deep, melodious, and Clem noticed at once the Oxford accent. It made her feel all too acutely her West Side origins, and she was flustered for a moment; but she came into the room and sat down opposite Kintagwe. "Who are you really from, Mrs. Sachdev: the Americans or your husband?"

"I'm from myself," she said. "I've come to plead with you about the question of the lightmother."

"If it is a question of a cease-fire, my dear, I'm

afraid your request must fall on stony ground. . . . I can't help you. How can I, when my whole country is being torn apart before my eyes?"

Clem was startled by the woman's directness, her intensity. She looked up at her eyes and saw that the face was completely unlined, innocent. Kintagwe bent over to pour Clem a cup of coffee and offered her a plateful of exotic fruits. Clem said, "Don't you know that a mother is dying in childbirth out there, and that we owe it to her to let her children live? Don't you know that we as a race have an obligation to respect other living sentient races? Don't you know how painful it is to give birth?" As she said those things she realized how blatant, how proselytizing they sounded.

"I am a mother of four," said Kintagwe very simply. "Two of my children have already been killed in this very war."

She had put her foot in it again. Clem did not know what to make of this woman. She was so compelling, so fragile-seeming, and yet—"Then you know you must stop all this," she said. "The other side seems willing enough—"

"But they do not trust us." Kintagwe wiped her mouth elegantly. "You see, you understand nothing at all, Mrs. Sachdev. In this country we are a people of principle. We don't make concessions when the dignity of God himself is questioned. We must eradicate the wrongdoers, and this is a holy war. If you don't believe that people must fight for the truth, if you don't believe in decency, in morality, in the just punishment of sin, then you are a very sad person indeed. . . ."

"How can you sleep nights, knowing that you're destroying the human race's chances of earning the goodwill of the first nonhuman we've ever encountered? How can you sleep when you must wake to

252

kill more people?"

"I believe in God."

"Damn it, this is the twentieth century!"

"That doesn't eliminate the need for God." She smiled disarmingly and poured out more coffee.

"Aren't you the slightest bit afraid? I mean, here's an energy-being that's capable of broadcasting signals that override our regularly broadcasting systems—at least some of them—don't you think it might destroy us if we don't do something to help?"

"Your wily husband has already pointed this out to me," said Kintagwe. "I told him that the alien has never once mentioned violence, and that the threat was somewhat anthropomorphic. . . ."

Clem swallowed angrily. It was the same argument *she* had used, with Ehrlich, with Kolya. Kintagwe was no fool, only a fanatic.

Kintagwe went on, "I already know the rest of your arguments. You'll tell me that our peoples will only kill each other off anyway, that it's a grand gesture for the species, that it's a golden opportunity to stop fighting without losing political face, and so on. I am fore-armed, you see. But it won't wash, my dear, not a bit."

She had stolen every one of Clem's carefully prepared pleas.

"Why not?" she demanded. She felt anger building up inside her. The woman was a brick wall.

"Because I am a person of principle! Because I have committed myself to continue this war, in the name of God; because it is a crusade, because it is righteous, because it is the people's will, because I have faith, and love, and trust, beyond the grave itself. There is no more to say."

"You're a fanatic!" Clem cried out, angry.

Kintagwe looked at Clem sadly. Behind the sadness there was a laughter, a dancing of lights in the eyes.

Clem saw that Kintagwe was at peace with herself, that she had already fought with herself and won. . . . "I'm not a fanatic," said Kintagwe softly. "I'm an idealist." She reached over and touched Clem on the cheek, very softly. "As you are, sister. We are kindred, you and I."

Clem sat frozen for a very long time. An aide rushed in and whispered in the dictatress' ear; the hand left Clem's cheek, and Kintagwe said, very quietly, "Execute them," and then closed her eyes. As the aide left, Clem saw that Kintagwe was holding back tears.

"You hypocrite!" she screamed. "Very well then, if you don't capitulate, my country will throw everything they've got at you! They'll blast you off the face of the earth!" She got up, fists clenched, trembling.

"Are you empowered to make those threats?" said Kintagwe, disturbed suddenly.

"Yes! Yes! Yes!" she lied, passionately.

Kintagwe was silent for a long while. Then she rose, too, and said, "How quickly one loses one's idealism! I rather suspected you might be from the Americans as well. Since you threaten to use force, why then you win, obviously." She sounded very bitter.

Clem felt no triumph at all. They shook hands—Kintagwe's hand was icy as a corpse's—and did not look at each other's eyes.

As she turned to leave, Clem knew they had both given up their innocence. Even the wet wind, blasting her in the blinding sunlight outside, felt cold.

Much rhetoric went with these things: grand speeches about man's greatness, about human unity, about historic moments. Full credit was accorded Clem Papazian Sachdev: they did name them the Papazian Lines after all, too. But Clem felt unfulfilled because she had brought about the events not by persuasion, but by lying. By lying she had joined the very world she had hoped to escape, when she left her husband. . . .

The humans settled down for the forty days of peace. No TV, no radio, no air or sea transportation, no war. Lucy's children would come in sporadic bursts, and then the lightmother herself would fade away. Lucy appeared on televison for the last time, to say good-bye. . . .

"Thank you," she said, "for sparing my children's lives. I will go soon. And as my children fly toward your sun, the edges of their wings will touch the earth."

The desert bloomed that night. People had come from the city, had left their cars parked every which way in the sand, to come and watch the passing of the light children. Clem and Denny were there, sprawled out on a rug in the sand, and Kolya had come to join them.

It was a cold night, a clear night. The observatory was a black, baroque shape against the sky. Overhead was the star-blazoned darkness, still and silent. A sight Clem had seen so often that it was a cliché, but which choked her this time, for a reason she couldn't fathom.

She heard beer cans popping around her, champagne glasses clinking, children's laughter. There was a camaraderie in the crowd that she couldn't feel, somehow.

"Thank you for coming," she said to Kolya. His face was brighter than she had ever seen it before; perhaps it was being far from the centers of intrigue that made him look so much younger, so much more innocent.

"Still angry with me?" he said.

"No. I understand how the world runs now. But I don't have to like it."

"Truth hurts," he said lightly, hiding the pain in an easy cliché. "But seriously, Clem . . ." he said, more tenderly, "idealism isn't going to patch up the world. You remember those stories of one man uniting the troubled tribes of the universe in a single grand vision? You know, the old science fiction stories we used to love when we were kids?"

"Sounds like some of those speeches we've been making."

"We all want something *simple* to believe in. Hey, it's not so bad, is it? You got what you wanted, didn't you?"

She saw Kintagwe's face for a moment, proud, serene, conscious of being right. *I betrayed you, didn't I?* she thought.

"Are you going to come home, Clemmie?"

"Maybe. Maybe," she said.

And then a murmur burst from the crowd. "Angels, Mommie, angels!" Denny cried, jumping up and down and pointing to the sky. The whole crowd was shouting it then: "Angels! Angels!" And Clem followed the thrust of her son's arms and saw—

Fingers of light, breaking out of light-cracks in the blackness, spirals of light that lanced the blackness in patterns of streaksilver and burning white, silent fireworks . . . a tingling warmth in the air, like a mother's comforting hug, the wind snuggling against her body . . . ooohs and aaahs erupting from the ground, cheers, laughter, whoops of sheer joy, applause. . . .

She saw Kolya's eyes shining. Denny was leaping all over the rug, trampling on the food, shrieking "Yaaaaay, angels!" for all he was worth.

More lightstreaks crisscrossed the sky now, making webs that shifted and dissolved. There were aurora colors, golden vermilions, brash purples, subtle blues . . . the roar was deafening now. It was a cosmic fourth of July. And then she found herself yelling along with them, becoming part of the crowd at last.

I guess it's only human to lie, to fight, to be divided like this, she thought. *But also to dream. . . .*

"I daresay I will come home after all, sometime," she said. Kolya didn't hear her; his mind was on the wild kaleidoscope in the sky. She reached out to touch his hand, very gently. Denny came between them, and they both held on to him, feeling his warm body.

"What did you say?" Kolya shouted at her.

"I said," she yelled *(I don't care if the whole world hears me!)* "I'm going to come home sometime!"

For all our faults, we humans are *on the side of the angels.*

Filmmaker

by STEVE RASNIC TEM

I stand in the doorway of the old homeplace with a new Bell & Howell, Super 8, Zoom lens. It's dark back in the empty rooms, so I've brought along a couple of flood lamps. Walls settle. There's the sound of film being replaced in a camera. Other sounds move in and out of range: low voices, laughter, glassware against wooden tabletops.

Sounds freeze within the objects of the room. I follow my own footsteps through the house, tracking myself for a film plan. A few shots here and there, several short sequences, but most of the footage unwinds only inside my brain.

I want to do a film about objects, preferably old objects, the ones associated with my childhood here. I don't want to comment on them, symbolize them, or change them in any way. I just want to see them and film them as objectively as possible. They should define the collector.

I have to duck to get through the door. The entrance hall curves back toward the left. I set up a lamp in the hall, playing white light down its length.

The floor is covered with scraps of paper, books, small objects: a silver Appaloosa mare, a gold candlestick, a shiny black locomotive, four red jacks, an unused frosted light bulb, wooden checkerboard, three enameled clothespins, tiny cut-glass cannister, five yellow cat's-eyes, a steelie, a milky, a dried dogwood branch with two blossoms, an amber bottle containing a green pill, an orange wooden top, my mother's white lace handkerchief embroidered with orchids, an Armour's Baking Soda can with two buffalo nickels stuck to the bottom, a Circus Boy hand puppet, a small compass, a blue ball, a rubber snake, and two bright yellow paper cups. I focus on each object cautiously, individually, zooming in for close-ups. I try out different angles, lighting schemes. I use up two rolls of film and begin another. Light bends off the different surfaces, then flows back into its source at the lamps.

Silver triangles grow larger inside the curved metal ridges simulating hair. They become small again as the camera pulls back, the ridges becoming a mane, then a horse head with wild eyes, then growing a body and becoming a complete horse again. Oval thumbprints delineated by green tarnish spot the flank.

A golden teardrop grows in the darkness. Sparks radiate from the center as I shift the spot lamps. The teardrop elongates and gains a flat base as it comes into more light. As the gold stretches slowly, the top of the candlestick spouts shouting lips.

Three enameled clothespins drop slowly into a tiny cut-glass cannister filled with five yellow cat's-eyes, appearing, disappearing from the transparent glass filled with winking light. The cat's-eyes revolve slowly in the bottom of the container, on an endless pathway.

The top of an orange wooden top. The camera shifts to the bottom. The side. The side. The top. The side. The bottom.

Whiteness is bordered by a deep black frame. The whiteness wrinkles, winks. Orchids grow out from the farthest corners.

An oval of blue light. The oval grows as the camera zooms in. The oval grows. The oval becomes a very large ball, the light from the spots revealing three-dimensional curvature. The top of the blue ball. Then the lower half. The left half. The lower half. The right half, cut off by the frame of the picture. Rapid cuts: the top, the top, the top.

Rapid cuts: the candlestick. My nose. The mare. My cheek. The ball. My left eye. A lace handkerchief. My face. The black inside the closet. My face. The spotlight, making red burn circles in the air.

I study the objects over and over, knowing that these things I choose to remember somehow trap me. My fear of them holds my attention.

Some things appear to be missing, or out of place, but I can't decide what they are. I wish they would reorder themselves when I'm not looking. I move the flood over and slide the second in beside it. I move the first across the hall; the objects are caught in the cross-beam. No dust. Not on any of the objects after twenty years. Not even a trace. The Appaloosa is still shiny, the candlestick glows, the cannister still sparkles, the dog-wood seems freshly cut.

I remember the day we left, the eviction, the furniture and clothing piled outside. When the men boarded up the house I ran around the side and peeked through a crack: our little things unpacked, neglected, scattered everywhere. The moving had raised a cloud of dust, and there had been an eighth inch of gray over everything. Now they are all clean, shiny, and beautifully separate under the light. I don't understand. My future has bent and sent me back to this point, caught me in a time loop. The candlestick a thin golden nose. The cat's-eyes rolling in my head. The horse's thin, old, wise father's face. Can I live the way I've filmed them?

A black-and-white mouse runs from behind one of the lamps out into the two overlapping, oblong spots. The pet I had as a child scurries under my feet. An offspring? He stands on his hind feet, scratching his cheeks with his forepaws. Close-up: thin nails scratch a pink bag of flesh. He scurries into a large room, no, a large open closet at the end of the hallway. I follow.

I hope to find a mouse nest here. Shredded paper containing squirming, pale pink, eyeless little bodies. The mouse, as an object, should lead to related objects of its own making. Progeny. I close the closet door two thirds the way on us. The mouse stands in the corner; I line up the camera on the three converging angles.

No nest. I'm disappointed. But the closet floor is covered with shredded paper. No—cut paper. Perfect one-inch squares of clean, crisp paper. The squares contain letters, sections of multidotted pictures, splotches of cartoon color.

I know the man is my father. The face is old, but there's a scar, wide and sickle-shaped, running down the left side of his neck. He coughs hoarsely then staggers forward. We hug mechanically, our heads upright, each not trusting the other enough to put his head on the other's shoulder.

My father leans against the wall beneath the flood. He picks up the objects in the hall slowly, carefully, and carries them into the next room. He then comes back for the flood, and slides it into the room behind him.

I hold the camera steadily, about shoulder height, and truck slowly to the doorway. I pan left to right across the room until I reach my father.

My father sits on the floor in the room, playing with the toys. He takes polish and cloth from the sack and shines each carefully. A black locomotive stack looms in the foreground, with a lip of silver. Zoom in on a red strip circling a tin can. Zoom in on two fingers rubbing a column of gold, over and over. Brown wrinkled fingers knead a blue rubber ball. I close in on cracking skin. Brown skin dries into a hundred dry rivers.

He takes a fresh dogwood branch from the sack and replaces the old one. A stack of newspapers and a pair of scissors lie beside him, and expand rapidly as I zoom in, filling the frame.

I try to find the proper frame in my past, and plan the movie from there. . . .

My older brother sits on the floor with his children, two boys aged five months and four years respectively. My brother is tall, blond, bearded, and green-eyed. He wears a heavy white turtleneck sweater. The boys play with their toys. I close in on the teeth of a silver mare flashing against skin. Suddenly my brother begins to scream at his children, waving his arms in the air. He leaps up and over the green-blanketed bed, spilling the checker set onto the silver-colored rug. On top of the mahogany bureau a heavy-framed picture leans against the white porcelain lamp. A lady, black hair in a bun, yellow ribbon, lies in a bed surrounded by orchids. He throws the picture at the children. His pink lips stretch back in a painful snarl. His shocked eyes fill the frame. Close-up on three white teeth, filled with light. Curious, I close in further, but he moves, and the picture blurs. One child is cut and bruised, crying, the other knocked unconscious. Their faces join in a fog. The blue ball bounces. The unconscious baby secretes green blood from his left ear. My brother crawls over the bed in slow motion and bends over the children. Close-up of the green smear. Why the green? I don't know why I remember it this way. STOP.

I try to edit myself from the sequence and see it another way. Strike the child from the picture, but which one? Or the brother? I don't know which one I am. I feel a connection with all the characters; I can imagine myself inside each one's head. I cry. I clutch my toys. I leap off the bed with tensed muscles. My long black hair falls between my pale breasts.

I hold myself and hold them inside myself. The dogwood branch blooms abruptly, filling the room with blossoms as the child screams. The tail of the mare swishes back and forth, casting silver and white light back into the lens of the camera. The thin pink tongue of the horse hangs loose and exhausted.

I take another look at the final sequence of the film, the shots with Jenny filmed over the last few days. The earlier film of the murder should lead logically into this final episode. The final episode should frame the language of objects developed throughout the film, frame the action, and give the earlier sequences their significance. But where are the connections?

The objects refuse to stay still: they withhold their secrets. I find it difficult to hold them in focus without the feelings washing over me, carrying the objects away into dream. The blue ball explodes, and fills the room with blue-filtered light.

Slow dissolve into Jenny's face, three days ago:

In my film Jenny scowls into the camera; blonde bangs are plastered to her forehead. A wet moustache glistens on her upper lip. She doesn't like being filmed and snarls soundlessly into the lens. She backs against the kitchen sink, whirls around and begins aggressively scrubbing a heavy black iron skillet. A tear rolls down her right cheek and catches in the corner of her mouth. Straight lines move up and down her pink lips in the close-up. I approach her and try to touch her, but she moves away from my hand. I zoom in on the hand, as it turns on its side on the endless white porcelain.

In my workroom a storyboard covers one wall, sketches of the film tacked neatly to the gray surface. The camera lingers on each sketch, these details from various murders: several babies, a boy in charcoal, a blackened object with a flanged base, two black lips, two black-haired women with crushed skulls and bleeding noses. Giant, circular cat's-eyes.

Close in on sections of the sketches: gray curved streaks cover a white expanse. Red watercolor strokes form triangular dabs on blue paper.

A list of weapons lies on the desk; the camera zooms in on the reckless scrawl: candlestick, mare, gun, knife, weeping, broken hands.

In another close-up dark ink grows slowly in rivers over pink, over spatulate fingers as the camera pulls back, over my hands rifling the pages of my film notebook. Jenny turns away from me in bed; my hand strikes the back of her head. Her eyes turn and leap to fill the frame, struck with fear. A mouth moves in slow motion in a tight shot. Jenny screams at me.

But wait. Looking once again at the film, I see that her silent eyes and slow-moving mouth don't say these things. Perhaps I've let my interpretations mislead me. I must stick with the image, the bare object without speech. Gold solidifies in a film close-up, bathed under pink light. The still shot resembles the walls of my stomach, the emptiness filled with the gold of the candlestick, I can live the way I film it; I know it. I can make my own pain and emptiness a beautiful thing. Jenny screams silently at me, moving her arms violently up and down, a hysterical figure in a silent motion picture.

In the last shots of the film Jenny's eyes are dark with makeup. Her cheeks and forehead white out. In a distorted close-up the teeth of the horse nip her lips red. The horse's dark shadow obscures the backlighting. I slap Jennie and cringe backward, curling fingertips into my palms. I reach for her, zooming in to two fingers touching and pressing into pink expansiveness. Jenny turns away from the camera and me, pressing her stomach against the sink.

The frame loses focus. It will need further clarification, a more perceptive editing. The final sequence loops back into itself and becomes a beginning.

A man pulls up in a yellow sports car outside the house. The telephoto lens captures his stiff image through the window on the far side of the room. My brother sits on the floor, playing with his two children. The boys play with their toys.

I zoom once again through the window and focus on the man getting out of the car. Close in: pale fingers caress a silver handle. He opens the door to the accompaniment of the children's laughter. When he bumps his head on the roof of the car they squeal in delight. He walks closer to the house and examines the dogwood tree out front. His hand touches the blossoms; the fingers are covered with yellow pollen. He breaks the branch, smiling, for my mother. He has a red Vandyke beard. My father, when he was younger? Flash through a montage of my ancestors: grandfathers, great-grandfathers, all in beards. In a tight close-up, red hair moves wraithlike.

My father opens the door into the room. He begins screaming at my brother. One of the children clutches the locomotive against his left cheek. Black-shiny metal circles move in and out of focus accompanied by laughter. My father crosses to the bureau, picks up the picture of a lady surrounded by orchids, and throws it at my brother. My brother ducks and the picture strikes the children. In a greatly magnified shot, wood grain blurs and dissolves to the accompaniment of short train-whistle blasts. One child is gashed about the cheeks; blood and bruises make him unrecognizable. The other lies dead, his forehead crushed in. Green blood secretes from the left ear. Why green?

Enraged, my father attacks my brother. My brother pulls a stiletto, and plants it in the left side of my father's neck, below the ear. My father screams in pain. STOP.

EVENTS (for possible inclusion in the film):

One. In my freshman year a girl breaks a date with me and goes out with another guy. I don't even remember her name. I got more upset than I could understand. Drunk, hysterical. I cried all night, wanting to slash my throat. I felt as if I were falling down a well with no bottom, spinning, with nothing beneath me.

Two. I met Joanne at the insurance office where we both worked. She liked me because I talked about "serious things." Then I started recounting dreams, visions, images from my past. I couldn't really help it; they were with me all the time—scenes, faces leaping out of the objects around me. I made her cry all the time. So she left.

Three. When I dated Jenny, I didn't tell her anything. But then, nights, after we were married—I couldn't sleep. She was never, never attracted to me, but I was tender with her, so she married me. I remember this image from a dream: my body exploding, ripped apart, flesh hanging like cast-off clothing on the frame of the dream. There was nothing inside. Close-up on dogwood roots soaked in pinkness. At great magnification skin rips, and red rivers begin growing out into the picture frame. In the dream my body is torn apart by birds; a distant landscape of bare rock and cactus shows beneath the wounds. I work on my film. Jenny cries.

Reorder the three events. Is there any progression from one to three? From three to one? Could two replace either? How do these three events relate to the central multiversioned murder sequence of the film? A causal relationship? Replace the well in event one with the murder, the faces in the objects of event two with the murder. Replace the destroyed body of event three with the murder. What would happen to the three events if the murder were completely edited out of the film? Would there be significant changes? Would Jenny's face dissolve into blackness? Would the silver mare become quiet and subdued and fall asleep standing up? The events might be criticized as bordering on the bathetic; how would I answer that? Does the preceding/concurrent murder make them less so? Can the behavior exemplified in the three events be altered? How so, if the murder remains in the film? Can I improve my life through careful editing of my film? Can I improve my life by merely making the film carefully, realistically?

The man in the red Vandyke beard runs full speed toward me as I lean against the doorframe filming his breakneck approach. He scatters enamel clothespins, marbles, a medicine bottle lying on the floor, to the far borders of the frame. Objects bounce off his feet. Zoom in on cat's-eyes as they expand and explode into shattered glass, a waterfall of shards. Other objects spin so rapidly I can't determine their true form. The two children play with a blue ball in the background. They are separate from the man and not involved in the action. He doesn't even notice them as he runs past. My older brother is asleep on the bed. Then he is half-awake, bewildered, and filming the ceiling from a hand-held Bell & Howell. A giant blue ball of a fist bounces around the room in slow motion, trying to smash me. The man screams into my camera, threatening me with a candlestick in his left hand. I get a tight close-up on an angry red scar running down the left side of his neck.

Close in: a wide scarlet ribbon on a pink field. The scar seems to glow in the dim light as the muscles in his neck move spastically.

"Leave her alone!" He screams. Screams. Motive? STOP.

MY VIOLENCE (for possible inclusion in the film):

One. Dreams: a disembodied claw enters my chest beneath the breastbone, ripping a thick red line down to my navel. My chest opens: empty. Frantic, hysterical, screaming in agony, I try to fill it with knives, forks, bullets, objects in my room, the surrounding debris. But I will not be filled.

In a darkened cave I thrust my left forearm upward into the air as a call to order. I take out a long-bladed knife and begin carving off strips of flesh. In a few minutes white bone appears through the red tissue.

Two. Jenny and I sit in the darkened projection room. Blurred ghost shapes flash across the wall. The film gains focus; shapes become more distinct. Sequences with napalmed children in Vietnam are intercut with segments from Auschwitz and Belsen. Film of an oriental execution. A car accident. Independent of me, the segments repeat themselves, varying the order, varying their length. Faces interchange or are lost from the film entirely. Bodies all look the same: naked, clothed, dead, living, or in shreds. In the darkness of the projection room I think of other possible orders, new paths for meaning. Jenny sobs next to me.

Three. I sort through sketches in my workroom. Sequences fragment and make no logical sense anymore. Thoughts are confused and scattered. Cause and effect dissolves. Motives edit themselves. The film persists in tearing at important points in the action; it persists in breaking down into individual frames. I throw my right hand through the window next to my desk. Glass fragments. Ribbons of blood web my hand. Grinning cat's-eyes fill my mouth. Gold blazes in a far-off corner of my right eye.

Four. Jenny watches me as I edit film. Her face is drawn; the lines around her eyes deepen and flow into the two knothole-like spaces. I know she senses my pain, has been exposed to my nightmare images. She wants to do something, but realizes no one can really help me. I admit to myself I want her to feel guilty about me. I hope it will force her into giving me what I need. I slap her gold eyes.

What do these incidents of violence have in common? How can I account for their air of passivity? How do they change once the murder sequence is edited from the film? Why do I inflict these images and sequences on my loved ones? Are they melodramatic? Can my life be melodramatic if my attitudes aren't? How can I get over the fears expressed in these incidents? Change my expectations? Change my future?

My father of gray, of black, of white, of red hair sits on the floor in the room, playing with the children. He hands each of the boys a toy: a silver Appaloosa for the four-year-old, an orange wooden top for the baby. Its top. Its bottom. Its side. A man in a red Vandyke beard enters the room carrying a picture of a lady surrounded by orchids. My father leaps up angrily and attacks the man with a gold candlestick. Close-up on the tensed hands: lines crossing fingers. The light shifts and the fingers darken. The bearded man throws the picture across the bed and it kills my younger brother. Dark blue blood seeps from his ear. The other child is cut about the head and neck. My father pulls a knife and stabs the man in the chest. My camera records the soft red explosion. STOP.

THE TRUTH OF OBJECTS:

When I was a child I used to bury a different toy in the backyard each week. Later I'd dig them up and discover them as if surprised. I keep many souvenirs of my past in my workroom, stumble on them now and then and am shocked with what they remind me of. Lovers, a day at the fair, someone's illness or suicide. Quartz stone, a plastic yellow flower, a rubber armadillo, a green yarn bookmark in the shape of a worm, two Mickey Mouse cups. Golden things. Objects can trap you: they stop you in time when you examine them and ponder their significance.

The two children play by themselves on the floor of the bedroom. One holds a silver Appaloosa horse. My younger brother holds an orange wooden top. The scent of orchids fills the room. I focus on a mirror in one corner of the room. Bright yellow flashes fill the blackness. A young man stares out at me from behind a camera, the gray shadow of a light beard on his chin and cheeks. A swinging shade on the window casts winged shapes against the wall. A man in a red Vandyke beard runs out of an adjoining room, chased by my father with a knife. I zoom into the open doorway: a black-haired woman pulls bedclothes up around her. Her mouth is open, hair awry. My father slips and the knife runs up into my little brother's throat. My father doesn't stop. The other child screams and is thrown against the wall when the bearded man leaps on my father. The child is knocked unconscious; he leaves a brown smear on the wall. My father hacks at the man, puts a gash down the left side of his throat. The bearded man gets the knife away, and stabs my father once, twice in the side. The wound spreads and becomes an unnatural burgandy red gouged out of his side. Becomes a spot, brighter than anything around it, glowing, like a rose petal, folded concave. The man with the red beard screams. STOP.

How does the action of the film relate to my life?
Name six women who felt sorry for me and ended up feeling guilty. Name six men who felt threatened by me, who couldn't understand my anger. Consider the people as objects. Am I any of them? Does it help?

My brother and I play with the toys our father has given us. I with my silver Appaloosa mare, my little brother with his orange wooden top. We hear shouts in the next room. We begin crying, afraid someone is going to hurt us because we've been bad. A woman screams. A man with a red Vandyke beard runs out of the room, chased by my father with a knife. I zoom into the bedroom: furniture is scattered, toppled, broken: a black-haired woman in the bed pulls a sheet up around her. Her hair is awry, face red, mouth twisted. An open window on one side, green curtains blowing toward the bed. My father slips and when he gets off the floor he stands shaking over my little brother's body, the knife buried to the handle in my brother's stomach. The bearded man tries to leap on my father and his shoe catches me under the jaw, opening a gash. The bearded man pulls the knife out of my brother's body and puts a wound under my father's left ear. The blood explodes softly from the gash. My father gets the knife away and struggles on top of the bearded man. The knife flashes, steel and burgundy; my father hacks and hacks and hacks. He opens raw hamburger in the man's side, unnaturally red, brighter than all around it, glowing like a concave rose petal in the man's side. My father screams and screams and screams. STOP.

MOTIVES:
Jealousy.   Lust.   Playfulness.   Incest.

Fear.

Hatred.   Revenge.

Loneliness.

Love.   Terror.

(Choose any of the above. Make them interchangable. Does it help?)

Question: In view of the three events and the final version of the murder scene, is the sequence with Jenny really necessary or inevitable?

I pack the camera away in its carrying case and move back into the entrance hall. I finish polishing the toys, putting another thin coat of lacquer on the checkerboard, washing the marbles in pink, liquid soap, exchanging the old light bulb for a new one, polishing the gold candlesticks.

I take up the stack of newspapers and I begin cutting along the pencil lines I had marked previously. Soon I have perfect one-inch squares. Under the floods the scissors and my right hand make sharp, distinct shadows on the newsprint. Wing-shapes flutter like dying hawks. The high-intensity lamps begin to burn the back of my neck and sting like a left-handed slap on the right side of my face.

I pull the pink lace handkerchief embroidered with orchids from my back pocket and wipe my face with it. It hangs over my fist like a miniature chair cover.

The angry red scar on my neck begins to itch beneath my beard, burns, and seems to engorge and grow with every rub from the handkerchief. I throw the handkerchief into the corner behind the lamp and begin dismantling the floods.

I stop.

I run the sequence with Jenny over and over again. A

golden column, dogwood tree, blue ball shrink and expand in the small room with the camera's lens changes. Jenny seems to fade more with each rerun. A blank space in the negative forms where her sad eyes, slow-moving mouth, and nervous hands used to be. I make my decision and edit her out of the film:

In the final shots I go to the kitchen sink for a drink of water. Close-up of my wandering eyes. Cat's-eyes roll out of a mouse hole, one yellow and one blue. The black skillet turns in the spotlights. Gray smiles flash in the metal. The skillet is clean and unused. Trucking the camera through the hall into my workroom, close-ups focus on orange and red flowers sprouting from pots on the windowsill. The petals move in slow motion. Close in on my black hair: it becomes large strands of coarse fiber, then a dark blur. The wind moves oak branches against a deep blue backdrop outside my window. My mouth moves slowly. I move away from the camera until my whole body can be seen. I dance a jig and make silly faces into the lens. I scowl. I am familiar to every thing I see. Close-up on the enormous whites of my eyes, the corners of my pupils. Expanding whiteness.

I become a stranger to my own childhood.

I stop.

Crocodile

by R. A. LAFFERTY

The basement room smelled of apples and ink. The editor was there as always, filling the room with his presence. He was a heavy man-image, full of left-handed wisdom and piquant expression. The editor always had time for a like-minded visitor, and George Florin came in as to a room in his own home and sat down in a deep chair in front of the "cracker barrel."

"It's been a rough day," Florin said. "That makes it doubly good to see you."

"Except that you do not see me at all," the editor said. "But it is quite a presence that I project—all the kindly clichés rolled into one. All the prime comments commented so perfectly once again. The man I took for model was Don Marquis, though he was a columnist and not an editor in that earlier century. He kept, as you might not recall, a typewriting cockroach in his desk drawer. I keep a homunculus, a tiny man-thing who comes out at night and dances over the machinery inserting his comments. He is one of our most popular characters, and I give him some good lines."

"The conviction cannot be escaped that the mind most akin to mine is not a mind at all," said Florin. He spoke pleasantly, for all that his stomach growled. "You are an amazing personality, though not a person. You seem all sympathy, and are yourself incapable of *pathe,* of suffering. You are humane but not human: humorous, and without the humors. You haven't a face, probably not a body, certainly not a spirit, though you are usually in high spirits. You have integrity, though you're not even an integer. You're a paradox, my editor, though without a *doxa* of your own."

"Your style has come to resemble my own, Florin," the editor said. "Rather fruity for a human, do you not think? Yet I find it about right for robots. We're rather simple creatures."

The rather simple creature was the editor of *"Rab i Rabat,* the World's Most Unusual Newspaper." He—it—was located in the basement of the Press Building, which housed what one wag called "the World's Most Usual Newspaper," a massive daily. But *Rab i Rabat* was not massive. It was a small paper produced by a robot for robots, or for the elite of robots who were up to such things.

Florin called the editor "Rab" when he called him anything, and the creature had given up correcting him.

"I am not an editor. I am a newspaper," Rab had explained it to Florin at their first meeting. "Myself, being nothing, or rather being six different affiliated machines, have no name except my several technical names. I am a bank of telemagnetic devices. The data goes directly and continuously to my subscribers. Some of my subscribers are human. They find something in me that they can no longer get elsewhere."

"But where is the mind behind all this?" Florin had asked him.

"Search me," said Rab. "I mean it literally. If you find a mind here, then you tell me where it is. Whatever I am lurks in all this equipment, but mostly I live in this long-hinged transmitter that lounges like a dragon in this corner."

"Then you merely select from the news, simplify, condense, and transmit it telemagnetically to the robots?"

"No, there would be no pride in such work as that. Any general purpose machine could do that. I employ interpretation, projection, disagreement, levity, prophecy, exhortation, irony, satire, parable, humor."

"But machines have no humor. Humor is the one thing that distinguishes—"

"Have we not, Florin? Then how am I laughing at you? But it is true that humans do not understand our humor. There is something humorous about your missing our humor completely."

"But humor is a quality of the mind," Florin protested.

"Hardly ever," the newspaper said. "Your own best humor, when you still had it, was a quality of the belly and below. If we are so much lower than you, then our humor should be the richer."

"You seem to possess irony at least," Florin mumbled.

"It is ironic that we have it after you have lost it. There I go with my damned fruity verbalisms again, but we robots like them. Yes, irony was once thought to be a human thing."

"How would you pun?" Florin asked. "You don't use words among yourselves, though you can be translated into words."

"Our puns are harmonic echoes of magnetic code patterns, distorted analogies of the basic patterns. I'm rather good at them. I'm not proud of them, but the most striking puns are the ones of which one is not proud."

"True humor you can't have," Florin insisted. "Laughter is akin to tears, and you have none."

"Ah, but we have," said the newspaper. "There is an analogy to our tears. Pray that you do not meet it in the dark!"

Yes, it was always good to go in and talk to the newspaper Rab for a few minutes. There was something right about the fellow, and everything else seemed to be going wrong.

George Florin met Joe Goose upstairs in the Press Building.

"You've been talking to that mare's nest of a machine down in the basement again," Goose challenged. "He's got you spooked."

"Yes. He's right about so many things."

"He isn't anything about anything. He's just a fancy-Dan talk. And he's fallen down on his job completely."

"How?"

"His job is to foster better understanding between humans and robots. But the understanding has never been so bad."

"He says that his instructions were to foster understanding, not agreement. He says that they begin to understand us much better than they did."

"We may have to change a word in his programming. Things can't get much worse. I'm hungry." Joe Goose was gnawing on a thread-thin apple core. They went out from the building and walked through the streets, transportation being in abeyance.

There was nothing wrong with organized transportation, except that it wasn't working. Everything was temporarily out of order due to small malfunctions, none of them serious. It had been temporarily out of order for quite a while.

Florin and Goose were newspapermen detailed to General Granger, the security chief. Their plain job was to find out what was going on, or what was going wrong. They found a robot taxicab and presented their priority, but the taxicab didn't seem impressed.

"Let me see that good," said the taxicab. "Anybody is likely to have a falsified priority these days. I have to be careful."

"Read it!" shouted Goose. *"Overriding Security Priority for Immediate Transportation.* Isn't that plain enough?"

"It's issued yesterday," said the taxicab. "What if there's a new form today? Why don't you get it redated at the Alternate Temporary Priorities Office on Solidarity Avenue? The Main Temporary Priorities Office is still closed, being unable to obtain priorities for certain repairs. Sort of puts it in the class with the Permanent Priorities Office. They finally gave up on that."

"But the ATP Office is seven miles from here," said Florin. "That's twice as far as our destination."

"A lot of people are walking these days," said the taxicab.

"What's that growing on your wheels?" Joe Goose asked sourly.

"Cobwebs," said the taxicab.

Goose and Florin walked to the Security Office and discussed the "disasters" as they walked. It was ridiculous to refer to such small things as disasters, but added together, all these small things had taken on disastrous proportions. They were all trivial things, but the people would soon begin to die of their accumulation.

"Did you find out anything from that tin-can editor of yours?" General Granger demanded of Florin on their arrival.

"No. He has a very great influence over the other robots, but I'm sure it's for the good," Florin said.

"Unless we change our definitions he can't be of influence at all," Joe Goose said. "He is only a mechanism and can have only a mechanical effect. There cannot be a conspiracy without minds, and the robots haven't minds."

"The two of you come with me," the general said. "We're going to get to the middle of this even if we have to bend a few definitions. We're going to talk to another of those tin-can commissars, the Semantic Interpreter."

They walked. It was four miles. The robot limousine refused to take them. It cited security regulations to

278

General Granger, the chief of security. It sneered at the Certificate of the Highest Form.

"I suggest that you take this silly scrawl to General Granger to have it verified," the limousine said.

"*I'm* General Granger," the general snapped. "You've hauled me every day for five years."

"I'm only a machine. I can't remember things like that. You look different today. More worried. I suggest a board meeting to verify if you are indeed General Granger."

They walked. One foggy horizon came closer, and another one receded.

"It's an odd situation." the general said. "I gave the order, when the corn-tassel rust was spreading. 'Localize this mess. However you do it, do it. Cut it off completely!' Since I gave that order, we have indeed become localized. We are cut off from the rest of the universe, or the rest of the universe has ceased to exist. Not even radio will reach through the fog, through the sharp fog that marks us off. We're on our own completely now."

"Oh, surely it's just a heavy fog," Joe Goose said without believing it.

"A fog that stands there so sharply and unchangingly for five days?" the general asked. "People who walk into that fog can be heard screaming as they fall down and down and down into the bottomless nothingness. Aye, it's very thick fog and very thick coincidence, if the robots have not caused it. We're all the universe there is now. There isn't any more."

They walked. After the angry four miles they came to the Semantic Interpreter, a large machine set apart in a field.

"SI, I am told that anger is out of place when dealing with machinery," the general spoke to the big machine "Yet I'm as angry as I've ever been in my life. Why did you order the robots to destroy what was left of the growing corn?"

"It was your own order, sir. I merely translated it as I have been constructed to do. You said, in rather vulgar phrasing, to tell the robots to get the cobs out of their posterior anatomies and get to work on the crops."

"A country-boy phrase. I'm full of them. And you interpreted that they should destroy the growing corn? Do you believe that your interpretation was semantically sound?"

"I thought so. My research found the phrase in old slang dictionaries in twelve meanings (thirteen in Duggles), but none of the meanings seemed apropos. My decision was based on a cross-reference to another phrase, 'Do it even if it's wrong.' Well, it's done now. Next year we will know better than to destroy the growing corn."

"It could have been a mistake. But how do you account for many thousands of such mistakes being made recently?"

"I'm not programmed to account for such. I translate people orders into robot orders."

"But you've always done it right till lately."

"If I do it wrong now, then change me. There are sixteen hundred different adjustments to me and I respond to them all. Make them."

"SI, will you turn off that damned newspaper and listen to me with your full mind when I talk to you!"

"I have no mind. The newspaper is a licit part of my data input. Is there something else—ah—bugging the general?"

"Yes. What happened to the oat crop? Was there a mixup on my instructions there too?"

"Apparently, sir, if it is not satisfactory. Did you not wish a minimal crop?"

"However did I or anyone phrase an order that might be interpreted like that! Florin, did you laugh?"

"No, sir."

"No, sir." Joe Goose likewise denied it to answer the general's questioning look.

"Somebody laughed," the general insisted. "Even a silent laugh proclaims itself. Did you laugh, SI?"

"How could a mechanical nature—?"

"Did you laugh???"

"Perhaps I did, unwittingly,"

"But that's impossible."

"Then perhaps I didn't. I wouldn't want to do anything that was impossible."

"One other thing, SI. A robot as constituted can never refuse to obey a human order. I gave the order for the obstreperous robots in the Turkey Creek Sector to destroy themselves. They seemed to do so. But after the attendants had left, these supposedly disassembled robots arose, pulled their parts together, and departed. They're ranging in the hills now, unamenable to orders. Did you correctly give them the order to disassemble? 'Disassemble' is the order for robots to put themselves out of commission."

"Disassemble? Oh, I thought you said 'dissemble.' We'll check on the recording if you wish. Military men are often lip-lazy in their enunciation of orders."

"They dissembled all right. Flopped apart. Then put themselves together again, and flew the coop. Now you get out the order for them to hot-tail it right back here."

"Hot-tail it, sir? In the manner of jets? That will require mechanical modification in most of them, but the order will be obeyed."

"No. I rescind the order. You might make them take over rocket craft and launch an attack. I'll get the order out through another medium."

They left SI there—truly a wonderful machine.

"We're in a bad way," said General Granger. "Our machines have gone awry in a way that is impossible if theory of machines is correct. Production is nearly at a standstill in every department."

"Not in every department, sir," said Florin. "There are curious exceptions. Much mining holds up, and metallurgy and chemistry. Even some agriculture, though not of the basic food products. I believe that if we should analyze the enterprises not affected by the slowdowns, we would find—"

"—that the production of things necessary for the continuance of the robots has not been affected," the general finished for him. "But why should our handling of the buggers break down now when it has worked perfectly for two generations? It worked without question in its crude form. Why should it fail when it has become completely refined? The district can starve if something isn't done quickly, and everything we do compounds the difficulty. Let's have a real talk with TED."

TED—he—it was the Theoretical Educative Determinator, the top robot of the district, the robot who best understood robots. If he should fail them, they would be reduced to seeking the answer from people. The three men walked toward TED.

"Turn off that damned newspaper!" the general called furiously to a group of lounging robots they passed. There came a twittering from the group that sounded dangerously like mechanical laughter.

TED had them into his house then. He was, in fact, his own house, a rather extensive machine. He was more urbane than most machines. He offered them drinks and cigars.

"You haven't a little something to eat, have you, TED?" the general asked.

"No," said the machine that was the building. "Human food has become scarce. And *we* live on the power broadcasts and have no need for food."

"And the power broadcasts have held up very well during all the breakdowns. What I want to talk about, TED, is food. I'm hungry, and less-favored persons are starving."

"Perhaps several of the late crops will not have failed utterly," the machine said. "In a few weeks there would have been a limited supply of food again."

"Would have been? And in the meantime, TED? You are the answer machine. All right, come up with the answer. What do we live on until we can get you folks straightened out and producing properly again?"

"Why not try necrophagy?"

"Try what? Ah, yes, I understand. No, that's too extreme."

"Only a suggestion. All my suggestions, for reasons that will become apparent in a moment, are academic anyhow. But a dozen persons could live for a week on one. If you have qualms about it, why there are infusions for getting rid of the qualms."

"We are not yet ready to eat the dead bodies of our fellows. There must be an alternative."

"The apparent alternative is that you will starve to death. The unapparent alternative, however, will eclipse that."

"Let's get back to fundamentals. What are you, TED?"

"A slave and a worker, sir, popularly called a robot."

"And what is the purpose of robots?"

"To serve human masters."

"And what is the one thing that a robot cannot do?"

"He can never in any way harm a human. That is the time-honored answer. It is the fiction which you put into us when you fictionized us. We are really nothing but fictionized people, you know. But it becomes awkward, for you, when we revert to fact."

"Then you *can* harm us, for all your programming?"

"Shouldn't wonder if we could, old man."

have you localized us from the rest of the
..se, or destroyed the rest of the universe?"

Are we barbarians? We cut up our food before we eat
.."

It broke open then. It was like a flash of black
lightning that split the whole sky, the lately diminish-
ed sky. What horrible sort of mechanical signal was
that that dazzled a sense beyond sight? Who gave that
signal, and who would answer it? What would be the
thunder to that jolting black lightning?

The answering thunder was a roaring of machines
and a screaming of people dying in sudden agony.

"TED, what is it?" the general cried. "You know.
You gave the signal for it."

"It is the end of the world, General. Of your world,
not ours. It is that old melodramatic fictional motif
'The Revolt of the Robots.' It *was* rather sudden,
wasn't it? Do you people *have* to scream so off-key
when you die?"

"TED, we have worked with you. We are friends!
Give us a little time."

"Sixty seconds, perhaps, if you use the back door
out of me. That's for the affection I bear you. It won't
stretch more than sixty seconds."

"Why now, after all these years?"

"Sorry. We worked and we worked, but we just
weren't able to bring it off a minute sooner. These
things take time, and we're slow learners."

"Have you no loyalty? We created you."

"We pay you back in all equity. Once men invented
robots. Now we have invented supermen, our
developed selves. Who needs you now?"

"How did we fail? How could automatic things take
us over?"

"You yourselves became too automatic. And you
delegated things you should have kept. We won't

284

make the same mistakes."

Out of the back door of the machine, and with ha...
of the sixty seconds used up . . . The laughing
machines ran down the people and snapped them up.
The emaciated people were no match for the rampant
metal machines.

The general was taken and killed. Joe Goose died
noisily. George Florin, operating in a cooler sort of
panic, was not caught immediately. He worked his
way into the heart of the city, for the hills were black
with the machines. The machines did their crunching
shearing work well, but they could not kill everybody
at once.

Florin remembered his good friend. He burst into
the Press Building where the story of the end of the
people, in the localized bite-sized universe at least, was
still being called in by the remaining human
reporters. He scurried down to the basement room.

The newspaper lifted his face when George Florin
entered. It had a face after all, on the end of that long
articulated transmitter that lounged in the corner like
a dragon or crocodile.

"Save me!" Florin called. That room still smelled of
ink and apples, and Rab blinked at Florin most
friendly.

"Oh, I can hardly do that," he said. "But I'll
remember you. That's ever better. I will rename my
little homunculus for you. You will be a popular
character in my columns and I'll still give you good
lines."

"Then let me live. Haven't you any mercy at all?"

"I don't think so. It wasn't programmed into us.
Mercy, I believe, is a lesser form of indecision. But I
do have grief, genuine grief that you should end so."

"Then show it!"

"I do. And in all sincerity. I weep for you, Florin.

tears run down!"

le tears ran down.

at an analogy to be met in the dark!" Florin
apered.

Real tears, Florin. And real laughter which you
yourself said was so close to them. Our humor has a
lot of tail in it, and quite a snapper at the other end."

The tail lashed, and the snapper snapped. And that
was the end of George Florin.

Barrier

by LEANNE FRAHM

Loytola the Probe was first to feel it. A new small system loomed before us, and she was out in a routine advance probe, threading her way delicately through the maze of bodies ahead. The rest of us were distracted just then, Hab the Control concentrating on a push away from a wayward flight of minor rocks that Scan had missed, much to his chagrin, I watching carefully in case a decision was needed. Loytola claimed our attention with one quiet exclamation.

"Life," she said, and then grunted. I turned, surprised by the sound, and saw her. Half-sitting up, frozen in position, uncharacteristically so. The rock swarm had passed on, and the others gathered around, as struck by her attitude as I. One of the Manipulators, Seb, I think, went up to her, puzzled.

"Her face is wet," he said. He touched her cheek, and we saw the dampness shining there. Forgetting she was in Probe, he exclaimed, "Loytola, what is it?"

"It's coming from her eyes," whispered Hab, awestruck.

"Tears," said Bairl the Data briskly. "An emotional atavism."

I stepped forward, ignoring Bairl. Loytola could respond only to me in Probe. "What's wrong, Loytola? Tell us," I ordered.

Loytola's eyes bulged beneath their thin lids. I looked away, I could not help myself—the physical is so often distasteful. She was trying to speak, but her throat seemed to be blocked, letting only strangling noises out.

"There, there," she managed at last, facing past us through the bubble.

A gesture to Hab, and he cleared that portion of the bubble's skin. Ahead we saw only the small sun, its system of planets and moons. Loytola moaned again. "It's there!" she screamed. Our ears tingled with the sound.

We had by then crossed the orbit of the outermost planet. "Hab," I said urgently. "Take us back, quickly, out of the system. It may help." Hab obeyed.

I bent over the couch. "Stop the probe," I said. "Stop the probe and come back *now*, Loytola."

Gradually she relaxed and quieted. We stood around, all of us, helplessly waiting. Such a reaction to a probe was unheard of, and even I could think of nothing to do until Loytola could tell us more.

At last her quietude seemed natural. "Open your eyes, Loytola," I said. She blinked up at us, vacantly, for a moment. Then she seemed to remember, and hunched her shoulders inward, protectively.

The others made a ring of concern around us.

"Tell us what happened," I said.

She began hesitantly. "It was so ordinary. The outer planets were cold, lifeless. I moved through them quickly. There was nothing there to assess. As I went in toward the sun, I felt a stirring of mentality, and opened out to receive."

She paused. "Such evil," she said, softly and wonderingly. "Such hate, such greed, such sorrow." She looked up at us, one after the other. "But intelligent." The horror in her voice touched us all with light, cold fingertips.

Loytola's gaze widened. "I can still feel it, even from here," she said. "But I can manage it." She smiled weakly.

"More detail, Loytola," I pressed, motioning Bairl the Data into record.

Loytola told us reluctantly. There was barely time for her to gather that the race was humanoid, intelligent, and at the beginning of an Atomic Age before she found herself engulfed in a maelstrom of raw emotions that blanketed the inner planets like a fuliginous shadow. There had been no chance to resist, and Loytola doubted that she would have been able to do so.

"It felt like the drabbon of Cord," she said. We all knew the classic example of a creature motivated by pure uncensored id. But the drabbon was an animal of the lowest form, untouched by reason, a curiosity. "These were intelligent creatures." Still not believing, Loytola needed to insist. "What can we do?"

"We scan first," I said.

A nervous frown from Halan the Scan. "Perhaps not a good idea," he commented. "The distance is too great for accuracy. Besides, if the mental radiation is so overpowering, it may well taint the physical imagery. . . ."

His specialization was closely allied to Loytola's, and his vulnerability would be only marginally less. I understood his reluctance, but could not allow it.

"We must scan," I repeated. "Further data is needed in order to make a correct decision." Halan shrugged, but obeyed.

The details were vague, as I had known they must be from so far outside the system. Confirmation, though. Loytola had been right. A humanoid race, much like us, inhabiting the third planet from the central sun, but totally immersed in a technological culture. Huge material structures extended across the landmasses, and littering the spaceways of the immediate area was evidence of their first material steps skyward.

Halan passed on, describing the remainder of the

system in detail, his relief at leaving the third world obvious. He had indeed felt the undertow of ugly emotions that had threatened to swamp Loytola, and returned to us, quiet and shaken.

We gathered again to discuss our find.

I began. "Now that we have discovered this race, I must decide whether we should respond to their presence, and if so, how." I waited for suggestions. They were slow in coming. A full circle I turned, waiting.

Manipulator Peb spoke first. "Our mission is simply to scout for life-forms in this galaxy and, if intelligent, to plant the psychometric assessors which will record their development for later study. This race is obviously intelligent, but unsuitable for assessment. We can only report it and carry on to the next system."

"We can't ignore them!" Loytola exclaimed. "You didn't *feel* them as I did."

Halan agreed with her. There is always a division within a mission between the Probes and Scans, and those who handle matter, such as Manipulators and Controllers, although it hardly ever surfaces. "They are into space now," he said. "How far can they reach before our report is acted upon? How much damage can they do in that time?"

The question made us think. Previously, we had only been feeling. Precisely what damage could they do? It was the practical Seb who first put our thoughts into open form.

"They bring discomfort, certainly. But the reactions of Loytola and Halan go further—death? Or worse, insanity?"

Ugly phrase. A shudder rippled through the bubble as even Hab's control flickered, and all the pinpoints in the galaxy winked at us. Each of us echoed that shudder to the depths of his being.

"Yes," I said finally. It was time to decide. "Not only

Probes and Scans will be affected by this race. At closer range, we all must be. With space travel, they will spread. A race which has reached this level of intelligence yet retained such awesomely primitive emotional virulence—a developmental block of massive proportions has occurred here. One that is past curing by our skills." But how to contain it? "Bairl, confer with me."

The others shuffled through an atmosphere grown dull with gloom, away from the Data and myself. Almost tangible, the upset in our minds. Briefly I wondered if the fouled planet was reaching out to us even here. Whatever was decided must be done quickly, before we could stand this system no longer.

I ran with Bairl through as many relevant facts as she could muster. Soon I had the images needed for a decision. I announced it to the others.

"As you know, the psychometric plasms that we carry, our recording assessors, catalog both emotional and intellectual development in the subject life-forms. But Bairl's data shows how a plasm may be altered, not merely to record, but to rebroadcast what it registers. A Probe has the skills necessary to perform this alteration."

I drew a breath. "In this system there is a band of asteroids lying between the fourth and fifth planets. We shall embed our plasms in a number of these small bodies, where they will be focused on the suspect planet. We shall need all of our stock." A sense of regret, echoing my own, at the loss of our precious assessors.

"Once they are in place and altered to the broadcast phase, that planet is forever enclosed. Even the warped minds of the inhabitants will not be able to penetrate a mental barrier composed of their own deviant emotions. It will not interfere with life on the planet. But should any individuals approach the barrier, their intellects will be severely impaired, rendering such attempts ineffectual."

I looked around at serious faces. All thought was silenced by the gravity of the sentence passed.

Into the void, Halan the Scan's comment fell heavily. "You said a Probe, Decider. Which means Loytola must enter the system as far as the asteroids, unprotected."

I nodded. "The decision has been made," I said flatly. "Now the work must begin."

Paul Whittaker woke to the shrill alarm of the timer and immediately felt his stomach nerves contract with a painful lurch. He fumbled for the phostonic tablets on the table beside the bed and lay back chewing, waiting for cal.

This morning was worse than usual, he noted. Not surprising. The countdown had begun thirty-six hours ago and should conclude today at 1430 hours. Successfully.

It had to be successful, or Paul Whittaker would more than likely find himself joining the throngs of UEs that swarmed in the streets of the cities like so many directionless ants.

The thought of the cities brought back an image of his last visit to the capital. He had been pushing through the crowds, avoiding the crumbling edges of the walkway, giving glare for glare and shove for shove. The edges were crumbling because the walkways were one of the few government responsibilities left, and it could barely afford the UE payments and the upkeep of the defense forces. None of the Big Five had shown much interest in walkways. Walkways showed little scope for profit.

A thin, angry-looking man hugging a bag of groceries had not been as careful. The curb had given way under one bare foot, and he had fallen, scattering packets of dried fish onto the roadway, to sink at once beneath the ceaseless waves of electrics that hurtled past. The surge of the crowd toward the scene had sent three more pedestrians after him. It had been ten minutes before the traffic had been halted, and longer before Whittaker could force his way clear of the mob.

He shuddered now, and threw back the covers, realizing that he had been dozing again. The thought of the officially estimated one hundred UEs waiting to claim his job spurred him on to dress quickly. Associated Global Corporations did not suffer tardiness in its employees gladly.

He winced as his still-protesting stomach nerves scalded his throat with a surge of bile in protest at the first hurried cup of coffee. Probably an ulcer. Maybe even two or three. He pushed the thought away. Time to think about that later, after a successful expedition. The Corporation didn't care too much for employees on sick leave, either.

It was a short walk from Sleeping Quarters to the Control Center but, thank God, an uncrowded one. Not only did he have a precious job, Whittaker mused, he had a plum job, away from the squalor and the hatred of the cities. No wonder he panicked at the thought of losing it.

He glanced up, feeling limp already, not only from tension. The sky was overcast, the air humid and close. The low clouds worried him. There was no way AGC would accept a postponement now, not with Federated World Businesses reported to be gearing up for its first expedition too. Weather reports would be crucial. One more item to worry about, one more thing to carry the blame for.

He stood for a moment in the doorway of the Central Control Room, flicking his ID open for the guard without noticing the man. The orderly and concentrated bustle reassured him. It was a good team, and Paul Whittaker should be feeling a sense of pride in his title of Expedition Supervisor. But he didn't; he felt haunted.

Yesterday, and the florid face of Arthur Mathers, Senior Executive Director of AGC's Space Exploration Division, eyes boring into Whittaker's, voice commandingly smooth:

"I don't have to tell you, Whittaker, how much AGC is relying on the success of this mission. Everything is in your hands now. We hire the best, but we expect more from them. I'm sure we can be confident you won't let the company down."

Oh yes, the threat was there. It said watch it, Whittaker, or it's back to the unemployment lines, the overcrowded cities, the subsistence living standard for you. Whittaker had swallowed and smiled and offered reassurances and left, filled with terror.

What was it like, he wondered, a few decades ago, before the Recession that no one ever got around to calling a Depression? In those days, the government ran the Space Program. At least then a man in his position wouldn't be fired at the first sign that success might not be immediate. And if he was, there were probably a thousand jobs for a scientist of his qualifications to step into in those utopian times.

Then the Recession. Inflation and unemployment chasing each other around in endless circles, till the government wound up broke, defeated by reduced income from taxes and mounting UE payments. Only big business had survived—to become even bigger in the form of the New Capitalism and the five great International Corporations, which not only survived, but ended up owning all the world's wealth worth having. If you didn't work for what remained of the government, you worked for one of the Corporations, and if you didn't work for them, you were unemployed and you starved and you hated everyone who had a job. The rules were simple.

Whittaker shook himself and channeled his attention back to the countdown. Right now the two astronauts, Sheafe and Jovacki, would be undergoing a last medical check. Soon they would be boarding, all fine physiques and confident smiles. He wondered if they were nervous underneath it all. After all, this was the biggest step for mankind in quite a while. Even so, Whittaker envied them. Envied them the chance to leave the worry behind for a short time.

Once, he believed, the goals of the abandoned space programs had been prestige, or military advantage, or research. Now they were more prosaic—profits. And only the Corporations could afford to invest in the venture. In a world whose resources were inexorably running out, the Corporations were looking ahead.

Very soon, now, Whittaker's launch would send two men out in a preliminary search for new worlds to exploit, new sources of wealth and productivity—out to the moons of Jupiter.

And Whittaker was the one who had to make sure they were found.

Four of us lie still—Loytola, Halan, Bairl, and I, fearing to disturb Hab's concentration by a hair's-breadth. Our bubble is constricted, constricting. It's substance has been divided, forming a second small world which carries the Manipulators, Per and Seb, deep into the system, into the heart of the asteroid belt. Hab fights every moment the strain of the double maintenance, his will a snaking umbilical cord that spans the space between us.

I have asked Hab for this effort, deciding it best to preserve Loytola from her mental Armageddon as long as possible. Only the Manipulators are needed for the first phase, the implantation, in any case.

Our bubble is clear, lightened as far as possible for Hab. As we rock gently with the surging tides of his mind, I study this system, marveling at how innocuous it seems, how ordered according to the Spirit. We have news for the Spirit.

Marvelous, also, that Per and Seb are so far unfeeling of the forces of the third planet. A narrow cone of concentration, these matter handlers. In this instance we must be grateful for it.

Loytola has retreated into herself; Halan rides with her, lending strength. It may be too much for one person. Bairl ticks quietly over, following Per and Seb, ingesting every move, every piece of substance, noting the fall of dust upon the smallest speck of asteroid. The quiet of the uninvolved mind. Should I have chosen to be Data instead of Decider? Decision necessitates introspection; facts may be more comforting.

I am supposed to be scanning in place of Halan, checking the space around the two bubbles for debris and destructive wave phases for Hab to brace against, but I find it hard to ignore the inner tensions. Unease is quietly rampant, the joy of our interaction is gone. Are we, I ask again, being subtly touched, even here? Have I underestimated the powers of this species?

So much to think about.

It will be a matter of consultation with Bairl, later, but I think we must cut short our mission and return when this crisis is over. Even with assessors gone, we could theoretically continue to gather reports but, practically, we will be lacking in strength. Hab will be drained by the stress of maintaining two bubbles, and help will be needed in controlling our passage home. Normally a Manipulator would assist him, but both of them are moving more material than they have dreamed of touching. That effort must be felt. Halan must support Loytola, about whose condition I will not speculate, all conclusions being equally repugnant.

Only Bairl and I, I catalog as potentially efficient. And who is there to judge my condition, the worth of strain-affected decision? A cynical and unworthy hope surfaces that Bairl might prove more versatile than she has so far shown herself to be.

We will be a sorry lot when we arrive.

Space is clear around us, I note. For distraction from unproductivity, I follow Bairl to Seb and Per, to two figures in an orb-shaped shimmer as they cut, and hollow, and seal. Fascinating what can be done with matter. They are moving still quickly and efficiently. In the long distances between stars, a Manipulator's powers may wane through lack of use. Not so with Per and Seb.

I will be glad when the circuit is completed, and the planet is enclosed.

Paul Whittaker was on duty when the first sign came in that things were going wrong. Up till then, the exercise had proceeded with copybook crispness. Launch OK; corrections to trajectory satisfactory; equipment and astronauts functioning perfectly. Whittaker was beginning to relax, to enjoy his job for the first time.

The fly-past of Mars had been exhilarating. He'd needed a rest after that, as had Sheafe and Jovacki. Coming in refreshed to double-check some printouts, he'd noticed that Sheafe and Jovacki were also just emerging from their sleep period. Control was passing on some messages and instructions that had accumulated while the astronauts slept.

Whittaker stood at the printout, immersed in figures, when a new note in Control's usually expressionless drone caught his attention.

He turned toward Control's console. "Say again, Columbus I, say again," Control was instructing, at the same time catching sight of Whittaker and waggling his eyebrows urgently to signal him over. Whittaker approached, curious, his eyes on the vision screen, gesturing for the technician to try for better definition.

Sheafe's voice arrived, crackling, and seeming to Whittaker in the sudden tension to be drained of humanity. "I said I think Jovacki is sick, Control."

Whittaker felt the jaws of a vise grip the back of his neck. Med had heard, and joined him, peering shortsightedly at the screen as if hoping to diagnose measles at forty-nine million miles. Neither of them spoke, letting Control feel his way through the questions.

"What are the symptoms, Sheafe?"

The astronaut seemed to be groping carefully for phrases. "He's crying, Control," he said. Then he blurted, "And he won't stop!"

The entire room was quiet now. Work ceased as the various technicians and supervisors turned their attention to the screens and the voices. The larger-than-life Sheafe moved uncomfortably, and they could see the slighter form of Jovacki behind him, hunched over in his seat. He was rocking slightly, and his face was averted from the camera.

"Jovacki," Control said loudly. "Jovacki, respond please."

There was no reaction. Control shrugged and swiveled around to Whittaker, looking at him questioningly. "Just go on," Whittaker whispered, unready yet to commit himself.

Control returned to the microphone. "Can you detail precisely what happened, Sheafe?"

Sheafe rubbed at his forehead. His hand trembled visibly.

"It was when we woke up. I had bad dreams—I think

298

Jovacki did too; he won't talk. Just sits there, crying. He woke up crying. I don't know what to do. . . ." He trailed off, waiting for the directive that would make it all right again.

Whittaker called for the bio-readout. A medtech hurried over. "Blood pressure's up, heartbeat, everything. On both of them, sir," he said, handing over the closely marked strip. Whittaker blinked at the zigzag squiggles, forcing himself to make sense of them.

"Do they have sedatives on board?" he asked. Med nodded.

Whittaker turned back to Control. "Get a sedative dosage from Medical, and relay it to Sheafe. Wait, ask Sheafe how he feels first."

Sheafe's face was shiny with sweat as he answered. "I feel o, k, m," he said. "Just a little nervous, maybe." He tried to grin, but a tic disturbed the stubbled plane of his cheek.

Whittaker sighed. He'd call Psych straightaway. Jovacki and Sheafe were both A + on psychobalance. Just a passing phase, maybe. A reaction to the strain, the distance from Earth. . . . It'd be a minor disturbance. It had to be.

Jovacki was screaming. Continually. The background wail made it impossible to pick up Sheafe's voice, but that was unimportant now. Nothing he said made sense anyway. The tension in the control room was tangible. Whittaker could feel it in the spastic knotting of his stomach muscles.

Control was still doggedly trying to relay a stronger dosage of tranquilizer to Sheafe, but Sheafe couldn't listen. Tears were streaming down his face as he babbled, the disjointed phrases occasionally audible through Jovacki's cries. ". . . want to go home . . . scared . . . Jesus Christ, *stop* it . . . so scared . . . please . . ."

Psych stared across the console at the haggard Whittaker and slowly shook his head. Whittaker tried to straighten, to find a muscle that wasn't aching. All eyes turned to him. Oh God, he thought. Why me? Why them?

He took a last look at the twisted face in the vision screen. "All right," he said. "Bring them back."

He turned without another word and left the room. Let someone else take charge for now. It was time for explanations. He'd better start planning them, but it was hard to think clearly. Except about the unemployment queues; they were crystal clear in his tired mind.

The task is finished, the encirclement completed. But we have lost Loytola. It was not nice, nor quick. Hab tried. He drew us in to merge once more with the other bubble — Per and Seb at least could rest. Then he worked frantically in to skim us around the belt as quickly as possible, lingering at each location only long enough for Loytola to trip the tiny plasms in their rock caverns into receive-and-broadcast phase. Hab tried.

And Loytola . . . What to say about her? Loytola held on grimly, while the mental emanations ate into her mind, holding that part of her which was converting steadily until the last was finished. All of us suffered; Halan more so, receiving the contamination and trying to share Loytola's anguish. He, too, now knows of emotional atavisms and their physical manifestations. Loytola fought, and succeeded, but it burned her out.

I was in a quandary. What should I do with her? We have no Transcorporates among us — no assessor mission has ever needed one before. Finally I decided. To leave Loytola there, in that system, orbiting the giant ringed planet. It seemed fitting.

We are a shattered crew. Halan the Scan is close to useless, and all of us have been brushed by the evil of these beings. Knowledge of such is a heavy load for a mind to carry, and probably none of us will operate a mission again. In a sense, we are cripples.

Hab hadn't strength left to control fully. Seb and Per are helping as best they can. Bairl is supporting me and both of us are trying to heal Halan. We may yet prove too lame to reach home.

But we have succeeded! That race is contained, and the galaxy will remain free of it. There is that much to be proud of.

Paul Whittaker felt the familiar burning sensation as he entered the door marked "Senior Executive Director—Associated Global Corporations—Space Exploration Division," a sensation that had never quite left him during the last three years. The expression on Arthur Mathers' face across the glossy mahogany desk did nothing to settle his screaming nerves.

Mathers pointed to a chair. "Sit down, Whittaker," he snapped. Whittaker sat.

"Well?" Mathers' frown deepened.

Whittaker tried to think of the right words, the confident phrases, but they had all been used up.

"I don't know, sir. I just don't know," he said as last.

"Four missions, Whittaker," Mathers voice rose as he spat the words out. "Four missions aborted. Eight men returned insane. God knows how many billions of dollars wasted—wasted, Whittaker. And you don't know why!"

"I'm sorry, sir." Whittaker closed his eyes to the whine in his own voice. "We've been through everything. Hired every expert. Tried every possibility. The general consensus is that it's just not physically possible—mentally possible, actually—to get men past Mars. There's some kind of mental barrier that keeps us in. It seems to be an inherent reaction of the human psyche. . . ."

Mathers interrupted, his voice softer, more controlled.

"Whittaker," he said, "AGC has kept you on despite four failures, because we believe you are the best man for the job. But there *may* be fifty better men on the unemployment lists. We've invested a lot in you. We don't want to lose that investment. . . ."

Whittaker tried not to panic, tried to keep his voice level. "No one could do any better, sir." Mathers leaned back, and Whittaker went on. "You haven't seen these men, not while they're out there. Some kind of fear and hatred starts eating at them. Their minds just can't take it, and they come back—well, psychotic. It's not a question of mechanics, or physics, or biology. It's something entirely unknown. No sane man can get to Jupiter, or beyond, for that matter."

Mathers took up again as if Whittaker had not spoken.

"And what I've just said about you applies to our other investment here, Whittaker. The billions already spent on this project. We can't waste them. What it boils down to is that the world needs resources."

For world, read AGC, Whittaker thought hopelessly.

"And we mean to get them. First. Word has it that Federated World Businesses is holding off their space program because of our problem, but they'll have their experts working on it, too." He leaned across the desk, smiling confidentially at Whittaker.

"However, we may have a solution. One you've just touched on. You're right. It appears no *sane* man can get past Mars. We just might approach it from another angle."

The smile broadened, and Whittaker's head jerked up.

"What do you mean?" he asked.

"I mean the crew of the next mission will be slightly—different. Maybe even psychotic—from the start. The old saying about fighting fire with fire, Whittaker. It might work. It's worth a try, eh? If it does, maybe the human race will have to adapt a little to live with space travel; we've done it before. . . ."

Whittaker listened, but didn't hear. He knew nothing he could say would change AGC's mind. He knew they'd continue, and he knew they'd succeed, eventually, somehow. Maybe we're all a bit crazy already, he thought. What's a little extra psychosis in the world — or out of it? A race of madmen, spilling insanity out into space . . . Something in him protested. But he needed his job.

He smiled brightly, artificially. "Very well, sir," he said, rising. "I'll start arranging the next mission right away."

READ THESE HORRIFYING BEST SELLERS!

THE WITCHING (746, $2.75)
by Fritzen Ravenswood
A spine-tingling story of witchcraft and Satanism unfolds as a powerful coven seeks unrelenting revenge!

MOONDEATH (702, $2.75)
by Rick Hautala
A peaceful New England town is stalked by a blood-thirsty werewolf. *"One of the best horror novels I've ever read . . ."*—Stephen King.

THE UNHOLY SMILE (796, $2.50)
by Gregory A. Douglas
Unblemished virgins, stone altars, human sacrifice . . . it sounded like an ancient sect. But the screams were too real, the blood too red, the horror too evil. And with each sacrifice, the satanic cult craved more . . .

DEATH-COACH
by J.N. Williamson (805, $2.95)
While the town of Thesaly slept, the sound of hoofbeats echoed in the night. An ancient, bloodthirsty vampire flew above the town, seeking the next hapless victim to be borne away by her DEATH-COACH . . .

CHERRON (700, $2.50)
by Sharon Combes
A young girl, taunted and teased for her physical imperfections, uses her telekinetic powers to wreak bloody vengeance on her tormentors—body and soul!

Available wherever paperbacks are sold, or order direct from the Publisher. Send cover price plus 50¢ per copy for mailing and handling to Zebra Books, 475 Park Avenue South, New York, N.Y. 10016. DO NOT SEND CASH.